熱門影集

[CONTENTS]

冰與火之歌
GAME OF THRONES
權力遊戲

Based on George R.R. Martin's [1]**epic** [2]**fantasy** series *Song of Ice and Fire*, **HBO**'s *Game of Thrones* is set in the [3]**medieval** world of Westeros, a continent of Seven Kingdoms ruled from the Iron [4]**Throne**. As the story begins, King Robert Baratheon has traveled north to ask his old friend Ned Stark, Lord of the North, to serve as Hand of the King. Learning that the former Hand, who was his mentor, died under [5]**mysterious** [6]**circumstances**, Ned agrees and travels south to King's Landing with his two daughters, one of whom is to marry Prince Joffrey, the king's son. Meanwhile, Ned's [7]**bastard** son Jon Snow goes north to serve on the Night's Watch, a **military order** that guards the Wall, a 700 ft. high ice [8]**barrier** that protects the Seven Kingdoms from [9]**wildling** attacks. Once there, he finds out that the wildlings aren't the only threat from beyond the wall.

《權力遊戲》是 HBO 根據喬治馬丁的奇幻史詩系列小說《冰與火之歌》改編的影集，場景設在維斯特洛的中古世紀世界，維斯特洛是一座由鐵王座統治的七大王國大陸。故事開始時，國王勞勃拜拉席恩前往北境請老朋友，臨冬城公爵奈德史塔克，擔任御前首相。奈德得知前首相，也是他的導師，神秘死亡後，同意與兩位女兒前往南境的君臨，他其中一位女兒會嫁給國王的兒子喬佛里。同時，奈德的私生子瓊恩雪諾往北擔任守夜人，加入守衛城牆的軍團。那道城牆是七百英尺高的冰牆，保護七大王國不受蠻族入侵。他在那裡發現蠻族不是牆外唯一的敵人。

© theglobalpanorama

On becoming King's Hand, Ned learns an [10]**explosive** secret—Prince Joffrey is the result of [11]**incest** between Queen Cersei Lannister and her twin brother Jaime—the same secret that got the former Hand murdered. When Ned [12]**confronts** Cersei, and the King dies in a hunting accident, a violent struggle for the throne between House Stark and House Lannister follows. Meanwhile, across the Narrow Sea in Essos,

another threat is ¹³⁾**brewing**. Prince Viserys Targaryen has arranged to trade his sister Daenerys in marriage to the Dothraki ¹⁴⁾**warlord** Khal Drogo in exchange for Drogo's army. Son of King Aerys, who was ¹⁵⁾**defeated** by Robert Baratheon, Viserys plans to use the army to retake the Iron Throne. Who will end up as ruler of the Seven Kingdoms? Let *Game of Thrones* take you on a journey that is shocking and violent, but never boring!

成為首相後，奈德得知一個震撼的秘密──喬佛里是王后瑟曦蘭尼斯特和她雙胞胎哥哥詹姆亂倫所生──而且前首相是因為這個秘密而被殺害。在奈德與瑟曦對質、國王死於狩獵意外之後，史塔克家族和蘭尼斯特家族之間的爭權之戰一觸即發。同時，狹海對岸的厄斯索斯的威脅也正在醞釀當中。韋賽里斯坦格利安王子安排妹妹丹妮莉絲嫁給多斯拉克部族的首領卡奧卓戈，用來交換卓戈的軍隊。伊里斯國王被勞勃拜拉席恩打敗後，他的兒子韋賽里斯計畫用這支軍隊奪回鐵王座。最後誰會成為七大王國的統治者？就讓《權力遊戲》帶你踏上驚心動魄、激烈打鬥、精彩絕倫的旅程！

HBO 家庭票房頻道

全名為 Home Box Office（意指「居家售票處」，在家就能輕鬆觀賞電影的意思），這家有線電視及衛星聯播網在美國擁有三千萬付費訂戶，在世界至少一百五十二國播出，訂戶超過一千萬名。其自行製播過的節目除了販售給其他電視網播出，也會推出 DVD 進入零售市場，或是放上網路影片租售平台。

中世紀歐洲軍事團體

military order 軍事修會

十二世紀前葉，羅馬天主教會為了協助十字軍東征（Crusades），建立了幾支由修士（fray）組成、軍事色彩濃厚的修會，第一支為聖殿騎士團，與後來的醫院騎士團、條頓騎士團並稱三大騎士團。

Chivalric order 騎士團

中世紀歐洲，各國王室及貴族會冊封騎士（knight），騎士必須加入其私有軍隊，對其效忠。十二世紀後，這些王室軍隊開始仿效軍事修會嚴明的制度，成為騎士團。

Vocabulary

1) **epic** [ˋɛpɪk] (a.) 史詩（般）的，宏偉的
   The people's epic struggle for freedom is finally over.

2) **fantasy** [ˋfæntəsɪ] (n.) 奇幻（作品），幻想，夢想
   Bobby likes reading science fiction and fantasy novels.

3) **medieval** [ˌmɪdɪˋivəl] (a.) 中古世紀的
   There are many medieval castles in Scotland.

4) **throne** [θron] (n.) 寶座，王位
   The king sat on his throne.

5) **mysterious** [mɪˋstɪrɪəs] (a.) 神祕的，使人摸不透的
   The walls of the temple were covered with mysterious symbols.

6) **circumstance** [ˋsɝkəmˌstæns] (n.) 情況，情勢
   Police are investigating the circumstances of the man's death.

7) **bastard** [ˋbæstəd] (n.) 私生子，王八蛋
   The king's bastard ended up on the throne.

8) **barrier** [ˋbærɪɚ] (n.) 障礙（物），阻礙
   The river forms a natural barrier between the two countries.

9) **wildling** [ˋwaɪldlɪŋ] (n.) 野生動植物（在此指「野蠻人」）
   Most wildlings live in small villages north of the Wall.

10) **explosive** [ɪkˋsplosɪv] (a. / n.) 爆炸性的，炸彈
    The terrorist was caught with explosives in his underwear.

11) **incest** [ˋɪnsɛst] (n.) 亂倫，近親通婚
    The young girl is a victim of incest.

12) **confront** [kənˋfrʌnt] (v.) 對付，面臨
    Police were sent to confront the demonstrators.

13) **brew** [bru] (v.) 形成，醞釀
    It looks like there's a storm brewing.

14) **warlord** [ˋwɔrˌlɔrd] (n.) 軍閥
    In the 1920s, most of China was controlled by warlords.

15) **defeat** [dɪˋfit] (v./n.) 戰勝，擊敗
    The Americans defeated the Japanese in World War II.

看影集

韋賽里斯安排妹妹嫁給卓戈，但她越來越不受控制，令韋賽里斯非常不爽。

Viserys: You would turn me into one of them, wouldn't you? Next you'll want to braid my hair.

Daenerys: You've no right to a braid. You've won no victories yet.

Viserys: You do not talk back to me! *[Viserys hit Daenerys]* You are a horselord's slut. And now you've woken the dragon ….

Daenerys: I am a **Khaleesi** of the Dothraki! I am the wife of the great **Khal** and I carry his son inside me. The next time you **raise a hand to** me will be the last time you have hands.

Dothraki language
多斯拉其語

在《冰與火之歌》原著小說中，Dothraki 是多斯拉其海當地居民的語言。為了拍攝《權力遊戲》，HBO 特別聘請語言學家利用小說中的一些單字與短語，創制一種虛擬語言（fictional language）。上面對白中的 Khal 是「統治者」，「統治者的妻子」就是 Khaleesi。二〇一一年該劇推出之後，隔年就有一四六名美國新生女嬰被命名為 Khaleesi，可見這個影集受歡迎的程度。

除了 Dothraki，《冰與火之歌：權力遊戲》還有 Valyrian languages（高地瓦雷利亞語）這支地方語系。

《冰與火之歌》作者
George R.R. Martin

©s_bukley / Shutterstock.com

韋賽里斯：妳想讓我變得跟他們一樣，對吧？接下來妳就會想替我編辮子了。

丹妮莉絲：你沒有資格編辮子。你沒打過勝仗。

韋賽里斯：不要頂嘴！（韋賽里斯掌摑丹妮莉絲）妳這個馬王的蕩婦。我這隻睡龍被你喚醒了……。

丹妮莉絲：我是多斯拉克族的卡麗熙！我是偉大卡奧的妻子，我懷了他的兒子。下次你再動手打我，你就會失去雙手。

學英文 🎧 3

raise a hand to/against sb. 動手打人

舉起手來對付人，就是打人的意思。也可說 lift a hand to/against。

A: Do you believe in corporal punishment?
你覺得體罰有其必要嗎？

B: No. I would never raise a hand to my children.
不。我絕對不會動手打孩子。

看影集

瑟曦綁架提利昂的妓女情人蘿絲作為要脅，這樣她的兒子喬佛里就不會被殺。

Cersei: Ser Mandon, bring in my brother's whore.

Tyrion: I'm sorry they hurt you. You must be brave. I promise, I will free you.

Ros: Don't forget me.

Tyrion: Never. *[to Cersei]* I will hurt you for this. A day will come when you think you are safe and happy, and your joy will **turn to ashes in your mouth**, and you will know the debt is paid.

瑟　曦：曼登爵士，把我弟弟的蕩婦帶進來

提利昂：我很抱歉他們傷害妳。妳一定要勇敢。我保證，我會把妳救出來。

蘿　絲：別忘了我。

提利昂：不會的。（轉向瑟曦）我會讓妳為此付出代價。總有一天，當妳自以為平安幸福時，妳的快樂會在妳嘴裡化成灰燼，到時妳就知道該還債了。

學英文 🎧 4

sth. turns to ashes (in one's mouth) 幻滅

形容成果化為灰燼，到嘴的鴨子飛了，讓人非常失落。

A: Why did the woman take her own life?
那個女人為什麼要自殺？

B: Because all her dreams turned to ashes.
因為她所有的夢想都破滅了。

看影集

艾莉亞在宮中跟西利歐上劍術課。

Syrio: You're not here. You're with your trouble. If you're with your trouble when fighting happens…*[Syrio puts Arya on her back]*… more trouble for you. Just so. How can you be quick as a snake, or as quiet as a shadow, when you are somewhere else? You are fearing for your father, hmm? That is right. Do you pray to the gods?

Arya: **The old and the new.**

Syrio: There is only one god. And his name is death. And there is only one thing we say to death: "Not today."

西利歐： 妳心不在焉。妳心煩意亂。妳出戰時若是心煩意亂……（西利歐把艾莉亞絆倒）……會惹來更多麻煩。就像現在。妳若是心不在焉，妳怎麼能跟蛇一樣迅速，或跟影子一樣安靜？妳在擔心妳父親，嗯？這是人之常情。妳會向神靈祈禱嗎？

艾莉亞： 舊神和新神都有。

西利歐： 世上只有一個神，就是死神。對死神，我們只有一句話：「今天不行。」

The Old Gods and the New Gods 新舊眾神

在《冰與火之歌》當中，史塔克家族信仰舊神教（Old Gods of the Forest），他們相信祖先登陸西方世界（Westeros）之前，這裡屬於森林之子（Children of the Forest，土石與樹木的神靈）以及巨人。後來東方世界（Essos）安達爾人（Andal）入侵西方世界，在當地推行七神教（Faith of the Seven），崇拜象徵七種德行的神祇，人們會依照所求的事物，向其中一個神明禱告，成為七大王國（Seven Kingdoms）的主流宗教。

© Helga Esteb / S

侏儒演員彼得汀克萊傑（ Peter Dinklage）把亦正亦邪的提利昂演得入木三分，為了補足外型上的缺憾，這位王子飽讀詩書，劇中說了許多相當雋永的台詞，例如：
"A very small man can cast a very large shadow."
「非常矮小的人能投射出非常大的陰影。」

© HBO

看影集

關於丹妮莉絲坦格利安的小會議。

Robert: The whore is pregnant.

Ned: You're speaking of murdering a child.

Robert: I warned you this would happen, back in the North. I warned you, but you didn't care to hear. Well, hear it now: I want them dead. Mother and child both, and that fool Viserys as well. Is that plain enough for you? I want them both dead.

Ned: You'll dishonor yourself forever if you do this.

Robert: Honor? I've got Seven Kingdoms to rule! One king, Seven Kingdoms! Do you think honor **keeps them in line**? Do you think it's honor that's keeping the peace? It's fear! Fear and blood!

勞勃：　那淫婦懷孕了。

奈德：　你談的是謀殺孩子。

勞勃：　在北境的時候，我警告過你會有這種情況。我警告過你了，但你不想聽。那你現在聽好：我要他們死。母子兩個，還有那個笨蛋韋賽里斯。夠清楚了嗎？我要他們兩人都死。

奈德：　假如你這麼做的話，你的名譽會永遠受損。

勞勃：　名譽？我統治七大王國！七大王國的唯一國王！你覺得名譽能讓他們聽話嗎？你覺得名譽能維持和平嗎？是恐懼！恐懼和流血才能！

看影集

奈德與瑟曦對質時，瑟曦告訴他有機會就該稱王。

Cersei: You should have taken the realm for yourself. Jaime told me about the day King's Landing fell. He was sitting on the Iron Throne and you made him give it up. All you needed to do was climb those steps yourself. Such a sad mistake.

Ned: I've made many mistakes in my life, but that wasn't one of them.

Cersei: Oh but it was. When you play the game of thrones, you win, or you die. There is no **middle ground**.

瑟曦：　你本來應該稱王的。詹姆告訴我君臨淪陷那天的事。他當時坐在鐵王座上，你逼他退位。你要做的，就只有登上王座。真是可悲的失誤。

奈德：　我這一生犯了不少錯誤，但那不是其中一個。

瑟曦：　但那的確是。當你加入權力遊戲時，不是贏，就是死，沒有中間立場。

學英文 🎧 5

keep...in line 讓……乖乖就範

字面上的意思是「讓……排成一列」，引申為讓一群人或動物聽從指揮。

A: What do you do to keep your kids in line?
你怎麼讓孩子們乖乖聽話的？

B: I threaten to take away their allowance.
我威脅要扣他們的零用錢。

學英文 🎧 6

middle ground 中間立場，中立

位於兩個極端之間，也就是妥協讓步的結果。

A: Have the two countries reached an agreement yet?
這兩個國家達成協議了嗎？

B: No. They're still seeking a middle ground.
沒有。他們還在尋求中間立場。

剛當上國王的喬佛里命人將羅柏史塔克的頭帶到君臨，要獻給前未婚妻珊莎，她即將嫁給提利昂。

Joffrey: Write back to Lord Frey. Thank him for his service and command him to send Robb Stark's head. I'm going to serve it to Sansa at my wedding feast.

Varys: **Your Grace**, Lady Sansa is your aunt by marriage.

Cersei: A joke. Joffrey did not mean it.

Joffrey: Yes, I did. I'm going to have it served to Sansa at my wedding feast.

Tyrion: No, she is no longer yours to torment.

Joffrey: Everyone is mine to torment. You'd **do well to** remember that, you little monster.

Tyrion: Oh, I'm a monster? Perhaps you should speak to me more softly then. Monsters are dangerous, and just now, kings are **dying like flies**.

喬佛里：回信給佛雷侯爵，謝謝他的幫忙，並命令他送回羅柏史塔克的頭，我要在我的婚宴上獻給珊莎。

瓦里斯：陛下，珊莎夫人現在是你的舅媽。

瑟　曦：他在開玩笑。喬佛里不是認真的。

喬佛里：我是認真的。我要在我的婚宴上將它獻給珊莎。

提利昂：不行，你已經沒有權利折磨她。

喬佛里：我有權利折磨任何人。你最好記住，你這小魔鬼。

提利昂：喔，我是魔鬼？那也許你該對我更加輕聲細語。魔鬼是很危險的，而且最近，國王就像蒼蠅一樣紛紛死去。

would do well to 最好能夠（做某事）

do well 是「老老實實的」，這個片語用來表示能夠怎麼做的話，會比較保險，或能得到好處。

A: The boss has been complaining about my tardiness?
老闆已經開始抱怨我經常遲到？

B: Yes. You'd do well to come in on time in the future.
是的。你以後最好能夠準時上班。

die/drop like flies 大量死亡

drop like flies 的說法較常用，這個片語字面意思是「像蒼蠅一樣成群死亡。」

A: They said on the news that the disease is spreading fast.
新聞上說那種疾病正快速擴散。

B: Yeah. People are dropping like flies.
是啊。已經造成許多人死亡。

飾演丹妮莉絲的艾米莉亞克拉克（Emilia Clarke），在劇中一頭接近白色的金髮，造型非常搶眼，婚禮上生食整顆馬心的戲更是令人印象深刻。

Style 榮銜與尊稱

在嚴格講究位階的王室、政界、法界、軍隊等場合，提到領導與上級時必須加上尊稱，如對白中稱呼國王 Your Grace（用於第三人稱則為 His Grace），就是英國亨利八世之前對國王的尊稱。常見的王室稱謂如下：

His / Her Majesty 國王／女王陛下

His / Her Highness 王子／公主殿下

His / Her Grace 公爵／公爵夫人

His / Her Excellency 閣下／閣下夫人

SHERLOCK
新世紀福爾摩斯

There have been many [1]**adaptations** of Sir Arthur Conan Doyle's famous [2]**detective** stories over the years, but BBC's *Sherlock* has a major difference. Sherlock Holmes is still an [3]**arrogant** genius who solves crimes with the assistance of his friend and roommate Dr. John Watson, but the [4]**setting** has changed from Victorian London to the London of the 21st century. Sherlock's pipe and [5]**magnifying glass** have been replaced by [6]**nicotine** [7]**patches** and a [8]**laptop**, and Watson is an army doctor who has returned to London after being wounded in Afghanistan.

多年來，柯南道爾爵士的知名偵探小說一直有許多改編版本，不過，英國廣播公司的《新世紀福爾摩斯》很不一樣。福爾摩斯依舊是個自負的天才，在朋友兼室友華生醫師的幫助下破案，但場景從維多利亞時代的倫敦，改成二十一世紀的倫敦。福爾摩斯的菸斗和放大鏡換成尼古丁貼片和筆電，而華生是位軍醫，在阿富汗戰爭中負傷後回到倫敦。

© BBC

SHERLOCK
"THE ABOMINABLE BRIDE"
1ST JANUARY 2016
© BBC

Running into an old [9]**colleague** in a park, Watson mentions that he can't afford London rents on an army [10]**pension**, and doesn't think anyone would want to share a [11]**flat** with him. His colleague says he knows someone in the same situation, and takes him to his hospital's [12]**morgue**, where Sherlock Holmes is beating a [13]**corpse** as part of an experiment. Holmes uses his powers of [14]**observation** to [15]**deduce** that Watson is an injured army doctor looking for a roommate, and tells him to meet him tomorrow at that famous address, 221B Baker Street.

華生在公園裡遇到以前的同僚，提到自己軍隊的退休金負擔不起倫敦的房租，也不認為會有人想和他一起合租公寓。他的同僚說，他認識一個情況和華生一樣的人，於是帶華生到他任職的醫院太平間，福爾摩斯正在那裡為了做實驗而鞭打屍體。福爾摩斯運用他的觀察力推斷華生是受了傷的軍醫，正在找室友，並要他隔天到那個知名的地址見他：貝克街 221B 號。

No sooner has Watson decided to move in than Holmes [16]**involves** him in a case—a series of suicides that appear to be related. At the crime scene, Sherlock deduces that the latest body is a victim of murder, not suicide, and that the killer has the victim's phone. Using [17]**GPS** to find the killer, Sherlock learns that he forces his victims to choose between two pills, one harmless and one poison, and then swallow it while he swallows the other. Sherlock is talked into playing the game, but is saved by Watson, who arrives just in time to shoot the killer. Just before he dies, the killer shouts the name of the man who ordered the murders: Moriarty, Sherlock's [18]**archenemy**!

華生才剛決定要搬進福爾摩斯的公寓，福爾摩斯就將他拉入一樁案件——一連串似乎互有關連的自殺案。福爾摩斯在犯罪現場推斷新發現的屍體是謀殺案的受害者，不是自殺，而且兇手拿了受害者的手機。福爾摩斯利用 GPS 找到兇手，並得知他逼迫所有受害者從兩顆藥丸選擇一顆，一顆沒毒，一顆有毒，然後一顆受害者吞掉，另一顆兇手吞掉。福爾摩斯被說服玩這個遊戲，但華生及時趕到，射殺兇手，救了福爾摩斯。兇手臨死之際，喊出了幕後主腦的名字：莫里亞蒂，福爾摩斯的死敵！

Sir Arthur Conan Doyle
柯南道爾爵士

原著小說中福爾摩斯自己的說法以及華森的描述，福爾摩斯閒來無事經常喜歡給自己來一針毒品！沒錯，福爾摩斯是偵探英雄，但也是個不折不扣的毒蟲！而且，以現今的標準來看，他慣用的毒品是今日列管為一級毒品的古柯鹼（cocaine）與嗎啡（morphine）。根據華森的描述，福爾摩斯吸毒的習慣已經有段時日，他不但會熟練地自行施打毒品，手臂上還「布滿了數不清的針孔」。

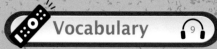

Vocabulary 9

1) **adaptation** [ˌædæpˈteʃən] (n.) 改編，改寫
   (v.) adapt [əˈdæpt]
   The director is working on an adaptation of *Macbeth*.

2) **detective** [dɪˈtɛktɪv] (n.) 偵探，警探
   My little brother likes to read detective stories.

3) **arrogant** [ˈærəgənt] (a.) 傲慢的，自大的
   It's arrogant to think you're smarter than everybody else.

4) **setting** [ˈsɛtɪŋ] (n.) 環境，背景
   A Ph.D. is necessary if you want to teach in a university setting.

5) **magnifying glass** [ˈmægnəˌfaɪɪŋ] [glæs] (n.) 放大鏡
   The teacher had us look at leaves with a magnifying glass.

6) **nicotine** [ˈnɪkəˌtin] (n.) 尼古丁，菸鹼
   The company now makes cigarettes that are lower in nicotine.

7) **patch** [pætʃ] (n.) 貼片，補丁
   The boy wore jeans with patches on the knees.

8) **laptop** [ˈlæpˌtɑp] (n.) 筆記型電腦
   I always take my laptop with me when I travel.

9) **colleague** [ˈkɑlig] (n.) 同事，同僚
   I'd like you to meet my colleague, Ed Roberts.

10) **pension** [ˈpɛnʃən] (n.) 退休金，養老金
    Does your company have a pension plan?

11) **flat** [flæt] (n.)（英國）一間公寓
    Renting a flat in London can be very expensive.

12) **morgue** [mɔrg] (n.) 太平間，停屍間
    The patient was declared dead and taken to the morgue.

13) **corpse** [kɔrps] (n.) 屍體
    The battlefield was covered with corpses.

14) **observation** [ˌɑbzɚˈveʃən] (n.) 觀察，瞭望
    The patient was kept at the hospital for observation.

15) **deduce** [dɪˈdus] (v.) 推論，推理
    The police detective deduced the identity of the murderer.

16) **involve** [ɪnˈvɑlv]（使）捲入，連累，牽涉
    Don't involve me in your argument!

17) **GPS** 即 **global positioning system**
    [ˈglobəl] [pəˈzɪʃənɪŋ] [ˈsɪstəm] 全球定位系統
    Do you have GPS in your car?

18) **archenemy** [ˌɑrtʃˈɛnəmi] (n.) 死敵，大敵
    Lex Luthor is Superman's archenemy.

 看影集

華生和福爾摩斯剛抵達貝克街 221B 號。

Watson: Well, this is a prime spot. Must be expensive.

Sherlock: Oh, Mrs. Hudson, the landlady, she's giving me a special deal. **Owes me a favor**. A few years back, her husband got himself **sentenced to death** in Florida. I was able to help out.

Watson: Sorry—you stopped her husband being **executed**?

Sherlock: Oh no. I ensured it.

華　　生：嗯，這是黃金地段。一定很貴。

福爾摩斯：喔，房東哈德森太太給了我優惠。她欠我人情。幾年前，她丈夫在佛羅里達州被判死刑。我幫了她忙。

華　　生：不好意思——你幫她丈夫免於死刑？

福爾摩斯：喔，不是。我協助定案。

📢 學英文 🎧 10

owe sb. a favor 欠（某人）一份情

favor 是「恩惠」的意思，owe sb. a favor 就是別人對你有恩的意思。

A: Are you sure Steve will let you borrow his car?
你確定史蒂夫會把車借給你嗎？

B: Yeah. He owes me a favor.
確定。他欠我一份情。

📢 看影集

福爾摩斯和華生坐計程車前往犯罪現場的途中。

Watson: Who are you? What do you do?

Sherlock: What do you think?

Watson: I'd say private detective ....

Sherlock: But?

Watson: But the police don't go to private detectives.

Sherlock: I'm a consulting detective. Only one in the world. I invented the job.

Watson: What does that mean?

Sherlock: It means when the police are **out of their depth**, which is always, they consult me.

Watson: The police don't consult amateurs.

death sentence 死刑判決

sentence 可作動詞「判刑」或名詞「判決」，說一個人「被判處死刑」就是 be sentenced to death。會被判死刑的犯罪類型隨各地宗教、風俗而有不同，最普遍的重罪包括「一級謀殺」（first degree murder）、「叛亂」（treason）。

execute 執行死刑，處決

作為一種終極的懲罰，死刑原始的用意是要給受刑人造成極大的痛苦，隨著人道主義日興，越來越多國家廢除（abolish）死刑，尚未廢除死刑的國家，也都改採快速死亡、較不痛苦的行刑方式，例如：

firing squad 槍斃
electric chair 電椅
gas chamber 毒氣室
lethal injection 毒物注射

華　　生：你是誰？是做什麼的？

福爾摩斯：你覺得呢？

華　　生：我想應該是私人偵探……。

福爾摩斯：但是呢？

華　　生：但是警察不會找私人偵探。

福爾摩斯：我是諮詢偵探。全世界獨一無二的，是我發明這份工作的。

華　　生：什麼意思？

福爾摩斯：警察力有不及時，總是會有這種情況出現，他們就來向我諮詢。

華　　生：警察是不會諮詢業餘人士的。

be out of one's depth 吃不消

depth 是「深度」，這句話用在表示一件事太過困難，讓人無法負荷。要注意主詞是吃不消的人，不是讓人吃不消的事物。

A: How come I didn't see you at Spanish class yesterday?
　昨天我在西班牙文課堂上，怎麼沒有看到你？

B: I was out of my depth, so I switched to a lower level.
　我學不來，所以轉到比較低階的班。

血字的研究
A Study in Scarlet

《血字的研究》（*A Study in Scarlet* ）是第一本以福爾摩斯為主角的作品，《新世紀福爾摩斯》的第一集，即改編自這個故事，劇名為 *A Study in Pink*。

在原著中，死者留下的血字 Rache 其實是德文「復仇」的意思，留下的物品是一枚戒指。到了現代版的詮釋，Rache 成為死者女兒的名字，還是打開手機的密碼。

A Study in Pink 播出之後受到極高評價，為《新世紀福爾摩斯》系列及後續電影版打下一片江山。

 看影集

福爾摩斯的哥哥邁克羅夫帶華生到一座空倉庫談論福爾摩斯。

Watson:　Who are you?

Mycroft:　An interested party.

Watson:　Interested in Sherlock? Why? I'm guessing you're not friends.

Mycroft:　You've met him. How many friends do you imagine he has? I am the closest thing to a friend that Sherlock Holmes is capable of having.

Watson:　And what's that?

Mycroft:　An enemy.

Watson:　An enemy?

Mycroft:　In his mind certainly. If you were to ask him he'd probably say his archenemy. He does love to be dramatic.

Watson:　Well thank god **you're above all that**.

華　　生：　你是誰？

邁克羅夫：利害關係人。

華　　生：　跟福爾摩斯有利害關係？為什麼？我猜你們不是朋友。

邁克羅夫：你認識他。你想他會有多少朋友？我是福爾摩斯的關係人當中，跟朋友最接近的一種。

華　　生：　那是什麼？

邁克羅夫：敵人。

華　　生：　敵人？

邁克羅夫：在他心中肯定是這麼認為。假如你去問他，他大概會說是死敵。他很愛把事情搞得戲劇化。

華　　生：　那感謝上帝，你不是這種人。

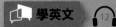

be above sth. 不屑

above 當介系詞有不願紆尊降貴的意思，be above sth. 表示不屑做某件事。

A: Janet caught her boyfriend cheating with another girl.
　珍娜抓到她男友劈腿。

B: Rick? I thought he was above that sort of thing.
　瑞克？我還以為他不屑幹那種事。

看影集

福爾摩斯和華生回到公寓討論案件。

Watson: Have you talked to the police?

Sherlock: Four people are dead. There isn't time to talk to the police.

Watson: So why are you talking to me?

Sherlock: Mrs. Hudson took my skull.

Watson: So I'm basically **filling in for** your skull.

Sherlock: Relax. You're doing fine.

華生：　　　你和警察談過了嗎？

福爾摩斯：有四人死了，沒有時間和警察討論。

華生：　　　那你為什麼跟我談？

福爾摩斯：哈德森太太拿走了我的骷髏頭。

華生：　　　所以我基本上是來替補你的骷髏頭。

福爾摩斯：不要緊張，你做得很好。

學英文 13

fill in for 代班，頂替

fill in for sb. 是暫時幫別人做他的工作，fill in for sth. 則是取代原本的東西。

A: Could you fill in for me while I go run an errand?
　　我去辦點事情，你能幫我處理一下工作嗎？

B: Sure, no problem. Take your time.
　　好啊，沒問題。你慢慢來。

© Joe Seer / Shutterstock.com (2)

儘管馬丁費里曼（Martin Freeman）在《新世紀福爾摩斯》當中，是班乃迪克康柏拜區（Benedict Cumberbatch）身邊的的最佳綠葉，但到了他後來擔綱主演的系列電影《哈比人》當中，兩人再度同台，只是康柏拜區完全沒得露臉，而是擔任巨龍 Smaug 及法師 Necromancer 的配音員。

另外值得一提的是，在《新世紀福爾摩斯》當中飾演他妻子的女星阿曼達艾賓頓（Amanda Abbington），就是他現實生活中的太太！

© Joe Seer / Shutterstock.com (2)

© Mr Pics / Shutterstock.com

患有絕症的兇手向福爾摩斯解釋他的動機。

Cabbie: When I die they won't get much, my kids. Not a lot of money in driving cabs.

Sherlock: Or serial killing.

Cabbie: You'd be surprised.

Sherlock: Surprise me.

Cabbie: I have a sponsor.

Sherlock: You have a what?

Cabbie: For every life I take, money goes to my kids. The more I kill, the **better off** they'll be. See? It's nicer than you think.

Sherlock: Who would sponsor a serial killer?

Cabbie: Who would be a fan of Sherlock Holmes?

計程車司機：我死後，我的孩子拿不到多少遺產。開計程車賺不了多少錢。

福爾摩斯：　連續殺人也是。

計程車司機：說了你會驚訝。

福爾摩斯：　那讓我驚訝吧。

計程車司機：我有贊助人。

福爾摩斯：　你有什麼？

計程車司機：我每殺一個人，我的孩子就會拿到錢。我殺的越多，他們就過得越好。懂吧？比你想的還好。

福爾摩斯：　誰會贊助一個連續殺人犯？

計程車司機：誰會是福爾摩斯的粉絲？

 學英文 🎧 14

better off 比較寬裕

well off 是「富裕」，better off 是其比較級。

A: Is Kevin well off now that he won the lottery?
凱文中樂透之後日子過得不錯吧？

B: Well, he's not rich, but he's better off than he was before.
他不算很有錢，但比起之前是寬裕多了。

福爾摩斯與雷斯垂德對話，推斷是華生將他從連續殺人犯手中救出，但不想讓他惹上麻煩。

Sherlock: The bullet they just dug out of the wall is from a handgun. A kill shot over that distance, from that kind of a weapon, that's a **crack shot** you're looking for but not just a **marksman**, a fighter. His hands couldn't have shaken at all so clearly he's acclimatized to violence. He didn't fire until I was in immediate danger though, so strong moral principle. You're looking for a man probably with a history of military service and…nerves of steel. Actually, do you know what? Ignore me.

福爾摩斯：他們從牆壁上挖出的子彈是從手槍發射的。遠距離射殺，又是用那種武器，你要找的是一個神槍手，但又不只是射擊手，而是個真正的戰士。他的手一點都沒有發抖；可見他是習慣暴力的。不過他等到我在千鈞一髮時才開槍，看來是非常講道義的。你要找的人應該有兵役背景，而且……意志堅強。其實，你知道嗎？當我沒說。

神射手

英文有很多字彙表示「槍法準的人」，對白中福爾摩斯用了 crack shot 和 marksman 這兩個字，其他還有 sharpshooter（也可以簡稱 shooter）、deadeye、shot 這幾個字。

若是強調槍手使用來福槍（rifle），就是 rifleman；藏身隱密處伺機射擊的「狙擊手」，就是 sniper。電影中謀殺政商領袖的刺客（assassin），就經常隱身高樓阻擊，從遠距離用來福槍行刺。

Breaking Bad 絕命毒師

Widely considered one the greatest TV series of all time, *Breaking Bad* tells the story of Walter White, a high school [1)]**chemistry** teacher who [2)]**transforms** into a [3)]**ruthless** criminal over the course of the show. Once a [4)]**promising** chemist, Walter makes so little teaching that he has to work part-time at a [5)]**carwash** just to make ends meet. And then, on the day after his 50th birthday, he [6)]**collapses** at the carwash and is rushed to the hospital, where the doctor tells him that he has stage-

Breaking Bad Season 2 poster

three lung cancer—even though he doesn't smoke. Although Walter quietly accepts that he doesn't have long to live, he worries what will happen to his family—his teenage son Walt Jr. is [7)]**handicapped**, and his wife Skylar is [8)]**pregnant** with a second child—after he's gone.

《絕命毒師》被許多人認為是有史以來最棒的電視影集之一，故事描述高中化學老師瓦特懷特隨著劇情發展變成殘忍的罪犯。瓦特曾經是位前途無量的化學家，靠著教書賺取微薄薪水，為了維持生計，還要在洗車廠兼差。然後，在他過了五十歲生日後的第二天，他在洗車廠倒下，被緊急送往醫院。醫生告訴他，他得了肺癌第三期——雖然他不抽菸。儘管瓦特默默地接受自己來日不多的事實，但他擔心自己過世後，家人以後該怎麼辦——正值青春期的兒子小瓦特是身障，而妻子絲凱勒正懷著第二胎。

[9)]**Recalling** that his [10)]**brother-in-law** Hank, a DEA [11)]**agent**, told him that $700,000 was seized at a recent meth [12)]**lab** [13)]**bust**, he agrees to go with him on a ride-along to another meth lab. When Walt sees a former student of his, Jesse, [14)]**fleeing** the scene, instead of telling Hank, he later goes to Jesse's house with a [15)]**proposition**: if he handles [16)]**distribution**, Walt will use his knowledge of chemistry to make the purest meth he's ever seen. With [17)]**equipment** stolen from Walt's high school and a used [18)]**RV** as a lab, the two become partners and start manufacturing and selling meth. But does Walt have the brains and ruthlessness

On March 8, All Becomes Crystal Clear
NEW SEASON SUNDAYS 10PM amc
EMMY-WINNING SER

I AM NOT IN DANGER
I AM THE DANGER

© luke.wanden / flickr

necessary to become a drug lord and make enough money to support his family after he dies? As it turns out, the answer is yes. But will he avoid being caught or killed in the process? There's only one way to find out!

他想起在美國緝毒署擔任探員的連襟漢克曾告訴他，最近一次在搜查安非他命製造工廠時，查扣了七十萬美元，於是答應跟他一起坐警車到另一間安非他命製造工廠。瓦特看到他以前的學生傑西從現場逃走，但他沒告訴漢克，之後前往傑西的住處，向他提議：假如他願意負責經銷，瓦特願意用自己的化學知識製作最純的安非他命，而且是他從沒見過的。倆人於是成為合夥人，利用瓦特從高中偷來的設備，把二手露營車當實驗室，開始製作和販賣安非他命。不過，成為毒梟要有頭腦，心也要夠狠，這樣瓦特才能賺到足夠的錢，讓家人在他死後無後顧之憂，他能做得到嗎？從結果看來，答案是肯定的。但在這過程中，他能逃過逮捕或追殺嗎？想知道答案，辦法只有一個！

Drug Enforcement Administration 緝毒署

簡寫為 DEA，隸屬於美國司法部（U.S. Justice Department），主要負責偵查和預防美國國內外大規模非法毒品之製造、走私（smuggling）等犯罪行為，並協助世界各國進行毒品危害防治，例如為了查緝毒品，DEA 就長年在哥倫比亞部署聯絡人力。

毒品相關英文

recreational drug 消遣用藥，是指非醫療需要，僅為娛樂放鬆而吸食、施打的藥品，簡稱 drug，是最常用來表示「毒品」的字。dope [dop] 和 drug 口語上用法相近，都是指會令人興奮或麻痺，進而上癮的藥品。常見毒品有：

methamphetamine 甲基安非他命，簡稱 meth，是一種中樞神經興奮劑，也稱 crystal meth。

amphetamine 安非他命
heroin 海洛因
ecstasy 搖頭丸
marijuana 大麻

cocaine 古柯鹼，是由可可樹液中提煉出的一種興奮劑，也稱為 crack（快克，一種點火吸食的高純度古柯鹼）。

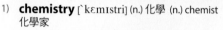

Vocabulary 16

1) **chemistry** [`kɛmɪstrɪ] (n.) 化學 (n.) chemist 化學家
Brian got a chemistry set for his birthday.

2) **transform** [træns`fɔrm] (v.) 改變，改觀
Technology has transformed the way we live and work.

3) **ruthless** [`ruθlɪs] (a.) 冷酷的，無情的 (n.) ruthlessness
The ruthless killer was given the death penalty.

4) **promising** [`prɑmɪsɪŋ] (a.) 有前途的，大有可為的
The young athlete has a promising career ahead of him.

5) **carwash** [`kɑr,wɑʃ] (n.) 洗車場
How much does it cost to get your car washed at the carwash?

6) **collapse** [kə`læps] (v.) 病倒，昏倒，累倒
The old man collapsed and died of a heart attack.

7) **handicapped** [`hændɪ,kæpt] (a.) 殘障的
Rob got a ticket for parking in a handicapped zone.

8) **pregnant** [`prɛgnənt] (a.) 懷孕的，懷胎的 (n.) pregnancy
The woman is pregnant with twins.

9) **recall** [rɪ`kɔl] (v.) 回想，想起
I can't recall the last time I had a meal this good.

10) **brother-in-law** [`brʌðɚ.ɪn,lɔ] (n.) 連襟，大伯，小叔，姐、妹夫
Do you get along with your brother-in-law?

11) **agent** [`edʒənt] (n.) 探員，特工
An FBI agent was sent to question the witness.

12) **lab** [læb] (n.) 藥廠，化學工廠，實驗室，即 laboratory [`læbrə,tɔrɪ] 的簡稱
The police found a drug lab in the suspect's basement.

13) **bust** [bʌst] (n./v.) 搜查，搜捕，逮捕
Six suspects were arrested during the drug bust.

14) **flee** [fli] (v.) 逃走，逃亡
The robber fled from the scene of the crime.

15) **proposition** [,prɑpə`zɪʃən] (n.) 提議
Have you thought about my business proposition?

16) **distribution** [,dɪstrə`bjuʃən] (n.) 經銷，配銷
Who owns the distribution rights to that product?

17) **equipment** [ɪ`kwɪpmənt] (n.) 設備，器材
The new equipment increased the efficiency of the factory.

18) **RV = recreational vehicle** [,rɛkrɪ`eʃənəl] [`viɪkəl] (n.) 休閒旅遊兩用車
We parked our RV at an RV park and spent the night.

© Pinkcandy / Shutterstock.com

看影集

在瓦特的生日派對上，電視新聞正在報導漢克的毒品搜查行動。

Walt: Hank, how much money is that?

Hank: Uh, it's about seven-hundred grand. A pretty good haul.

Walt: Wow. That's … unusual, isn't it—that kind of cash?

Hank: Um, it's not the most we ever took. It's **easy money**, till we catch you.

瓦特：漢克，那是多少錢？

漢克：呃，大約有七十萬元。很大一筆。

瓦特：哇。那真是……少見，不是嗎——這麼多的現金？

漢克：嗯，那不是我們查到最多的。這種錢賺得毫不費力，只要沒被我們逮到。

學英文 🎧 17

easy money 不勞而獲，不義之財

得來全不費工夫的錢，若不是靠天外飛來的好運，就往往需要牽涉非法行為了。fast buck 也是同樣的意思。

A: Did you hear about Tommy winning the lottery?
你有聽說湯米中樂透嗎？

B: Yeah. I wish I could make some easy money like that.
有啊。真希望我也能天外來一筆橫財。

看影集

在醫院裡被診斷出癌症後。

Dr. Belknap: You understood what I just said to you?

Walt: Yes. **Lung cancer**, inoperable.

Dr. Belknap: I just need to make sure you fully understand.

Walt: **Best-case scenario**, with **chemo**, I'll live maybe another couple years.

癌症相關字彙

根據衛生署的資料，目前癌症位居國人十大死因之首，而致死率排名前十的癌症為：

· lung cancer 肺癌
· liver cancer 肝癌
· colorectal cancer 大腸癌（又稱結腸、直腸癌）
· breast cancer 乳癌
· oral cancer 口腔癌
· stomach cancer 胃癌
· prostate cancer 攝護腺癌
· pancreatic cancer 胰臟癌
· esophageal cancer 食道癌
· cervical cancer 子宮頸癌

癌症在臨床上分為四期，隨癌症發生的部位不同而略有不同：

· stage 0 原發性期：表示腫瘤是出自該處組織惡性變化而來，但尚未侵犯到更深部組織或轉移到別處。

· stage 1 第一期：腫瘤侷限一處，沒有擴散跡象。

· stage 2 第二期：腫瘤已擴散到鄰近的淋巴結，但尚未波及其他器官或組織。

· stage 3 第三期：腫瘤已波及附近器官或組織。

· stage 4 第四期：腫瘤已擴散到遠處的部位。

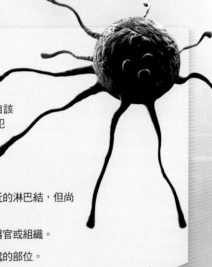

貝爾納普醫師：我剛剛說的你聽懂了嗎？

瓦特：　　　是。肺癌，無法動手術。

貝爾納普醫師：我只想確定你都懂了。

瓦特：　　　最好的情況，用化療，我也許可以再活
　　　　　　一、兩年。

學英文 🎧 18

best-case scenario　最好的情況

scenario [sɪˋnɛrɪˏo] 源自義大利文「劇本，情節」的意思，
引申為事態發展。best-case scenario 表示「所能預期最
好的情況」。反之，worst-case scenario 就是「最糟的情
況」了。

A:　What's the best-case scenario for the economy?
　　預估最好的經濟情況會是如何？
B:　I think the best we can hope for is a mild recession.
　　我看能夠只是小幅衰退就要偷笑了。

毒癮相關英文

rush　快感
在口語中，rush 有「刺激、興奮」的意思，指吸食毒品之後帶來
的亢奮及快感。rush 也常與帶有刺激性的食品連用，像喝濃咖啡
的 caffeine rush 或是抽菸之後的 nicotine rush，就是指食用咖啡因
和尼古丁帶來的快感，有提振精神的效果。

addiction　癮
毒品成癮是 drug addiction，其他還有：Internet addiction「網路成
癮」、porn addition「色情成癮」等。「成癮的人」是 addict。

dependence　依賴
指對藥物的過度依賴，導致成癮。

rehab　勒戒（所）
rehabilitation 或 rehabilitation center 的簡稱。

in recovery　在恢復、勒戒中
這個片語可以表示傷病後逐漸康復，或者是正在戒酒或戒毒。也
被用來揶揄某些過度依賴的狀況，像是網路、電動等等。

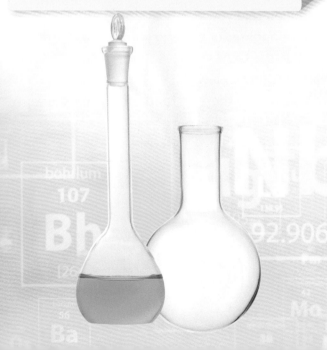

常見癌症治療方式

chemotherapy 化學治療
為治療癌症的方式之一，有時也直接簡稱為 chemo。是透過口服或注
射的方式讓藥物進入病人體內，以減緩癌細胞生長。

surgery 外科手術
直接切除癌症部位。

radiation therapy 放射療法
利用放射線所攜的能量來破壞染色體，使癌細胞停止生長，可用於對抗
快速分裂的癌細胞。

immunotherapy 免疫療法
利用增強免疫系統的機制來治療癌症。

targeted therapy 標靶療法
藉由藥物阻斷癌細胞的增殖與擴散，抑制腫瘤血管生長，使癌細胞停止
繼續增生或繁殖。

📺 看影集

瓦特來到傑西的住處，向他提議。

Walt:　You lost your partner today. What's his
　　　name? Emilio? Emilio is going to prison.
　　　The DEA took all your money, your lab.
　　　You got nothing. **Square one**. But you
　　　know the business, and I know the
　　　chemistry. I'm thinking … maybe you
　　　and I could partner up.

Jesse: You want to cook crystal meth? You and,
　　　uh … and me?

Walt:　That's right … or I turn you in.

瓦特：　你今天失去了你的搭檔。他叫什麼名字？艾米利
　　　歐？艾米利歐要去坐牢。緝毒署沒收了你所有錢
　　　和你的實驗室。你現在一無所有。要從頭來過。
　　　但你知道怎麼交易，而我懂化學。我在想……也
　　　許我們可以合作。

傑西：　你想做安非他命？你和，呃……我？

瓦特：　沒錯……不然我就告發你。

學英文 🎧 19

square one　起點，起頭

玩大富翁時，大家都要從第一格（square one）出發，抽
命運牌若遭遇不幸，會被罰回到第一格重玩，因此 back
to square one 引申為「前功盡棄」，一切要「從頭來
過」。

A:　I hope our new plan works.
　　希望我們的新計畫順利。
B:　Me too. Otherwise we'll have to go back to square one.
　　我也是。不然我們就得從頭開始了。

© Doug Kline

看影集

瓦特給傑西看他從學校偷來的設備。

Walt: You wouldn't apply heat to a volumetric flask. That's what a boiling flask is for. Did you learn nothing from my chemistry class?

Jesse: No, you flunked me. Remember? You prick! Now let me tell you something else. This ain't chemistry—this is art. Cooking is art. And the **shit** I cook is **the bomb**, so don't be telling me.

Walt: The shit you cook is shit. I saw your set-up—ridiculous. You and I will not make garbage. We will produce a chemically pure and stable product that performs as advertised. No adulterants, no baby formula, no chili powder.

Jesse: No, no. Chili p is my signature!

Walt: Not anymore.

瓦特：容量瓶不能加熱。所以才會有長頸燒瓶。你在我的化學課上什麼都沒學到嗎？

傑西：沒有，你把我當掉了。記得嗎？你這混蛋！讓我告訴你另一件事。這不是化學──這是藝術。製毒是藝術。我製的毒超勁爆的，所以輪不到你來教我。

瓦特：你製的毒是垃圾。我看過你的設備了──根本是亂搞。你和我合作不能做出垃圾。我們要製作化學性質純淨、穩定的毒品，效果就跟宣傳相符，不摻假，不加嬰兒奶粉，不加辣椒粉。

傑西：不行，加辣椒粉是我的招牌！

瓦特：不再是了。

學英文 20

shit 玩意兒，東西

shit 就是 stuff 的粗俗講法，可以指任何東西，像是Get your shit off the couch.「把你放在沙發上的東西拿走。」

A: Have you bought weed from Anton before?
　　你有跟安東買過大麻嗎？

B: Yeah. He sells some pretty good shit.
　　有啊，他的貨很不錯。

be (the) bomb 棒透了

bomb 在口語中表示「很酷炫、很棒的東西」。

A: Have you heard Eminem's new album yet?
　　阿姆的新專輯你聽過了嗎？

B: Not yet, but I hear it's the bomb.
　　還沒，但我聽說很棒。

看影集

傑西從絲凱勒那裡得知漢克是緝毒署探員之後。

Jesse: You got a brother in the goddamned DEA?!

Walt: What?

Jesse: You said you were just doing some ride-along! Yes or no—do you have a brother in the DEA?

Walt: Brother-in-law.

Jesse: Oh, now there's **a load off my mind**.

傑西：你有個兄弟在該死的緝毒署？！

瓦特：什麼？

傑西：你說你只是跟來巡邏體驗的！是或不是──你有個兄弟在緝毒署？

瓦特：是連襟。

傑西：噢，那我就放心了。

a load off one's mind 放心

解除心頭大患,就跟胸口壓一塊大石頭被移開一樣,終於能鬆一口氣。也可以說 a weight off one's mind。

A: I'm so glad dad's operation was successful.
　我真是太高興了,爸爸的手術很成功。
B: Yeah. That's really a load off my mind.
　是啊。我終於能夠放心了。

©️ 看影集

瓦特和傑西在討論如何擴大經營。

Jesse: You may know a lot about chemistry, but you **don't know jack** about *slinging dope.

Walt: Well, I'll tell you, I know a lack of motivation when I see it. You've got to be more imaginative, you know? Just think outside the box here. We have to move our production bulk wholesale now. How do we do that?

Jesse: What do you mean? To, like, a distributor?

Walt: Yes. Yes, that's what we need.

We need a distributor now. Do you know anyone like that?

Jesse: Yeah. I mean, I used to until you killed him.

傑西:你或許很懂化學,但你對販毒一竅不通。
瓦特:我這麼跟你說吧,你根本就是不夠積極。你要有點想像力,好嗎?你要跳出框架思考。現在我們必須將毒品批發販售。我們要怎麼做?
傑西:什麼意思?像是交給批發商?
瓦特:對,沒錯,這就是我們要的。我們現在需要批發商。你認識這樣的人嗎?
傑西:是啊。我是說,我本來認識,但被你殺了。

＊slinging（俚）販毒,即 selling (drugs)。

🔊 學英文 🎧22

not know jack (about) 一竅不通

在俚語中有「極少量」或「少到無價值」的意思,not know jack (about) 就是對某件事完全不懂、一竅不通。

A: Dan said he could help me fix my car.
　阿丹說他可以幫我修車。
B: Don't believe him. He doesn't know jack about cars.
　別相信他。他對車子一竅不通。

布萊恩克萊斯頓(Bryan Cranston)在《絕命毒師》當中飾演冷酷毒梟老師瓦特懷特,但頭髮留長、鬍子一刮,根本就是個溫文的歐吉桑。二〇一四年艾美獎上,《絕命毒師》是當晚的大贏家,布萊恩也得到戲劇類影集最佳男主角獎。當晚他和女演員茱莉亞路易卓佛擔任頒獎人時,揭露十多年前曾在《歡樂單身派對》(Seinfeld)軋過一角,飾演一名牙醫,還跟茱莉亞演過吻戲。當晚稍後,茱莉亞也因《副人之仁》(Veep)獲得喜劇類影集最佳女主角,上台領獎前,兩人深情一吻,成為二〇一四年艾美獎最經典的畫面。

萬惡 GOTHAM 高譚市

© FOX

23

Since Batman was created by DC Comics over 70 years ago, there have been countless adaptations, including a radio show in the 1940s, a hugely popular TV series in the 1960s, and eight films, including the [1)]**acclaimed** Dark Knight [2)]**Trilogy**. It may seem like there are no more Batman stories left to tell, but the new Fox series *Gotham* does just that—by exploring the backstory of the Batman Universe. Because Bruce Wayne is still a child at the time, *Gotham* focuses on a [3)]**rookie** police detective named Jim Gordon, who will eventually become [4)]**Commissioner** Gordon, one of Batman's most trusted allies.

DC 漫畫公司自七十多年前創造出《蝙蝠俠》後，就出現無數個改編作品，包括一九四〇年代的廣播節目、一九六〇年代廣受歡迎的電視影集，還有八部電影，其中包括備受好評的《黑暗騎士》三部曲。關於蝙蝠俠的故事似乎已經翻不出什麼新花樣了，但福斯電視網的《萬惡高譚市》藉由挖掘蝙蝠俠世界的背景故事推陳出新。由於布魯斯韋恩當時還是個小孩，因此《萬惡高譚市》將焦點放在菜鳥警探吉姆戈頓身上，他就是後來的戈頓局長，是蝙蝠俠最信任的盟友之一。

As the show opens, a young thief with catlike grace—the future Catwoman—steals a bottle of milk to feed cats in an alley, where she witnesses a double [5)]**homicide**. A masked man steals a wallet and pearl necklace from a well-dressed couple, and then murders them in front of their young son. When Jim Gordon arrives with his partner Harvey Bullock, he learns that the man was wealthy [6)]**philanthropist** Thomas Wayne, and promises his son Bruce that he'll find the killer. With no [7)]**leads**, Bullock takes Gordon to see Fish Mooney, a member of the Falcone [8)]**mob** who controls the local [9)]**turf**. At Mooney's nightclub, Gordon is [10)]**dismayed** to see one of her [11)]**underlings**, nicknamed the Penguin—yes, *that* Penguin—beating an employee accused of stealing. He's also dismayed that Bullock and Mooney are friends, as it means he's a [12)]**corrupt** cop.

超級英雄漫畫

DC Comics DC 漫畫
隸屬於華納兄弟公司，這系列漫畫還有超人（Superman）、神力女超人（Wonder Woman）、綠光戰警（Green Lantern）和閃電俠（Flash）等超級英雄。

Marvel Comics 漫威漫畫
隸屬於華特迪士尼公司，旗下有蜘蛛人（Spider-Man）、X 戰警（X-Men）、鋼鐵人（Iron Man）、浩克（Hulk）、美國隊長（Captain America）、雷神索爾（The Mighty Thor）、驚奇四超人（Fantastic Four）及夜魔俠（Daredevil）等。

© FOX

劇情一開始是一位身手像貓一樣優雅的年輕女賊——未來的貓女——偷了一瓶牛奶要餵巷子裡的野貓，她在巷子裡目睹一樁雙屍命案。一位蒙面男子從一對穿著考究的夫妻身上偷走錢包和珍珠項鍊，然後在他們的兒子面前殺了他們。吉姆戈頓和他的搭檔哈維布洛克抵達現場時，得知死者是富有的慈善家湯瑪斯韋恩，他向韋恩的兒子布魯斯保證會找出兇手。在毫無線索的情況下，布洛克帶戈頓去見費雪穆妮，她是控制該地盤的法爾科集團一員。在穆妮的夜店中，戈頓驚訝地看到她的手下之一，綽號企鵝人——沒錯，就是那個企鵝人——正在毆打一位被指控偷東西的員工。他也驚訝地發現布洛克和穆妮是朋友，這表示他是個腐敗的警察。

The connection, however, 13)**pays off**. Mooney tells them a 14)**thug** named Mario Pepper tried to sell the pearl necklace to one of her 15)**fences**. Bullock later kills Pepper in a 16)**shootout**, and the partners are praised for bringing the Waynes' murderer to justice. But then the Penguin, who is after Mooney's territory, reveals that she used the necklace to frame Pepper. Unfortunately, before the partners can 17)**apprehend** Mooney, she has her men hang them up in a meat locker. But just as they're about to be 18)**butchered**, they get rescued by crime boss Carmine Falcone, who has most of the police force on his 19)**payroll**. Falcone then orders Gordon to kill the Penguin to prove his loyalty, but Gordon lets him go before visiting the Wayne mansion, where he promises Bruce that he'll find the real killer.

不過，這樣的人脈是有好處的。穆妮告訴他們，有個名叫馬利歐佩帕的流氓想將一條珍珠項鍊賣給她手下一名黑市商人。布洛克後來在一場槍戰中殺了佩帕，他和搭檔因為將殺害韋恩夫婦的兇手繩之以法而受到讚揚。不過，覬覦穆妮地盤的企鵝人後來揭露，穆妮用項鍊陷害佩帕。不幸的是，這對搭檔在逮捕穆妮前，她已經讓手下將兩人吊在肉類冷藏櫃中。就在他們差點要被宰掉時，幾乎收買了整個警察局的黑幫老大卡麥法爾科將他們救出。然後法爾科命令戈頓殺掉企鵝人以證明自己的忠誠，但戈頓放了他，之後前往韋恩莊園，向布魯斯保證他會找到真兇。

Vocabulary 🎧 24

1) **acclaimed** [ə`klemd] (a.) 受到讚揚的
The acclaimed orchestra is performing at the concert hall tonight.

2) **trilogy** [`trɪlədʒi] (n.) 三部曲
Have you read the Lord of the Rings trilogy?

3) **rookie** [`rʊki] (n.) 新兵，新手，菜鳥
The team has added several rookies this season.

4) **commissioner** [kə`mɪʃənə] (n.) 官員，長官，委員
A new police commissioner will be appointed next month.

5) **homicide** [`hɑmə,saɪd] (n.) 殺人
The woman's death was ruled to be a homicide.

6) **philanthropist** [fɪ`lænθrəpɪst] (n.) 慈善家
Bill Gates is one of the world's leading philanthropists.

7) **lead** [lid] (n.) 線索，提示
The police are investigating a new lead in the murder case.

8) **mob** [mɑb] (n.) 犯罪集團，（大寫）黑手黨
The mob boss was murdered by a rival gang.

9) **turf** [tɜf] (n.) 地盤，勢力範圍，草皮
The two gangs are involved in a turf war.

10) **dismay** [dɪs`me] (v.) 使驚慌，使失望，使氣餒
Dana's parents were dismayed by her decision to leave school.

11) **underling** [`ʌndəlɪŋ] (n.) 小嘍囉，手下
The manager blamed the error on one of his underlings.

12) **corrupt** [kə`rʌpt] (a.) 貪污的，腐敗的
The corrupt official was sentenced to life in prison.

13) **pay off** [pe] [ɔf] (phr.) 得到好結果，取得成功
I hope all our hard work pays off.

14) **thug** [θʌg] (n.) 惡棍，流氓，歹徒
The victim was robbed and beaten by a group of thugs.

15) **fence** [fɛns] (n./v.) 買賣贓物的人；買賣贓物
The fence was caught with millions in stolen goods.

16) **shootout** [`ʃut,aʊt] (n.) 槍戰
The suspect was killed in a shootout with police.

17) **apprehend** [,æprɪ`hɛnd] (v.) 逮捕
The murderer was apprehended while trying to cross the border.

18) **butcher** [`bʊtʃə] (v./n.) 屠宰，殘殺；屠夫
Many villagers were butchered by enemy soldiers.

19) **payroll** [`pe,rol] (n.) 發薪名單，（公司）薪資總額，員工總數
The company added hundreds of new employees to its payroll last year.

看影集

© FOX

在警察局裡，有個嫌犯奪走一位警察的槍，並用槍頂著那位警察的頭，結果戈頓把槍搶回。

Bullock: What the hell are you doing? We **had the drop on** him.

Gordon: Yeah, well, he's dropped, isn't he?

Bullock: You could've gotten hurt. Rookie mistake. Next time, shoot the son of a bitch.

Gordon: If I shoot, that sets everybody off. Gunfire **every which way**.

Bullock: Somebody takes a **cop**'s gun, you shoot him. That's basic.

布洛克：你在做什麼？我們已經瞄準他了。

戈　頓：是啊，他已經被制伏了，不是嗎？

布洛克：你這樣很容易受傷。這是菜鳥才會犯的錯。下次直接開槍殺那個混蛋。

戈　頓：假如我開槍，大家都會跟著開，那子彈就滿天飛了。

布洛克：只要有人奪警槍，你就對他開槍。這是基本的。

學英文 25

have the drop on sb. 先發制人

這句話是指「先一步拿槍指著對方」，被槍指著的人自然是動彈不得了，引申為「先發制人，佔上風」。也可以說 get the drop on sb.。

A: How do you get the drop on your competitors?
你們是怎麼贏過競爭對手的？

B: We offer fast, free delivery.
我們提供快速且免費的配送。

every which way 到處亂跑

字面上的意思是「四面八方到處都是」，也表示「完全失控」。

A: What's it like driving in Manila?
在馬尼拉開車是什麼樣子？

B: It's pretty scary. You have cars and scooters coming at you every which way.
相當恐怖。到處都是汽車、機車朝你衝過來。

看影集

戈頓和布魯斯說話，並保證會找出殺害他父母的兇手，布洛克為此斥責他。

Bullock: Listen, hotshot. Do me a favor. Don't start talking to witnesses until I say so.

Gordon: What's your problem?

Bullock: My problem, soldier boy, you just caught us a gigantic flaming ball of crap.

Gordon: Oh, yeah? How's that?

Bullock: You never heard of Thomas and Martha Wayne?

Gordon: Yeah, sure. The Wayne Foundation.

Bullock: Yeah, two of the richest and most powerful people in Gotham. You can't begin to imagine the pressure if we don't close this thing quick.

這些字都是「警察」

cop 是「警察」（police officer）最常見的口語說法。cop 是從 copper 這個字而來，cop 當動詞有「逮住」的意思，copper 即「抓（壞蛋）的人」，但現在 copper 這個字已經不再使用。除此之外，**the fuzz**、**the heat**、**pig(s)**、**bacon**、**po-po** 也都是警察的俚語說法。

Five-O 警察
源出於一九七〇年代極受歡迎的影集《檀島警騎》（*Hawaii Five-O*），講述夏威夷（美國第五十州，五十即five-o）一個地方警局的故事。

narc 臥底緝毒警員
是指 narcotics agent。

Fed 聯邦執法人員
即 federal law enforcement personnel，如 FBI 幹員、聯邦法警等。

rent-a-cop 保全人員
字面上是「租來的警察」。

Gordon: So let's close it quick.
Bullock: Yeah, right. This is a random street robbery, Holmes. **Perp** could be any one of 10,000 **mopes** out there.

布洛克：聽著，高手。幫幫忙。除非我說可以，否則不要跟目擊者說話。

戈　頓：你有什麼問題？

布洛克：我的問題，阿兵哥，就是你害我們接到一個燙手山芋。

戈　頓：喔，是嗎？怎麼說？

布洛克：你沒聽過韋恩夫婦湯瑪斯和瑪莎嗎？

戈　頓：當然聽過。韋恩基金會。

布洛克：沒錯，高譚市最有錢、最有權勢的兩個人。我們要是不盡快破案，你無法想像這壓力會有多大。

戈　頓：那我們就快點破案。

布洛克：最好是。這是街頭隨機搶劫案，福爾摩斯先生。在街頭遊蕩的那一萬個無賴都有可能是犯人。

看影集

布洛克想請警長准許他換搭檔。

Captain: First a crime wave and now this. You take all the people and resources you need. You just close this case.
Bullock: Yes, Captain. Jim, will you give us a minute?
Gordon: Captain. *[leaves office]*
Captain: The answer is no. **Teach him the ropes**.
Bullock: On a weak case?
Captain: Yes.

警　長：先是犯罪率激增，現在又出了這事。需要多少人力和資源都可以給你們。只要能破案。

布洛克：是的，警長。吉姆，能讓我跟警長單獨談談嗎？

戈　頓：警長。（離開辦公室）

警　長：答案是不行。教他怎麼做。

布洛克：用這麼難破的案子？

警　長：對。

學英文 26

teach/show sb. the ropes 帶某人入門

以前船上的菜鳥水手都必須跟老鳥學打好幾十條桅繩來固定船隻，ropes 因此引申為「特殊的程序及相關細節」。這句話表示帶領人了解一項工作的技巧，或是做某件事的方法，

A: Can you show me how to use this software?
你可以教我使用這種軟體的方法嗎？
B: I'm no expert. You should ask Jerry in IT. He can show you the ropes.
我不是專家。你該問資訊技術部門的傑瑞。他會教你。

等到技藝學成就是老手了，learn the ropes 就表示「掌握訣竅」，也就是「上手」。

A: I had a really bad first day at work.
我工作的第一天超級不順的。
B: Don't worry; things will get better after you learn the ropes.
別擔心，等你上手後就會好轉了。

警用俚語

perp 犯案者
perp 即 perpetrator 的簡稱。perp walk 則是指警方移送嫌犯過程中，押著嫌犯讓媒體進行拍照。

mope 流浪漢
mope (around) 是「鬱悶，無精打采的閒逛」，當名詞就是處於這種狀態的人，是美國東岸警察的俚語。

bracelets 手銬
字面上是「手鐲（複數）」，即 handcuffs 的意思。

ex-con 前科犯
con 是 convict「罪犯」的簡稱。

rap sheet 前科紀錄
rap 是指法官宣判之後敲小木槌的聲音，因此 rap sheet 就是被判犯罪的紀錄。

B&E 非法入侵
breaking and entering，是指入侵他人房屋或產業非法取得財物，等於 burglary。

the farm 勒戒所
戒毒療養中心，即 rehab。

pat sb. down 搜身
字面上是「把一個人從頭到腳拍一遍」，也就是檢查身上是否藏有武器、毒品等等。

hinky 有嫌疑的
這個字當形容詞有「怪怪的」意思。

collar 逮住
這個字就是「狗項圈」，當動詞表示「逮住」，也可以說 hook「勾住」。

看影集

企鵝人帶著情報來找重案組的警探蒙托亞和艾倫。

© FOX

Penguin: Mario Pepper was framed by Fish Mooney and the cops. I saw Ms. Mooney with Martha Wayne's necklace. She was discussing how to get it into Pepper's home, inside a bag of drugs. This was shortly after she met with Detectives Bullock and Gordon from the homicide squad.

Allen: Mooney works with Carmine Falcone's mob. You saying Falcone had the Waynes killed?

Penguin: I'm just telling you what I saw.

Montoya: Why snitch on your own boss?

Penguin: I confess. That poor orphan boy **pricked my conscience**.

Allen: Nah. You want to push Fish out, huh?

Penguin: That's **beside the point**. I've done my civic duty. Good day to you both.

企鵝人：馬利歐佩帕被費雪穆妮和警察陷害了。我看到穆妮手上有瑪莎韋恩的珍珠項鍊。她在討論怎麼把項鍊放在一袋毒品中送到佩帕家裡。這件事發生在她跟命案小組的警探布洛克和戈頓見面後不久。

艾　倫：穆妮是幫卡麥法爾科集團工作的，你是說法爾科叫人殺了韋恩夫婦？

企鵝人：我只是告訴你們我所看到的。

蒙托亞：為什麼要告發你老闆？

企鵝人：我承認。那個可憐的孤兒讓我良心發現。

艾　倫：不對。你想除掉費雪，對吧？

企鵝人：那不是重點。我已經盡我市民的義務了。告辭了，兩位。

歷屆貓女比一比

© Helga Esteb / Shutterstock.com

卡麥蓉畢坎多瓦（Camren Bicondova）在《萬惡高譚市》當中飾演十四歲的貓女。

© Featureflash Photo Agency / Shutterstock.com

蜜雪兒菲佛（Michelle Pfeiffer）在一九九二年電影《蝙蝠俠大顯神威》飾演大導演提姆波頓（Tim Burton）版的貓女。

© s_bukley / Shutterstock.com

荷莉貝瑞（Halle Berry）在二〇〇四年電影《貓女》當中的造型，應該是影視史上穿著最清涼的。

© Everett Collection / Shutterstock.com

安海瑟薇（Anne Hathaway）是二〇一二年電影《黑暗騎士：黎明升起》的優雅貓女。

prick one's conscience 讓人良心發現

conscience 是「良心,道德感」,當你說 have a clean/
clear conscience,表示「問心無愧」。prick 表示「刺
(激)」,prick one's conscience 就是使人拿出良心。

A: Why did you donate money to that charity?
　　你為何捐錢給那個慈善機構?
B: Seeing those photos of starving children pricked my
　　conscience.
　　看到那些飢餓孩童的照片讓我良心發現。

beside the point 無關緊要

point 是「重點」,beside the point 表示沒有針對問題的
重點,也可以說 beside the question。而 to the point 就是
「切中要點」了。

A: But what I did isn't illegal.
　　但我做的事又沒違法。
B: That's beside the point. It's still wrong.
　　那不是重點。錯就是錯。

📷 看影集

布洛克開車載戈頓到碼頭,打開後車廂,戈頓發現企鵝人在
裡面。

Penguin: Please, please, I beg of you!
Bullock: Shut up! This is the fool that snitched
to Montoya and Allen. Falcone wants
you to walk him to the end of that
pier and put a bullet in his head.
Then everybody knows you're **with
the program**.
Gordon: And if I don't?
Bullock: Then I'm supposed to take you out,
and him too. And here's the thing,
Jim. I like you. I might **not have the
stomach** to do it, but I'll try.

企鵝人: 拜託,拜託,我求你!
布洛克: 閉嘴!就是這個笨蛋向蒙托亞和艾倫告狀。法
爾科要你帶他走到碼頭的盡頭,然後朝他的頭
開槍。這樣大家就會知道你很配合。
戈 頓: 假如我不做呢?
布洛克: 那我就得殺了你,還有他。讓我告訴你,吉
姆。我欣賞你。我可能沒膽這麼做,但我會盡
量做。

重案組

Major Crimes Unit 也叫 Major Case Squad,隸屬於各郡
(county)或城市的警察局(PD),負責偵辦重大案件,
但各地 Major Crimes Unit 的職掌範圍並不相同。以 NYPD
(紐約市警察局)為例,重案組要負責的是藝術品竊盜
案(art theft)、搶劫銀行(bank robbery)、勒索銀行
(bank extortion)、綁架(kidnapping)、公路搶劫貨車及
貨物(hijacking)、商業盜竊(commercial burglary)等重
大犯罪。

get with the program 配合,識時務

program 就是一套做事的計劃,get with the program 表
示遵守規則做該做的事,或是因應眼前的新局勢做調
整。

A: You look depressed. What's wrong?
　　你看起來不太開心。怎麼了嗎?
B: The boss told me I'd better get with the program if I
　　want to keep my job.
　　老闆說如果我想保住工作,就要好好配合。

not have the stomach 沒那個膽子(做某事)

中文用膽子代表勇氣,英文則可用stomach「胃」來代
表。可以說 not have the stomach for sth. 或 to do sth.。

A: Do you want to see that new horror movie with me
　　tonight?
　　你今晚想跟我一起去看那部新的恐怖片嗎?
B: Ooh, no. I don't have the stomach for scary movies.
　　才不要。我沒那膽看恐怖片。

另一個類似的片語是 not have the heart to...,這可不是
無心做某件事,而是太有同理心以致於「不忍心」去做
某件事。

A: Do the kids know that you had to put Princess to sleep?
　　孩子們知道你不得不讓公主(編註:寵物名)安樂死嗎?
B: No. I didn't have the heart to tell them.
　　不知道。我不忍心告訴他們。

CSI: CYBER
CSI 犯罪現場：網路犯罪

CSI: Crime Scene Investigation, the police drama about a team of Las Vegas crime scene investigators, was so popular that it ran for 16 seasons and [1)]**inspired** several [2)]**spin-offs**. First came *CSI: Miami* in 2002, then *CSI: New York* in 2004. And now there's *CSI: Cyber*, which follows an [3)]**elite** team of Washington-based FBI agents responsible for investigating Internet-related crimes all over the country. Led by [4)]**behavioral** [5)]**psychologist** Dr. Avery Ryan, the team includes ex-[6)]**Marine** Elijah Mundo, white hat hacker Daniel Krumitz, and Raven Ramirez and Brody Nelson, former black hat hackers now working for the good guys.

The team's first case begins when six-month-old Caleb Reynolds is [7)]**kidnapped** in Baltimore, Maryland. When the team arrives in Baltimore, they don't have much to work with—the Reynolds heard foreign voices coming from their Natal-Cam baby monitor, and the neighbors' kid Denny saw a woman enter a waiting car. But the wife is acting [8)]**suspicious**, so Avery has a DNA test done and discovers that Mr. Reynolds isn't the baby's father. Mrs. Reynolds has been having an [9)]**affair** with Bill Hookstraten, who

　　關於拉斯維加斯一個鑑識科團隊的警匪劇，《CSI：犯罪現場》，因為大受歡迎而播映長達十六季，並衍生出各種系列作品。首先是二○○二年的《CSI 犯罪現場：邁阿密》，然後是二○○四年的《CSI 犯罪現場：紐約》。現在又有了《CSI犯罪現場：網路犯罪》，敘述華盛頓聯邦調查局的一個菁英探員團隊，負責調查全美各地的網路犯罪案。由行為心理學家艾芙莉萊恩博士為首，團隊成員有前海軍陸戰隊成員伊利加孟多、白帽駭客丹尼爾克萊姆茲，還有曾經是黑帽駭客，現在改邪歸正的蕾文拉米瑞茲和布洛迪奈爾森。

網路犯罪相關字彙

cybercrime 網路犯罪
cyber- 這個字首表示「電腦的」，當名詞是指使用者之間透過網路密集互動的虛擬空間。cybercrime 也稱作 computer crime，是指透過網路從事犯罪活動，因此利用 chat room（網路聊天室）、e-mail、social media（社群網站）、行動電話都涵蓋在內。

hacker 駭客
由於現在政府、金融機構作業都已電腦網路化，駭客入侵（hacking）這類網路犯罪行為能造成極嚴重的危害，因此政府單位會招募訓練網路高手擔任 white hat hacker（白帽駭客），維護資訊系統的安全。而利用網路技能犯罪的駭客，就是 black hat hacker（黑帽駭客）。

malware 惡意軟體
即 malicious software，透過軟體安裝毀壞或變更作業系統，輕者只是藉此在網頁上插入廣告，重者可竊取電腦中的資訊。

identity theft 竊取個人資料
identity 是「身分」，identity theft 是竊取帳號、密碼、信用卡號、身分證號碼等個人資料之後，冒用他人身分進行違法行為。

[10)]**installed malware** on her computer to see photos of his baby. Avery and Elijah rush to Bill's boat shop, where they find him holding a baby, which the [7)]**kidnappers** gave him in exchange for $75,000. There's only one problem—the baby isn't Caleb!

　　本劇的第一樁案件是六個月大的迦勒雷諾茲在馬里蘭州的巴爾的摩市遭到綁架。當團隊抵達巴爾的摩時，他們得到的線索不多——雷諾茲夫婦聽到嬰兒監視器傳出說外語的聲音，鄰居的小孩丹尼則看到一名女子進入一輛等在路旁的汽車。但由於雷諾茲太太的行為可疑，因此艾芙莉做了DNA檢測，發現雷諾茲先生不是嬰兒的父親。雷諾茲太太一直與比爾胡斯川廷有婚外情，他在她的電腦裡安裝惡意軟體，好觀看他孩子的照片。艾芙莉和伊利加趕到比爾的小艇工場，發現他抱著一名嬰兒，是綁匪以七萬五千美元賣給他的。不過，問題是，這名嬰兒不是迦勒！

From a [11)]**fingerprint** Avery finds on the baby's diaper, they identify one of the kidnappers, and Raven and Brody use **social media** to track down her and her boyfriend. As they make the arrest, however, a [12)]**sniper** takes them both out. Caleb isn't there, but they find the memory card from the baby monitor, which reveals that a criminal gang is [13)]**hacking** into Natal-Cams to find kidnapping targets and selling the babies to international [14)]**bidders**. When they have the Natal-Cam **network** shut down, the gang sends a video of Caleb to Denny's video game [15)]**console**, threatening to kill the baby if they don't [16)]**restore** the network. Luckily, the team is able to use a [17)]**safeguard** in the console to trace the gang to a [18)]**warehouse** in New Jersey, and Caleb is safely returned to his parents.

　　根據艾芙莉在嬰兒尿布上找到的指紋，他們確認其中一名綁匪身分，蕾文和布洛迪則用社群媒體追蹤綁匪和她的男友。但是當他們在逮捕綁匪時，一名狙擊手出現，將兩名綁匪殺了。迦勒不在現場，但他們找到嬰兒監視器的記憶卡，發現有一個犯罪集團駭入嬰兒監視器，尋找綁架目標，然後將嬰兒賣給出價的國際買家。當他們關閉嬰兒監視器網絡時，犯罪集團將迦勒的影片傳送到丹尼的電玩主機，威脅若是不恢復網絡系統，就會撕票。幸好團隊利用主機的防護裝置追蹤犯罪集團，發現他們藏身在紐澤西州的一座倉庫，於是迦勒安全回到父母身邊。

© CBS

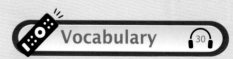
Vocabulary 🎧 30

1) **inspire** [ɪn`spaɪr] (v.) 賦予……靈感，激勵
The novel was inspired by the author's childhood experiences.

2) **spin-off** [`spɪn،ɔf] (n.) 衍生劇，副產品
American Idol is a spin-off of the British show *Pop Idol*.

3) **elite** [ɪ`lit] (n.) 菁英的，頂尖的
Lionel Messi belongs to an elite group of world-class athletes.

4) **behavioral** [bɪ`hevjərəl] (a.) 行為的
Behavioral problems can affect children's ability to learn.

5) **psychologist** [saɪ`kɑlədʒɪst] (n.) 心理學家，心理醫師 (n.) psychology 心理學
Paul is seeing a psychologist to deal with his depression.

6) **marine** [mə`rin] (n.) （常大寫）海軍陸戰隊隊員
Justin has wanted to be a Marine ever since he was a little boy.

7) **kidnap** [`kɪd،næp] (v.) 綁架 (n.) kidnapper 綁匪
A group of tourists was kidnapped in the Philippines.

8) **suspicious** [sə`spɪʃəs] (a.) 多疑的，可疑的
The villagers are very suspicious of strangers.

9) **affair** [ə`fɛr] (n.) 婚外情
Roger divorced his wife after he found out she was having an affair.

10) **install** [ɪn`stɔl] (v.) 安裝，設置
Can you help me install this program?

11) **fingerprint** [`fɪŋgə،prɪnt] (n.) 指紋
The suspect's fingerprints were found on the murder weapon.

12) **sniper** [`snaɪpə] (n.) 狙擊手，狙擊兵
The candidate was shot and wounded by a sniper.

13) **hack (into)** [hæk] (v.) 駭客入侵（電腦、語音信箱等）
The criminals hacked into the bank's computer system and stole millions of dollars.

14) **bidder** [`bɪdə] (n.) 買家，出價競標者 (v.) bid 投標，喊價
The painting will be sold to the highest bidder.

15) **console** [`kɑn،sol] (n.) 主機，遊戲機，控制台
Which game console do you have?

16) **restore** [rɪ`stor] (v.) 復原，修復
How do I restore the original settings on my computer?

17) **safeguard** [`sef،gɑrd] (n./v.) 防護裝置、措施；防護，保護
A healthy diet is a safeguard against illness.

18) **warehouse** [`wɛr،haʊs] (n.) 倉庫
The company's warehouse is located near the harbor.

© CBS

看影集

艾芙莉和伊利加抵達辦公室，他向她報告綁架案。

Elijah: I put Caleb Reynolds' photo out on the wires, notified **TSA**, contacted Baltimore **PD**. It took me a bit, but I finally **got** Detective Cho **on the horn**. CSI has already processed the perimeter. He's gonna hold the rest of the crime scene for us—so he says. State Police, Highway Patrol have already mobilized check points. **Amber Alert** has been issued as well.

Avery: Morning.

Elijah: Morning.

伊利加：我將迦勒雷諾茲的照片放上網絡，通知了運輸安全局，也聯絡了巴爾的摩警局。我花了點時間，但終於和卓警探通上電話。鑑識科已經處理了現場周遭。他會替我們保留犯罪現場的其他部分，這是他說的。州警和公路巡警已經動員設置檢查站，安珀警報也已經發佈了。

艾芙莉：早安。

伊利加：早安。

學英文 31

(get sb.) on the horn 跟人通電話
horn 有「電話」的意思，on the horn 就是「接通電話」。

A: Is Daniel coming with us on the sales call?
丹尼爾要跟我們一起去拜訪客戶嗎？

B: I'm not sure. Let me get him on the horn and ask him.
不確定耶。我去打電話問他。

看影集

艾芙莉、丹尼爾和布洛迪剛抵達雷諾茲一家的住處。

Avery: Krumitz, head up to the nursery. Nelson will be right in.

Daniel: What? You're sticking me with newbie Nelson? The guy I busted?

Brody: Hey, chubby, keep my name out of your mouth. I'm not your braces.

Avery: Enough. Nelson, **zip it**. Krumitz, **game face**. A baby's life's **at stake**. Focus.

Brody: That's the guy that busted me?

Avery: Krumitz—he's the best white hat hacker in the world. You hack it, he will come.

Brody: So is that why the judge sent me to you?

Avery: The judge sent you to me in the hopes

you wouldn't spend the rest of your life behind bars. The rules are simple.

Brody: Yeah, I know. Hack for good, prove my worth? Obey all orders? Yeah, I got it.

Avery: You're forgetting the **fine print**. One mistake—federal **pen**, five years.

艾芙莉：克萊姆茲，到育嬰房。奈爾森等一下就去。

丹尼爾：什麼？妳要把新人塞給我？我逮到的傢伙？

布洛迪：喂，胖子，別把我的名字掛在嘴邊。我不是你的牙套。

艾芙莉：夠了，奈爾森，別說了。克萊姆茲，正經點，有個嬰兒命在旦夕，專心點。

布洛迪：逮到我的就是那傢伙？

艾芙莉：克萊姆茲，他是這世上最厲害的白帽駭客。你非法侵入，他就來抓你。

布洛迪：所以法官才把我送到妳這裡？

艾芙莉：法官把你送到我這裡，是希望你不要下半輩子在牢裡度過。規則很簡單。

布洛迪：好了，我知道。當個好駭客，證明我有價值？遵守所有命令？好了，我知道了。

艾芙莉：你忘了還有附註條款。一犯錯，聯邦監獄，五年。

game face 正經點
是指比賽前換上認真嚴肅的表情及態度，不要嘻皮笑臉。

fine print 附屬細則
也寫做 small print，合約、聲明書等文件的詳細條件及規定，會以極小的字體附加在文件後面，常引申為「細節」的意思。

© CBS

學英文 32

zip it 閉嘴

等於 zip your lips，字面意思是「把嘴唇的拉鍊拉上」，當然就是「閉嘴」了。也可以說 zip it up。

A: Daddy, daddy, I want some ice cream!
爸爸，爸爸，我要吃冰淇淋！

B: Zip it, Billy. No dessert till you finish your dinner.
閉嘴，比利。要等到你吃完晚餐才能吃甜點。

at stake 處於危急關頭，吉凶未卜

stake 有「危險、風險」的意思，某樣人事物處於 at stake 的狀況，就代表前途不明，有遭逢厄運的危險。

A: The town should be evacuated before the hurricane hits.
這個鎮應該在颶風侵襲前撤離居民。

B: I know. Thousands of lives are at stake.
對啊。成千上萬的生命遭受威脅。

看影集

艾芙莉和上司賽門討論綁架案。

© CBS

Avery: So let's say that the kidnappers did steal **Baby Doe** and Caleb. Why sell Hookstraten the wrong baby?

Simon: OK. Maybe this **bait and switch** was on purpose. They know Hookstraten is desperate. He buys the wrong baby. He realizes it's not his. The kidnappers turn around and sell him the real one, but for more money.

Avery: I don't know. It doesn't **add up**.

Simon: No, I know. It doesn't add up, because… how can a second baby go missing and nobody even phones it in?

Avery: Well, law enforcement, somewhere, must've **dropped the ball**. We should've been notified by now.

艾芙莉：假如綁匪真的綁走了無名嬰兒和迦勒，為什麼要把錯的嬰兒賣給胡斯川廷？

賽　門：好，也許掉包嬰兒是故意的。他們知道胡斯川廷在情急之下會贖回錯的嬰兒，等發現不是他的孩子後，綁匪會帶著真的孩子回來找他，但會要求更高的贖金。

艾芙莉：我不知道。這聽來不合理。

賽　門：我知道這不合理，因為……有另一個嬰兒失蹤了，怎麼沒有人報警？

艾芙莉：嗯，執法單位在某個地方一定有所疏忽。我們不應該到現在都還沒接到通知。

Baby Doe 身份不明的嬰兒

在身份尚待查證或必須保密的情況下，男性會以 John Doe 代稱，女性會以 Jane Doe 代稱，也常指身份不明的屍體。對白中則以 Baby Doe 代稱身份不明的嬰兒。

學英文 33

add up 說得通

字面上的意思是「加起來」，如果加起來的數目跟總計相合，就是正確無誤，引申為「合理，說得通」的意思。這個說法一般用在否定句。

A: Why do you think the victim's boyfriend is the one who killed her?
你為何覺得被害者的男友就是殺害她的人？

B: Something about his story just doesn't add up.
他的一些說詞根本說不通。

drop the ball 失誤

該接住的球卻掉到地上，也就是「未能達成任務」或「沒有把握機會」的意思。

A: Why are you so nervous about this project?
這個專案為什麼讓你這麼緊張？

B: Because the boss said he'd fire me if I dropped the ball.
因為老闆說要是搞砸了，他會開除我。

看影集

一名醫生給艾芙莉和賽門看女綁匪屍體的掃描圖像。

Doctor: Found unusual scar tissue under both breasts. If there was an enhancement or a reduction, I'd expect to see a single scar. Your kidnapper had at least a dozen procedures.

Avery: She was **muling** drugs.

Doctor: Probably carrying them in her silicone implants. You can see here where they cut her open and sewed up her breasts to transport the drugs.

Simon: Both a **mule** and a saddlebag. It's a tough way to make a living.

Avery: No wonder she wanted out. Explains why she and Ricky **went rogue**; sold

the Harrisburg baby to Hookstraten;
cross their boss, which got them killed.

Doctor: Sounds like he'll stop at nothing to
keep his business going.

Simon: We're looking for a target who
graduated from **drug trafficker** to
child trafficker.

醫　生：兩個乳房下方都發現奇怪的疤痕組織。假如做
過隆乳或縮乳手術，應該只有一道疤痕。你們
的綁匪做過至少十幾次手術。

艾芙莉：她在運毒。

醫　生：應該是用植入的矽膠夾帶毒品。你們看，他們
在乳房這裡開刀後縫上，運送毒品。

賽　門：不但要運送毒品，還要充當藏毒容器。這樣討
生活還真不容易。

艾芙莉：難怪她想逃出來。所以她和瑞奇鋌而走險，把
海瑞斯堡的嬰兒賣給胡斯川廷。和他們的老大
作對，害死了自己。

醫　生：聽起來他會不惜代價，繼續做他的買賣。

賽　門：我們要找的目標已經從毒品走私犯變成嬰兒走
私犯了。

bait and switch 上鉤再掉包法

bait 是「（放餌）引誘」，這種商業手法是以廣告宣傳超低價，把人
吸引上門之後，再想辦法說服顧客買高價品。儘管多少涉及廣告不實
（false advertising），但已經被廣泛採用，幾乎所有打超低價的廣告，
背後目的都是要 bait and switch，例如用賠錢的價格廣告某樣商品做為
「帶路貨」（loss leader），客人到店之後才發現該商品早就賣完，
只好改買其他產品，或是吸引消費者上門購買商品的延後提貨券（rain
check），也會順便買其他東西。

© CBS

 學英文 🎧 34

go rogue 鋌而走險

rogue 有「離群猛獸（尤其是公象）」的意思，go rogue
因此表示不再聽從指揮，獨自行動。

A: Why was the dog put to sleep?
為什麼讓那隻狗安樂死？

B: Because it went rogue and started attacking people.
因為牠兇性大發，開始攻擊人類。

走私及運毒相關字彙

mule 走私闖關者

mule「騾子」要馱著 saddlebag「馬鞍兩邊掛的貨物袋」跋山涉水，用
來形容夾帶違禁品（contraband）闖關的人，再適合也不過了。這個字
也可以當動詞，指「走私闖關」。將物品塞在行李或車廂當中，或是藏
在身上走私（smuggle）的人，都叫 mule。運毒者（drug mule）經常
將裝有毒品的小容器吞到肚子裡，或塞到肛門裡，闖關之後再排出或取
出，也稱為 drug trafficker。

human trafficking 販賣人口

透過綁架、拐騙或脅迫將人運送他處販賣，大多成為娼妓或奴隸，甚至
遭人摘取器官。受害者大多為婦女及兒童，現已成為僅次於毒品、槍枝
走私的全球第三大非法交易。

派翠西亞艾奎特（Patricia Arquette）在《CSI 犯罪現場：網路犯罪》飾演的艾芙
莉萊恩是科學辦案的 FBI 幹員，有趣的是，她上一次主演電視影集《靈媒緝兇》
而大獲好評的角色，卻是以通靈能力協助檢察官辦案的靈媒。

出身演藝世家的派翠西亞最為人津津樂道的，就是一家三代都是藝人，含她在內
一共五個兄弟姐妹全部進入演藝界，影集《六人行》裡飾演莫妮卡的寇特妮考克
斯（Courteney Cox）還是她的弟媳。想像一下他們家吃年夜飯的場景，真是星光
閃閃啊！

唐頓莊園
DOWNTON ABBEY

© ITV

Set during the [1)]**reign** of King George V in the early 20th century, the acclaimed British series *Downton Abbey* is a historical drama about the lives of the [2)]**aristocratic** Crawley family and their [3)]**domestic** servants. Downton Abbey is the [4)]**seat** of Lord Robert Crawley, [5)]**Earl** of Grantham, who married a rich American [6)]**heiress**, Cora Levinson, to save his [7)]**estate** from [8)]**financial** [9)]**ruin**. Unfortunately, an **entail**—a type of traditional trust—requires that the estate can only be [10)]**inherited** by a male heir, and the Crawleys only have three daughters.

英國影集《唐頓莊園》是一部備受好評的歷史劇，場景設在二十世紀初英王喬治五世的統治時代，是關於貴族世家考利一家和家僕的生活。唐頓莊園是格蘭特罕伯爵羅伯考利的宅邸，為了挽救陷入財務困難的莊園，他娶了一位富裕的美國女繼承人珂拉萊文森。不幸的是，限定繼承──一種傳統的信託──規定莊園只能由男繼承人繼承，而考利家只有三個女兒。

It seems that Lord Grantham has solved this problem by arranging for his oldest daughter Mary to marry her cousin Patrick, but as the first episode begins, a cable arrives with news that Patrick and his father have died in the sinking of the Titanic. Lord Grantham's mother Violet feels that the entail should be broken so that Mary can inherit the estate, a

© ITV

entail 限定繼承

限定繼承是以不容後人更改條件的嚴格方式將財產傳下去。在封建時期歐洲，為了確保家族地位顯赫，都會將財富及土地集中於族長一人手中，以免子孫代代分割財產，偌大家產最終化為烏有。如果族長有能力掙得額外財富，就有資格處分自己那份財產，否則限定繼承來的財產，只能繼續限定繼承下去。根據英國法律，一九九六年之後就不再有限定繼承的遺囑，entail 這個字眼也只會出現在電影、小說中了。

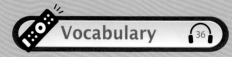

Vocabulary 36

1) **reign** [ren] (n.) 統治
The king's reign lasted for 30 years.

2) **aristocratic** [ə,rɪstə`krætɪk] (a.) 貴族的，有貴族氣派的，儀態高貴的
Christina comes from an aristocratic family.

3) **domestic** [də`mɛstɪk] (a.) 家庭的，家務的
The woman was a victim of domestic violence.

4) **seat** [sit] (n.) 宅邸，所在地，活動場所
The Hague is the seat of the Dutch government.

5) **earl** [ɝl] (n.) 伯爵
The Earl of Southampton was Shakespeare's patron.

6) **heiress** [`ɛrɪs] (n.) 女性繼承人，男性繼承人為 heir
Joan Kroc was heiress to the McDonald's fortune.

7) **estate** [ɪ`stet] (n.) 莊園，地產，遺產
The estate includes a big house, a tennis court and swimming pool.

8) **financial** [faɪ`nænʃəl] (a.) 金融的，財務的
There's a rumor that the company is having financial difficulties.

9) **ruin** [`ruɪn] (n./v.) 傾家蕩產，崩潰；使破產，毀滅
Venezuela is facing economic ruin.

10) **inherit** [ɪn`hɛrɪt] (v.) 繼承，遺傳
William inherited the business from his father.

11) **prospect** [`prɑspɛkt] (n.)（成功的）可能性、期望，前景，前途
Doctors say there is little prospect of saving the patient.

12) **suitor** [`sutɚ] (n.) 追求者
The pretty girl was always surrounded by suitors.

13) **duke** [duk] (n.) 公爵，女公爵、公爵夫人為 duchess
The duke and duchess live on a large estate.

14) **dalliance** [`dæliəns] (n.) 短暫戀情、性關係
The mayor's dalliance with a married woman caused a scandal.

15) **quarter** [`kwɔrtɚ] (n.) 住宿，住處（固定用複數）
The host showed us to our quarters.

16) **sabotage** [`sæbə,tɑʒ] (v./n.) 破壞，妨害
The opposition party tried to sabotage the negotiations.

17) **kindhearted** [,kaɪnd`hɑrtɪd] (a.) 好心的，仁慈的
The orphan was adopted by a kindhearted couple.

[11)]**prospect** that attracts a new [12)]**suitor**, the young [13)]**Duke** of Crowborough. But the Duke has also come to Downton to see footman Thomas Barrow, who he had a previous "[14)]**dalliance**" with in London, and when Lord Grantham tells him that he doesn't plan to fight the entail, he cuts his visit short.

為了解決這個問題，格蘭特罕伯爵已安排他的大女兒瑪麗嫁給堂哥派翠克，但在第一集當中，一份越洋電報帶來消息，派翠克和他的父親因搭乘沉沒的鐵達尼號而喪生。格蘭特罕伯爵的母親薇樂認為應該打破限定繼承的規定，讓瑪麗繼承莊園，而這樣的可能性引來新的追求者，是年輕的克羅伯勒公爵。不過，克羅伯勒公爵到唐頓莊園還有另一個目的，是來看男僕湯瑪斯巴洛，是他曾經在倫敦的「露水情緣」，而當格蘭特罕伯爵告訴克羅伯勒公爵，他不打算打破限定繼承的規定時，公爵便很快離去。

Meanwhile, down in the servants' [15)]**quarters**, Lord Grantham's new valet, John Bates, arrives to begin work. Mr. Carson, the butler, worries that his bad leg—which was injured when he served with Lord Grantham in the Boer War—will affect his duties, but housemaid Anna takes a liking to him. Thomas, who wanted the position for himself, plots with Cora's maid, O'Brian, to [16)]**sabotage** him. They nearly succeed in getting him fired, but at the last minute, the [17)]**kindhearted** Lord Grantham decides to give him another chance. When it comes to the entail, however, his mind is made up. The episode ends with Matthew Crawley, a young Manchester lawyer and distant cousin of Lord Grantham, receiving a letter informing him that he is heir to the Grantham estate.

同時，在僕人的樓下起居場景中，格蘭特罕伯爵的新貼身男僕約翰貝茲報到並開始工作。管家卡森先生擔心他跛腳——在波耳戰爭中服侍格蘭特罕伯爵時受傷的——會影響工作，但女僕安娜喜歡上他。覬覦貝茲職位的湯瑪斯，與珂拉的女樸歐布萊恩一起設計陷害他。他們差點害他被解雇，但在千鈞一髮之際，好心的格蘭特罕伯爵決定再給他一次機會。不過，在限定繼承方面，他已經做好決定。第一集結束時，住曼徹斯特的年輕律師馬修考利，也是格蘭特罕伯爵的遠房堂弟收到一封信，通知他是格蘭特罕莊園的繼承人。

© ITV

看影集

湯瑪斯在格蘭特罕伯爵的更衣室解說貝茲先生的工作內容。

Thomas: There's some cedar-lined cupboards in the attics for things that aren't often worn, travelling clothes and such. Mr. Watson used them to rotate the summer and winter stuff. I'll show you later.

Bates: What about **studs** and **links**? Do I choose them, or does he?

Thomas: Lay them out unless he asks for something in particular. These for a ball, these for an ordinary dinner, these only in London.

Bates: I'll **get the hang of** it.

Thomas: Yeah, you'll have to.

湯瑪斯：閣樓有一些雪松木櫃，用來放不常穿的衣物，像旅行用的衣服等。沃森先生用它們來更換夏季和冬季的衣物。我等一下帶你去看。

貝　茲：飾紐和袖扣呢？是要我選，還是他來選？

湯瑪斯：將它們擺出來，除非他特別要求要哪一組。這些是舞會用的，這些是一般晚餐用的，這些只有去倫敦時用。

貝　茲：我會學起來的。

湯瑪斯：是啊，你必須學起來。

學英文 🎧 37

get the hang of… 抓到……的竅門

hang有「竅門」、「做法或用法」之意，片語 get / have the hang of … 即指「抓到……的竅門，對……上手」。

A: Can you eat with chopsticks?
你會用筷子吃飯嗎？

B: Not very well, but I'm starting to get the hang of it.
不是很會用，不過我越來越上手了。

西裝飾品配件

studs 飾紐，用來扣住襯衫胸前的特殊扣孔（這種襯衫沒有釦子）。穿這種襯衫時要打 **bow tie**（蝴蝶領結），才不會把飾紐擋住。

links 袖扣，是 cufflinks 的簡稱，用來扣住襯衫袖口，必須是袖口兩邊都是扣孔（沒有釦子）的襯衫才能使用。

珂拉和薇樂在討論限定繼承引起的問題。

Cora: Now a complete unknown has the right to pocket my money, along with the rest of the swag.

Violet: The problem is, saving your dowry would break up the estate. It would be the ruin of everything Robert's given his life to.

Cora: And he knows this?

Violet: Well, if he doesn't, he will.

Cora: Then there's no answer.

Violet: Yes, there is, and it's a simple one. The entail must be smashed in its entirety, and Mary recognized as heiress of all.

Cora: There's nothing we can do about the **title**.

Violet: No. She can't have the title. But she can have your money, and the estate. I didn't run Downton for thirty years to see it go **lock, stock, and barrel** to a stranger from **God knows where.**

Cora: Are we to be friends, then?

Violet: We are allies, my dear, which can be a good deal more effective.

珂拉：現在一個陌生人有權侵吞我的財富，還有其他財產。

薇樂：問題是，挽救妳的嫁妝會讓莊園破產。羅伯特一生的心血都會付諸流水。

珂拉：他知道這點嗎？

薇樂：就算他現在不知道，遲早也會知道的。

珂拉：結果還是無解。

薇樂：有解，而且很簡單。限定繼承必須打破，讓瑪麗成為繼承人。

珂拉：但爵位的問題無法解決。

薇樂：沒辦法。她無法繼承爵位。但她可以繼承妳的財產，還有莊園。我經營莊園三十年，不是為了看到它全部落入不知道從哪冒出來的陌生人手裡。

珂拉：那我們現在要成為朋友了嗎？

薇樂：我們是站在同一陣線，親愛的，這樣會更有效率地達成目標。

lock, stock, and barrel 一股腦兒全部

這三個字分別是早期毛瑟槍（musket）的三個部分 lock「擊槌」、stock「槍托」、barrel「槍管」，加起來就是整把槍，引申為「全部」。

A: Did you lose anything in the fire?
你們在那場火災中有損失嗎？

B: Yes. We lost everything—lock, stock, and barrel.
有囉。我們變得一窮二白——什麼都沒了。

God (only) knows... 天曉得⋯⋯

God knows 表示「（除了上帝之外）沒人曉得」，God knows where 就是「來路不明」的意思，God knows 後面可以接任何 wh- 疑問詞（when、what、why、who、how 等）。heaven (only) knows 的意思與用法完全相同。

A: I can't figure out what Alison sees in her husband.
我真不懂艾莉森看上她先生哪一點？

B: Me neither. God only knows why she married that jerk.
我也不懂。天知道她為何要嫁給那個混蛋。

英國世襲貴族爵位

duke 公爵	duchess 公爵夫人
marquess 侯爵	marchioness 侯爵夫人
earl 伯爵	countess 伯爵夫人
viscount 子爵	viscountess 子爵夫人
baron 男爵	baroness 男爵夫人

英國的貴族大致分為世襲貴族（hereditary peerage）和終身貴族（life peerage）。世襲貴族所生的子女皆會自動繼承爵位，同時也具有上議院（House of Lords）議員的身分，但在一九九九年上議院法令修正之後，大部分的世襲貴族已失去上議員資格。

要注意的是，男爵／女爵並非全為世襲，這個爵位雖為王室中最低的位階，卻是終身貴族中的最高位置。英國規定上議院議員必須有男爵以上爵位，為了讓一些人，如大法官，進入上議院，會將他們冊封為終身制男爵。

終身貴族的稱號無法繼承給子女，且只授予男爵爵位，受封者除了因特殊成就、高尚品行而獲得此殊榮，也有些特殊職位通常會在任期結束後得到此身分，如首相、下議院（House of Commons）議長、坎特伯里大主教、財政大臣、內政大臣，或是首席法官等人。

對公爵及夫人的尊稱是 Your / His / Her Grace，其他爵位的統稱 Your Lord / Lady、His Lordship、Her Ladyship。在《唐頓莊園》中，由於裡面的僕從都是在 Lord Grantham 的領地討生活，因此會聽到僕從以 milord / milady 稱呼家裡的老爺夫人，也就是 My Lord/Lady 的意思。至於男爵以下位階的貴族，就以 Sir 稱呼。

看影集

歐布萊恩和湯瑪斯在討論家庭律師喬治穆瑞到訪的目的。

O'Brien: Well, Murray didn't stay long.

Thomas: Does Her Ladyship know how they left it?

O'Brien: No. They talked it all through on their way back from the church.

Thomas: If I was still his **valet**, I'd get it out of him.

O'Brien: Bates won't say a word.

Thomas: He will not? I bet you a tenner he's a spy in the other direction. I wanted that job. We were all right together, His Lordship and me.

O'Brien: Then be sure to **get your foot in the door** when Bates is gone.

Thomas: Can't get rid of him just 'cause he talks behind our backs.

O'Brien: There's **more than one way to skin a cat.**

管家及僕從

butler 管家，在過去皆為男性，為男性僕人（male servant）的總管。

valet 男主人的貼身男僕。

footman 馬車隨扈，跟著馬車跑的壯丁，在可能發生翻車的地方（陷入溝渠、卡到樹根等等）穩住車輛，並在快到目的地時，先跑去主人下榻處預作準備。由於用到 footman 的機會不多，男僕薪資又高過女僕，備有 footman 就成為一個家庭財力的象徵。

housekeeper 家務長，在過去皆為女性，為女性僕人（female servants）的總管。

lady's maid 女主人的貼身女僕。

housemaid 資深女傭，依照負責區域分為各種資深女傭，如：

· **parlor maid** 打理客廳及起居室

· **chamber maid** 打理房間，確保壁爐用火安全，供應熱水

· **laundry maid** 負責寢具、毛巾及全屋上下所有人衣物的清洗及熨燙

nursery maid 育嬰室女傭，打理育嬰室

cook 廚師，負責準備餐點

kitchen maid 廚娘，協助廚師管理廚房，有時會負責煮員工餐

· **scullery maid** 廚房清潔婦，負責清洗鍋碗瓢盆、刷廚房地板

歐布萊恩：嗯，穆瑞沒有待太久。

湯瑪斯：格蘭特罕夫人知道他們怎麼談的嗎？

歐布萊恩：不知道，他們從教堂回來一路上都在談。

湯瑪斯：假如我還是他的貼身男僕，我會打探出來的。

歐布萊恩：貝茲什麼都不說。

湯瑪斯：他不說？我打賭十英鎊，他是另一邊的間諜。我本來要那份工作。我們相處融洽，伯爵大人和我。

歐布萊恩：那麼貝茲離開時你自己找機會。

湯瑪斯：用他在我們背後說壞話的理由趕不走他。

歐布萊恩：要達到目的，辦法有很多種。

學英文 39

get one's foot in the door 搶佔先機

這個說法源自推銷員的技巧，登門推銷十之八九會吃閉門羹，但若一開始就把腳踩進門口，讓門關不起來，就能開始推銷，增加成功的機會。引申為搶佔先機、創造機會。

A: Why are you willing to accept such a low salary?
你為什麼願意接受這麼低的薪水？

B: I just want to get my foot in the door. That company has plenty of chances for advancement.
我只是想要搶佔先機。這間公司有很多升遷機會。

more than one way to skin a cat 方法多的是

字面上是「剝貓皮的方法不只一種」，表示要達到目的有很多辦法。

A: How can I afford to buy a house if the bank won't give me a loan?
如果銀行不貸款給我，我哪有能力買房子？

B: Don't worry. There's more than one way to skin a cat.
別擔心。方法多的是。

看影集

湯瑪斯向克羅伯勒公爵要求一份工作，這樣他們就能在一起。

Thomas: I want to be a valet. I'm sick of being a **footman**.

Duke: Yeah, Thomas, I don't need a valet. I thought you were getting rid of the new one here.

Thomas: I'll have done it, but I'm not sure Carson's gonna let me take over. And I want to be with you. *[they kiss]*

Duke: I just can't see it working, can you? We don't seem to have the basis of a **servant** / master relationship, do we?

© Twocoms / Shutterstock.com

皇家雅士谷賽馬於每年六月下旬舉辦五天，吸引超過三十萬人前來，是歐洲最大規模的賽馬會。主辦單位規定參加者必須遵守嚴格的服裝規定，而且不論男女都必須配戴大於十公分的頭飾，因此男士都戴上大禮帽，女性都會戴頭飾，尤其第三天 Ladies Day「仕女日」更是活動最高潮，現場女性無不極盡誇張之能事，在頭頂爭奇鬥豔。

逍遙音樂節每年夏天在皇家阿爾伯特音樂廳舉辦八週。這個古典音樂節會場不設座椅，參加民眾可以隨著樂曲和聲哼唱，在場內隨意走動，故稱 promenade「散步、兜風」。

© Twocoms / Shutterstock.com

伊麗莎白二世偕夫婿菲利浦親王出席皇家雅士谷賽馬。

© Bikeworldtravel / Shutterstock.com

以前，英國上流社會大多住在鄉間，國會開議等重大政治、社交活動，都安排在倫敦氣候最宜人的春、夏兩季。王公貴族過完耶誕節後紛紛回到城內，在私人大宅裡開舞會，或參加各種社交俱樂部的活動，適婚貴族男女也會趁機到處串門子，尋找結婚對象。到了隔年六月底，大家就趁天氣轉涼之前打道回府，一年的倫敦社交季節於焉落幕。

這種風氣在十九世紀達到鼎盛，二十世紀初第一次世界大戰期間，大部份貴族都將倫敦大宅脫手，貴族在私宅舉辦社交活動的做法已不復見，但上流社會仍保留大型聯誼的傳統，即便是在倫敦以外舉辦，也都被視為倫敦社交季節的一環，而且種類五花八門，如逍遙音樂節（Proms）、溫布敦網球錦標賽（Wimbledon）、切爾西花卉展（Chelsea Flower Show）、皇家雅士谷賽馬（Royal Ascot）等等都是。

湯瑪斯：我想當貼身男僕。我不想再繼續當侍從了。

公　爵：好了，湯瑪斯，我不需要貼身男僕。我以為你要趕走這裡新來的那個。

湯瑪斯：我會趕走他的，但我不確定卡森會不會讓我接手。我想跟你在一起。（兩人接吻）

公　爵：我看不到我們的未來，你呢？我們的主僕關係似乎無法發展，不是嗎？

© 看影集

湯瑪斯和公爵繼續他們的對話。

Thomas: You came here to be with me.

Duke: Among other reasons. And **one swallow doesn't make a summer**.

Thomas: Aren't you forgetting something?

Duke: What? Are you threatening me? Because of a youthful dalliance? A few weeks of madness in a **London season**?

湯瑪斯：你來這裡，就是為了跟我在一起。

公　爵：還有其他原因。不要太樂觀了。

湯瑪斯：你是不是忘了一件事？

公　爵：什麼？你在威脅我嗎？因為年少時那段風流事？倫敦社交季時，那幾個星期的瘋狂之事？

學英文 🎧 40

one swallow doesn't make a summer
不要太樂觀

字面上是「看見一隻燕子，不代表夏天來了」，表示只有一件好事發生，不代表整個情況就會改觀，這句諺語是要人不要過度樂觀。

A: Did you see how well the stock market did today? Maybe the recession is ending.
你有看到今天股市的亮麗表現嗎？不景氣可能要結束了。

B: Well, maybe. But one swallow doesn't make a summer.
哎，或許吧。但你別過度樂觀。

© Mystic Soul Fan Art / Flickr

the BiG BANG THEORY 宅男行不行

In an age where [1)]**geeks** are cool, it's not surprising that *The Big Bang Theory* is one of the most popular [2)]**sitcoms** on TV. What's so funny about geeks? Well, not much…until they start trying to [3)]**interact** with the opposite sex, that is. Leonard Hofstadter and Sheldon Cooper are both brilliant Caltech [4)]**physicists**—they have a combined I.Q. of 360—who share an apartment in Pasadena, California. They're [5)]**content** to spend their free time reading comic books and playing video games, until they return home one day to find a pretty [6)]**blonde** named Penny moving into the apartment across the hall. Developing an instant [7)]**crush**, Leonard invites Penny over for lunch, where they learn that she's a Cheesecake Factory waitress and [8)]**aspiring** actress, and she learns that they're *"Beautiful Mind* [9)]**genius** guys."

在這個當宅男才酷的時代，《宅男行不行》理所當然成為最受歡迎的情境喜劇之一。宅男有什麼好玩的？這個嘛，其實沒什麼好玩的……除了他們想跟異性互動的時候，這就好玩了。倫納德霍夫斯塔特和謝爾頓庫珀都是絕頂聰明的加州理工學院物理學家——兩個人的智商加起來是三百六十——他們在加州帕沙第納市合租一間公寓。他們平常有空時樂於看漫畫、打電玩，直到有天回到家時，發現對面搬來一位名叫佩妮的金髮美女。倫納德瞬間為之傾倒，邀請佩妮到家裡吃午餐。他們於是得知佩妮在起司蛋糕工廠（編註：美國連鎖餐廳）當服務生，也一心想成為演員。佩妮也得知他們都是「《美麗境界》的天才」。（編註：《美麗境界》敘述患有精神疾病的數學家約翰奈許的故事，由羅素克洛主演）

Penny also gets to meet Leonard and Sheldon's two other [10)]**nerd** friends—also Caltech scientists—when they drop by with a

Big Bang 大爆炸

又稱「大霹靂」，是受到普遍支持的宇宙誕生理論，簡單來說，就是宇宙是由一個密度極大、溫度極高的大爆炸而來，爆炸之後宇宙不斷膨脹至今日的狀態。

Stephen Hawking 史蒂芬霍金博士

英國物理學家史蒂芬霍金患有漸凍症（ALS），他最廣為人知的著作，就是全球暢銷書《時間簡史：從大爆炸到黑洞》（*A Brief History of Time: from the Big Bang to Black Holes*）。霍金不只著作受到大眾歡迎，還曾在影集《宅男行不行》當中客串演出。他與第一任妻子珍王爾德（Jane Wilde）的故事，更被改編成賣座電影《愛的萬物論》（*The Theory of Everything*）。

" [11]**fantastic**" **Stephen Hawking** video. While Howard tries to impress Penny with [12]**creepy** [13]**pick-up lines**, Raj is so shy around women that he doesn't say a word. Will Penny be able to bring this group of geeks out of their shells? In Leonard's case—he's [14]**determined** to win Penny's heart—the answer is yes. "Our babies will be smart and beautiful," he says, to which Sheldon responds "Not to mention [15]**imaginary**." And Raj's silence turns out to be an advantage—a girl he meets at Penny's Halloween party thinks he's a "good listener," and ends up in his bed. Penny also sets Howard up with a co-worker who's working on her Ph.D. in [16]**microbiology**, but Sheldon, who has [17]**OCD** and doesn't like [18]**physical** contact, is a more difficult case. Will he ever find—or even touch—a woman? You'll have to watch *The Big Bang Theory* to find out!

倫納德和謝爾頓另外兩個宅男朋友——也是加州理工學院的科學家——帶著「一級棒的」史蒂芬霍金影片來找他們家時，佩妮也因此認識了這倆人。霍華德想用怪怪的搭訕開場白引起佩妮注意，拉傑卻只要在女人旁邊，就害羞到說不出話來。佩妮有辦法讓這群宅男敞開心扉嗎？以倫納德來說——他下定決心要贏得佩妮的芳心——答案是肯定的。倫納德說「我們的寶寶一定會聰明又漂亮。」對此謝爾頓的回答是：「而且只存在於你的想像中。」拉傑的沉默寡言到頭來變成優點——他在佩妮的萬聖節派對上認識的女孩覺得他是個「很好的傾聽者」，後來還跟他上床。佩妮還撮合霍華德和她正在攻讀微生物學博士學位的同事。不過，謝爾頓就比較難了，因為他有強迫症，不喜歡跟別人身體接觸。他到底能不能找到——甚至是碰觸——女人呢？那你就得收看《宅男行不行》才能知道了！

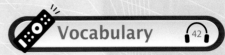

1) **geek** [gik] (n.) 科技迷，宅男
   All the geeks at our school hang out at the computer lab.

2) **sitcom** [ˈsɪtˌkɑm] (n.) （電視）情境喜劇，為 situation comedy 的簡稱
   Friends is my favorite sitcom.

3) **interact** [ˌɪntɚˈækt] (v.) 互動，互相影響
   In small classes, students can interact more with their teachers.

4) **physicist** [ˈfɪzɪsɪst] (n.) 物理學家；physics [ˈfɪzɪks] (n.) 物理學
   The physicist spent years studying the properties of light.

5) **content** [kənˈtɛnt] (a.) 滿意的，滿足的
   If you're not content with your marriage, you should get a divorce.

6) **blonde** [blɑnd] (n.) 金髮女人（金髮男人為 blond）
   Is Shelly a natural blonde?

7) **crush** [krʌʃ] (n.) （口）迷戀，迷戀的對象
   Have you ever had a crush on one of your teachers?

8) **aspiring** [əˈspaɪrɪŋ] (a.) 有抱負的，有志氣的，有意成為……的
   Most aspiring authors never get their books published.

9) **genius** [ˈdʒinjəs] (n.) 天賦，天才
   Mozart was a musical genius.

10) **nerd** [nɝd] (n.) 宅男，書呆子
    Those glasses make you look like a nerd.

11) **fantastic** [fænˈtæstɪk] (a.) 了不起的，極好的
    We had a fantastic time at the resort.

12) **creepy** [ˈkripi] (a.) （口）怪怪的、令人反感的
    Why does Susan always go out with such creepy guys?

13) **pick-up line** [ˈpɪkʌp][laɪn] (n.) 搭訕把妹的開場白（pick up 即「把妹」的意思）
    Do you know any good pick-up lines?

14) **determined** [dɪˈtɝmɪnd] (a.) 有決心的
    I'm determined to finish writing this report before I go home.

15) **imaginary** [ɪˈmædʒəˌnɛri] (a.) 想像的，虛構的
    The movie is set in an imaginary world.

16) **microbiology** [ˌmaɪkrobaɪˈɑlədʒi] (n.) 微生物學
    The researcher is an expert in microbiology.

17) **OCD** [ˈoˈsiˈdi] (n.) 強迫症（即 obsessive-compulsive disorder）
    Some cases of OCD can be treated with therapy.

18) **physical** [ˈfɪzɪkəl] (a.) 身體的，肉體的
    All students are required to take physical education.

© Doug Kline / flickr

看影集

倫納德與佩妮在走廊上初次見面。

Leonard: We don't mean to interrupt, we live across the hall.

Penny: Oh, that's nice.

Leonard: Oh…uh…no…we don't **live together**…um…we live together, but in separate, **heterosexual** bedrooms.

Penny: Oh, OK, well, guess I'm your new neighbor, Penny.

Leonard: Leonard, Sheldon.

倫納德：我們無意打擾，我們就住在對面。

佩　妮：喔，那很好啊。

倫納德：噢……呃……不是……我們不是同居……嗯……我們是住在一起，但睡不同房間，是異性戀。

佩　妮：喔，好，我想我是你們的新鄰居，我叫佩妮。

倫納德：我叫倫納德，他是謝爾頓。

學英文 43

live together 同居

上面的對白中，倫納德結結巴巴是因為 live together 本身有兩個涵義，其一是與人合住一房，其二是未婚同居。現今的社會風氣開放，不論是何種性別組合、哪種關係同居，外人都無法置喙，但對佩妮一見鐘情的倫納德怕跟另一個男人同居，會影響到他對佩妮的追求，只好努力解釋。

A: Did you and Mom live together before you got married?
你跟媽結婚之前就同居嗎？

B: No. Things were much more conservative back then.
沒有。過去的民風比現在保守多了。

sexual orientation 性傾向字彙

在現今風氣自由開放的社會中，大眾對於多元的性傾向，態度從反彈、歧視逐漸轉而寬容、接受。orientation 是「方向，傾向性」的意思，sexual orientation 則是指一個人在情感和生理上會被男性或是女性吸引。

heterosexual 異性戀

heterosexual [ˌhɛtərəˋsɛkʃʊəl] 是由代表「相異、不同」的 hetero- 組成。

straight 異性戀

雖然異性戀的正式說法是 heterosexual，但口語上更常用 straight。

homosexual 同性戀

homosexual [ˌhoməˋsɛkʃʊəl] 是由代表「相同、相等」的 homo- 組成。同性戀的其他說法：

queer [kwɪr] 原本有歧視意味，但後來同志開始以此自稱，顛覆其負面意涵。

fag 是 faggot [ˋfægət] 的簡稱，帶有貶義，不可用這個字稱呼同志。

LGBT 同志族群及非異性戀者

LGBT 指的是 lesbian、gay、bisexual 和 transgender 這四個字的英文縮寫。因為原先的「同性戀」一詞被認為含義太狹窄，所以在一九九〇年代 LGBT 一詞逐漸普及，泛指同志族群以及所有的非異性戀者。

lesbian 女同性戀

中文的「蕾絲邊」亦是源出此字，dyke [daɪk] 也代表女同志，和 queer 一樣原本帶有歧視意味，後來開始有女同志以此自稱，雖然如此，但還是儘量不要用這個字來稱呼。若要細分女同志的角色，butch [butʃ] 和 bull dyke 指的就是比較陽剛的女同志，也

就是台灣常說的 T，這個說法是從 tomboy「有男生氣息的女生」而來的，但其實這個字在英文中並不會和女同志做聯想，單純是台灣人的說法。比較柔性的女同志，則稱做 femme [fɛm]，相當於台灣說的「婆」。

gay 男同性戀

這個字原本是「開心，無憂無慮」的意思，後來逐漸轉為指同志（尤其是男同志）。在英文中，形容男同志的說法有很多，例如 bear [bɛr] 指的就是體型壯碩、毛髮較多的男同志，twink [twɪnk] 是體型纖細、年輕的男同性戀者，還有俗稱男同志的「一號」為 top，「零號」則是 bottom。

bisexual 雙性戀

不僅被單一性別對象給吸引，對於男、女皆會產生愛戀者。

transgender [ˌtrænsˋdʒɛndə] 是指不認同自己性別的人，許多有變裝甚至變性的行為，但跨性別者不一定是同性戀。

Battlestar Galactica《星際大爭霸》

《星際大爭霸》最初是一九七八年於美國廣播公司（ABC）播映的科幻戰爭影集，由環球影業製作。Battlestar Galactica「銀河號」是人類十二艘戰星（battlestar，即「太空母艦」）當中，唯一未被機器人敵軍賽隆人（Cylons）殲滅的，其任務是要保護僅存的人類艦隊在宇宙中航行，找到傳說中的第十三個殖民地，也就是地球。

這部影集很受歡迎，但在電腦動畫技術尚未普及的年代，儘管片中不斷重複使用許多特效鏡頭，每集成本仍是天價，ABC 於七個月後播映二十一集後停播該節目，憤怒的影迷甚至跑到公司總部外抗議。

而對白中謝爾頓和倫納德談論的，是二〇〇五年起在科幻頻道（Syfy Channel）播出的同名影集重製版，不論編劇、特效、音效都很精良，水準遠高於原作，獲得許多獎項，至二〇〇九年第四季全劇播畢。

© danieldoan / flickr

一九七八年版的銀河號模型，陳列於科幻小說博物館（Science Fiction Museum）

© s_bukley / Shutterstock.com
2009 年試映會上提供拍賣的賽隆人機器人偶。

🄫 看影集

倫納德與謝爾頓回到公寓。

Leonard: Should we have invited her for lunch?

Sheldon: No. We're going to start Season Two of *Battlestar Galactica*.

Leonard: We already watched the Season Two DVDs.

Sheldon: Not with commentary.

Leonard: I think we should be good neighbors, invite her over, make her feel welcome.

Sheldon: We never invited Louis/Louise over.

Leonard: Well, then that was wrong of us. We need to widen our circle.

Sheldon: I have a very wide circle. I have 212 friends on Myspace.

Leonard: Yes, and you've never met one of them.

Sheldon: That's **the beauty of it**.

倫納德：我們該請她吃午餐嗎？

謝爾頓：不用，我們要開始看《星際大爭霸》第二季。

倫納德：我們已經看過第二季的 DVD 了。

謝爾頓：幕後評論還沒看過。

倫納德：我覺得我們應該做個好鄰居，請她過來，讓她感覺賓至如歸。

謝爾頓：我們從來沒請路易斯／蘿依絲（編註：Penny 那間房原本住了一位變性人，Louis/Louise 發音相近，是前鄰居變性前後的名字）過來。

倫納德：那個，那是我們的錯。我們應該擴大我們的交友圈。

謝爾頓：我的交友圈已經很大了。我的 Myspace（社群網站）上有兩百一十二個朋友。

倫納德：是啊，但你一個都沒見過。

謝爾頓：這就是它的美妙之處。

💬 學英文 🎧 44

the beauty of something 美妙之處

這裡的 beauty 不是指外觀的美醜，而是指一件事物讓人愉悅的部分。

A: Your cousin is defending you for free?
你的表哥要免費幫你辯護？

B: Yeah. That's the beauty of having a lawyer in the family.
是啊。家裡出了個律師就是有這種好處。

© BagoGames / Flickr

SONY PICTURES CLASSICS

THE I

© Helga Esteb / Shutterstock.com

吉姆帕森斯（Jim Parsons）（左）在片中飾演天才物理學家謝爾頓，他在片中的女性朋友愛咪是一位智力與他不相上下的腦神經科學家。有趣的是，飾演這位絕頂聰明女性的演員馬伊姆拜力克（Mayim Bialik）（右）真的是畢業於洛杉磯大學的腦神經學博士！

看影集

佩妮到倫納德和謝爾頓的公寓吃午餐。

Leonard: Do you have some sort of a job?

Penny: Oh, yeah, I'm a waitress at the Cheesecake Factory.

Leonard: Oh, OK. I love cheesecake.

Sheldon: You're **lactose intolerant**.

Leonard: I don't eat it. I just think it's a good idea.

倫納德： 妳有在做什麼工作嗎？

佩　妮： 喔，有啊，我在起司蛋糕工廠當服務生。

倫納德： 噢，好，我很喜歡起司蛋糕。

謝爾頓： 你有乳糖不耐症。

倫納德： 我不吃起司蛋糕，我只是欣賞這個概念。

---

lactose intolerant 乳糖不耐症

lactose intolerant [ˋlæktos] [ɪnˋtɑlərənt] 是形容詞，指因身體的乳糖酶（lactase）不足，無法有效消化乳糖，而產生脹氣、腹瀉等腸胃不適，名詞為 lactose intolerance。由於這並不是免疫系統反應，不應稱其為對牛乳過敏（milk allergy）。

嬰兒很少出現乳糖不耐症，基因缺陷造成先天乳糖酶缺乏的嬰兒無法進食乳汁，在早年死亡率很高。然而一般人到成年之後，發生乳糖不耐的比例大增，這是由於大多數人在斷奶後，體內的乳糖酶就開始大幅減少，這種情況在很少食用乳製品的亞洲及非洲尤其明顯。

看影集

倫納德、佩妮、謝爾頓和拉傑在玩《最後一戰》。

Sheldon: OK, that's it, I don't know how, but she is cheating. No one can be that attractive and be this skilled at a video game.

Penny: Wait, wait. Sheldon, come back. You forgot something.

Sheldon: What?

Penny: This plasma grenade. [explosion] Ha! Look, it's raining you!

Sheldon: You laugh now. You just wait until you need tech support.

Penny: Gosh, he's kind of a **sore loser**, isn't he?

Leonard: Well, to be fair, he is also a rather unpleasant winner.

謝爾頓： 好了，受夠了，我不知道怎麼回事，但她作弊。不可能有人長得這麼美，又這麼會玩電動玩具。

佩　妮： 等等，謝爾頓，回來。你忘了一個東西。

謝爾頓： 什麼東西？

佩　妮： 電漿手榴彈。（爆炸）哈！看，我把你弄得粉身碎骨！

謝爾頓： 妳就笑吧，等妳需要技術支援時我就不理妳了。

佩　妮： 天哪，他有點輸不起，是吧？

倫納德： 嗯，說句公道話，他就算贏了也一樣討人厭。

sore loser 輸不起的人

sore 在口語中有「惱怒的」意思，loser 是「輸家」。輸了不向獲勝者道賀，也不摸摸鼻子自認技不如人，反而在那邊發脾氣，就是輸不起。

A: Rob got really mad when he lost the game.
羅勃輸掉比賽時非常生氣。

B: I'm not surprised. He's a sore loser.
不意外。他那個人輸不起。

看影集

倫納德和謝爾頓沒有從佩妮前男友那裡拿回電視後。

Leonard: I've learned my lesson. She's **out of my league**. I'm done with her. I've got my work, one day I'll win the Nobel Prize and then I'll die alone.

Sheldon: Don't think like that. You're not going to die alone.

Leonard: Thank you, Sheldon. You're a good friend.

Sheldon: And you're certainly not going to win a Nobel Prize.

倫納德：我學到了教訓。我高攀不上她。我放棄她。我有自己的工作，有一天我會得諾貝爾獎，然後我會孤老到死。

謝爾頓：別這樣想。你不會孤老到死的。

倫納德：謝謝你，謝爾頓。你真是好朋友。

謝爾頓：而且你絕對不會得諾貝爾獎的。

out of one's league 高攀不上

league [lig] 表示競賽時的等級，當我們說某人是out of one's league 時，表示某人配不上。口語常用來表示想交往的對象高攀不上，或是東西太貴買不起。

A: Do you think Christina will go out with me?
你覺得克莉斯提娜會跟我出去約會嗎？

B: No way, dude. She's way out of your league.
老弟，不可能。她是你高攀不上的。

nerd、geek 與 blonde 的刻板形象

nerd 書呆子

描寫美國青少年的電影中都會有 nerd，這種男孩會戴粗框大眼鏡（因為被欺負時眼鏡經常折斷，有時鏡架還會用膠帶黏著固定）、戴牙套（braces）、褲頭拉得老高或是穿吊帶褲，更慘一點的還滿臉青春痘（pimples）。他們常被描繪成不擅長體能活動、死讀書、喜歡下棋的社交障礙者，一般都是白種人或亞裔。

geek 電腦怪咖

geek 和 nerd 所描述的人造型很像，但 geek 更強調他們只顧著鑽研科學、電腦、科技，因此跟外界格格不入的生活方式。隨著電腦產業及網際網路的興起，往日的 geek 現已撐起世界經濟半邊天，而善於抽象思考、鑽研高深學問的 nerd 更能晉升政經學術高層，因此這兩個字已不再有那麼深的貶義。

jock 鮮肉男

相對於 geek 和 nerd 的不修邊幅與笨拙，jock 是高壯帥氣的體育健將，而且是那種頭腦簡單四肢發達、覺得所有女生都喜歡自己的草包，因此也有 dumb jock「笨伯」的說法。

blonde 金髮美女

在歐美社會當中，金髮（blond hair）的女性被視為性感美麗的象徵，身材尤其火辣的還被叫做 blonde bombshell「金髮尤物」，在影視節目中，他們的智力往往受到歧視，因此有 dumb blonde「傻大姐」的說法。相對於金髮美女被視為腦袋空空，被稱作 brunette 的「棕髮美女」往往被塑造成低調優雅的角色。

how i met your mother
追愛總動員

這部情境喜劇描述一群住在曼哈頓的朋友，這聽起來可能沒什麼創意，不過這部獲得艾美獎的影集有個出乎意料的轉折。就如片名所暗示的，《追愛總動員》是關於其中一位主角，名叫泰德莫斯比的建築師，如何認識他未來的妻子。《追愛總動員》的與眾不同之處在於以一連串的倒敘手法，由泰德向他的孩子們說故事。泰德的兒子和女兒當然知道他們的媽媽是誰，但觀眾卻不知道。

A sitcom about a group of friends living in Manhattan may not sound very original, but the **Emmy Award**-winning *How I Met Your Mother* has a 1)**twist**. As the title 2)**implies**, the show is about how one of the main characters, an 3)**architect** named Ted Mosby, meets his future wife. What makes *How I Met Your Mother* different is that the story is told by Ted to his children as a 4)**series** of 5)**flashbacks**. Ted's son and daughter, of course, know who their mom is, but the audience doesn't.

The story, as told by Ted to his son and daughter in 2030, starts back in 2005. At the time, 27-year-old Ted is sharing an apartment with Marshall, his best friend from college. Everything is going fine until Marshall **drops a bombshell**—he's going to 6)**propose** to his college 7)**sweetheart** Lily, who works as a kindergarten teacher. Realizing that it's time for him to find 8)**Miss Right**, Ted heads to the local bar with his

Emmy Award 艾美獎

為美國電視圈的年度重要盛事，其中又細分為黃金時段艾美獎（Primetime Emmy Award）、日間時段艾美獎（Daytime Emmy）及運動節目艾美獎（Sports Emmy）等類別，皆由分屬於不同機構的會員投票選出。

其他著名影視獎項：
Academy Awards 學院獎，通稱奧斯卡金像獎或奧斯卡獎（Oscars）。
Golden Globe Awards 金球獎，被稱為「奧斯卡的風向球」。
BAFTA Awards 英國影藝學院獎，由英國影劇學院（British Academy of Film and Television Arts）頒發，這個獎相當於美國的奧斯卡。
Sundance Film Festival 日舞影展，以獨立製片（independent film）為影展特色。

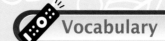

Vocabulary

1) **twist** [twɪst] (n.)（意外）轉折
The mystery novel is full of plot twists.

2) **imply** [ɪmˋplaɪ] (v.) 意味著，暗示
Are you implying that I'm the one who ate your ice cream?

3) **architect** [ˋɑrkɪˌtɛkt] (n.) 建築師
We hired an architect to design our new house.

4) **series** [ˋsɪriz] (n.) 連續，系列，一連串
A series of tests was performed on the patient.

5) **flashback** [ˋflæʃˌbæk] (n.) 倒敘法
The movie uses flashbacks to explain the killer's motives.

6) **propose** [prəˋpoz] (v.) 求婚
When are you going to propose to your girlfriend?

7) **sweetheart** [ˋswitˌhɑrt] (n.) 情人，心上人
Stella and I were childhood sweethearts.

8) **Miss Right** [mɪs] [raɪt] (phr.) 理想對象（男的為 Mr. Right）
Alan is still waiting for Miss Right to come along.

9) **playboy** [ˋpleˌbɔɪ] (n.) 花花公子
Bill Clinton is known as a playboy.

10) **break up** [brek] [ʌp] (phr.) 分手，拆夥
Debra broke up with her boyfriend last week.

11) **legendary** [ˋlɛdʒənˌdɛri] (a.) 傳說中的，著名的
The steaks at that restaurant are legendary.

---

9) **playboy** friend Barney, who tells him to "suit up!" After **striking out** with a Lebanese girl, Ted sees a beautiful woman across the room, and it's love at first sight.

泰德在二〇三〇年向兒女述說從二〇〇五年開始發生的故事。當時二十七歲的泰德和大學時代最好的朋友馬修合租公寓。一切都一如往昔，直到馬修投下了一顆震撼彈——他要向幼稚園老師莉莉，也就是他大學時期的戀人求婚。泰德意識到自己是時候找個真命天女了，於是跟花花公子朋友巴尼前往附近酒吧，而且巴尼要他「穿上西裝」！在泰德被一位黎巴嫩女孩拒絕後，他看到房間另一頭有位美麗的女人，並對她一見鍾情。

Robin, a reporter for a local TV station, agrees to go out with Ted the following night, but he scares her by telling her that he loves her on their first date. Ted and Robin decide to be friends, and later start dating again, but 10) **break up** after a year and start seeing other people. Will Ted ever get back together with Robin, or will he end up marrying one of the many other women he dates? If you want to find out, you'll have to watch all nine seasons—but don't worry, it'll be 11) **legen**…wait for it…**dary**!

地方電視台記者羅賓同意隔天晚上和泰德出去約會，但泰德在第一次約會就向羅賓表白，嚇到了她。泰德和羅賓決定先做朋友，後來又開始約會，但一年後分手，開始各自找其他對象。泰德最後會跟羅賓復合嗎？還是跟後來的眾多約會對象之一結婚？結婚？你想知道的話，就要看完所有九季的節目——不過別擔心，這將會是傳奇中的……聽好囉……傳奇！

編註：legen… wait for it… dary 是劇中丑角巴尼經常說的口頭禪，用來加強語氣，帶有「這是傳奇中的傳奇」的意味。

strike out 失敗，搞砸

原本是指棒球打擊手連續三個好球沒揮出安打，被「三振出局」，引申為「失敗」。
A: Did you manage to get that girl's phone number?
你有要到那個女生的電話嗎？
B: No. I totally struck out.
沒有。我完全失敗了。

drop a bombshell 宣布驚人消息

也可以說 drop a bomb，字面意思都是「投下震撼彈」，也就是所發佈的消息大出眾人意料，聞者無不震撼。
A: Tom really dropped a bombshell today.
湯姆今天宣布的消息真是驚人。
B: Yeah. I never thought he would get divorced.
是啊。我從沒想過他會離婚。

看影集

泰德在幫馬修練習求婚。

Marshall: *[opens wedding ring box]* Will you marry me?

Ted: Yes, perfect! And then you're engaged, you pop the champagne, you drink a toast, you have sex on the kitchen floor—don't have sex on our kitchen floor.

Marshall: Got it. Thanks for helping me plan this out, Ted.

Ted: Dude, are you kidding? It's you and Lily! I've been there for all the **big moments** of you and Lily: the night you met, your first date, other first things….

Marshall: Ha-ha, yeah, sorry. We thought you were asleep.

Ted: It's physics, Marshall—If the bottom bunk moves, the top bunk moves too.

馬修： （打開婚戒盒子）妳願意嫁給我嗎？

泰德： 很好，完美！然後你們就訂婚了，你開香檳，你們舉杯慶祝，在廚房地板上做愛——不要在我們廚房地板上做愛。

馬修： 知道了。謝謝你幫我計畫這些，泰德。

泰德： 兄弟，你在開玩笑嗎？是你跟莉莉耶！你跟莉莉的重要時光我都有參與：你們認識那一晚，你們第一次約會，還有其他第一次……。

馬修： 哈哈，是啊，不好意思。我們以為你睡著了。

泰德： 這是物理學，馬修——假如下舖在動的話，上舖也會跟著動。

學英文 🎧 50

big moment 重要時刻

畢業、求婚、結婚、生子、嫁女兒等等，這類人生重大經歷，或是期盼已久終於到來的時刻，都可稱為 big moment。

A: Why is Rachel taking so long to plan her wedding?
瑞秋為什麼要花這麼久準備婚禮？

B: It's her big moment. She wants to make sure nothing goes wrong.
這是她期盼已久的時刻。她要確定一切完美。

big time 非常多地，嚴重地

注意 big time 是副詞片語，等於 very much 的意思。

A: I couldn't have passed that class without your help.
要不是你的幫忙，我那門課一定不會過。

B: Yeah. You owe me big time.
對啊。你欠我的可多了。

看影集

巴尼和泰德在酒吧聊天。

Barney: Have you forgotten what I said to you the night we met?

[flashback to same bar, years earlier]

Barney: Ted, I'm going to teach you how to live. *[Ted is confused]* Barney, we met at the urinal.

Ted: Oh, right. Hi.

Barney: Lesson one: lose the **goatee**. It doesn't go with your suit.

Ted: I'm not wearing a suit.

Barney: Lesson two: get a suit. Suits are cool. *[points to self]* **Exhibit A.**

© CBS

各式各樣的鬍子

© Allan Bregg / Shutterstock.com

moustache 鬍髭。修得細細的短髭叫 pencil moustache「小鬍子」，若是左右各粗粗一撇，鬍梢還讓它往上翹，就是 handlebar moustache「八字鬍」。

© Helga Esteb / Shutterstock.com

soul patch 靈斑。下唇下面中間一小撮鬍子。

© Jaguar PS / Shutterstock.com

sideburns 鬢角。是將耳際的鬢毛連著兩腮的鬍子剃出形狀。

© Helga Esteb / Shutterstock.com

stubble 鬍渣。stubble 是「稻／麥田收割之後留在田間的稻／麥桿」。這種造型是指沒有刮鬍子，或是早上刮過，但忙了一天鬍子又長出來的樣子，因此也稱作 five o'clock shadow「下午五點的鬍渣」。為了製造這種慵懶粗獷的造型，現在已有附專用刀頭的刮鬍刀，能在刮鬍子時故意留下短短一截。

© Chesi - Fotos CC

mutton chops 羊排落腮鬍。細細的鬢角連結兩腮大片鬍子，下巴刮淨，從正面看就像兩根羊排的樣子，如電影《X 戰警》當中的金剛狼。

© Denis Makarenko / Shutterstock.com

Van Dyke 范戴克鬍。得名自十七世紀法蘭德斯畫家 Anthony van Dyck（安東尼范戴克），這種造型在當時的歐洲很流行，不論是在他的畫作或是自畫像中都能看到。范戴克鬍基本上是鬍髭加下巴的山羊鬍（goatee），也可以將山羊鬍再修出一塊靈斑。

© Denis Makarenko / Shutterstock.com

full beard 大鬍子。只要先天條件許可，全臉的鬍子放著不管，最後就會變成大鬍子。但還是要適當修剪才有型。

巴尼：你忘了我們認識的那天晚上，我對你說的話？
（回到幾年前，在同一家酒吧）
巴尼：泰德，我要教你怎麼過日子。（泰德一臉困惑）
　　　我是巴尼，我們在廁所見過。
泰德：喔！對。嗨。
巴尼：第一課：剃掉山羊鬍，它跟你的西裝不搭。
泰德：我沒穿西裝。
巴尼：第二課：買西裝。西裝才酷。（指指自己）這就是現成的例子。

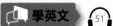 學英文 51

exhibit A 這就是現成的證明
這種說法源自在法庭上端出呈堂證物，第一個證物就稱作 exhibit A。日常生活中，當你要拿身邊的事物舉例時，就可以用上這個詞。

A: Good-looking guys never go out with ugly girls.
　　俊男絕不會跟醜女約會。
B: Sure they do. Paul and Ellen are exhibit A.
　　當然會。保羅和艾倫就是現成的例子。

看影集

莉莉回到家，發現馬修在廚房。

Lily: Ugh, I'm exhausted. It was Finger Painting Day at school, and a five-year-old boy got to **second base** with me. *[removes coat to reveal purple print on her chest]* You're cooking?

Marshall: Yes, I am.

Lily: Aw. *[they kiss]* Are you sure that's a good idea after last time? You looked really creepy without eyebrows.

莉莉：唉，我累壞了。今天學校是手指作畫日，有個五歲的男孩跟我進展到第二壘。（脫掉外套，露出胸前的紫色指印）你在煮飯啊？

馬修：是啊。

莉莉：噢。（倆人接吻）經過上次之後，你確定這還是個好主意嗎？沒有眉毛的你看起來真的很怪。

Sexual Bases
你們上幾壘了？

1st base 一壘打：親到嘴，甚至舌吻。

2nd base 二壘打：愛撫。

3rd base 三壘打：碰觸到性器官，但未性交。

home run 全壘打：性交。

上面對白中，莉莉說她跟五歲男孩「上二壘」，是拿她襯衫胸部被小孩蓋上手印這件事開玩笑。

求婚相關字彙

propose 求婚
這是動詞，名詞是 proposal。

pop the question 求婚
這裡的 question 當然就是 Would you marry me?

ask for one's hand (in marriage) 求婚
完整說法應為 ask for one's hand in marriage，但現今多將 in marriage 省略，指「男方向女方求婚」，另外要提醒一下這裡的 hand 要用單數形態表示。

engagement ring 訂婚戒指
一般只有女性在訂婚後配戴訂婚戒指，這枚戒指會戴在無名指上，因此無名指叫做 ring finger。跟 wedding ring「結婚戒指」不同的是，engagement ring 一般會有鑽石，而婚禮上雙方互換的 wedding ring 則是造型簡潔（經常無寶石）的黃金或白金環，也叫 wedding band。

fiancé 未婚夫，**fiancée** 未婚妻
發音均為 [ˌfiɑnˋse]。

wedding rings

看影集

馬修向莉莉求婚後，在廚房地板上做愛。

Marshall: I promised Ted we wouldn't do that.

Lily: Did you know there's a Pop-Tart under your fridge?

Marshall: No, but **dibs**. Where's that champagne? I want to drink a toast with my **fiancée**.

Lily: Aw.

馬修：我跟泰德保證過不這麼做的。

莉莉：你知道你家冰箱下面有果醬吐司餅乾嗎？

馬修：不知道，但現在歸我了。那瓶香檳呢？我要跟我的未婚妻乾杯。

莉莉：噢。

學英文 52

dibs 我的！
這是美國小孩玩耍或搶東西時會用到的話，用來宣示主權，表示某樣東西現在歸他了。

A: There's only one slice of pizza left.
   只剩一片披薩了。

B: Ooh, dibs!
   喔，我的！

泰德和羅賓在酒吧聊天。

Ted: So, what do you do?
Robin: I'm a reporter for Metro News 1.
Ted: Oh.
Robin: Well, **kind of** a reporter. I do those dumb little **fluff pieces** at the end of the news, you know, like, um, a monkey who can play the ukulele, but I'm hoping to get some bigger stories soon.
Ted: Bigger, like a gorilla with an upright bass? Sorry, you're really pretty.

泰德： 那妳是做什麼的？
羅賓： 我是都市新聞一台的記者。
泰德： 喔。
羅賓： 嗯，算是記者吧。我在新聞結尾報些無聊的小趣聞，你知道，就像，呃，會彈烏克麗麗的猴子，但我希望很快有天能追到更大的新聞。
泰德： 更大的新聞，就像大猩猩會拉低音提琴？不好意思，妳真的很美。

fluff (piece) 趣聞報導
新聞價值不高的溫馨故事及趣聞，在電視新聞當中一般安插於結尾，也可指報紙上的生活新知或地方趣聞。

 學英文 53

kind of 在某種程度上，有一點
kind of 表示看起來似乎是，但又不完全是。用在不想講得太白、想講卻又不知如何拿捏，或是沒有十足把握的時候。也可以說 sort of。

A: What was it like running into your old boyfriend?
碰到前男友感覺如何？
B: It was kind of strange to see him again.
再見到他感覺有點怪怪的。

尼爾派屈克哈里斯（Neil Patrick Harris）是一位多才多藝的演員，能歌善舞，身兼製作人、主持人（四次主持東尼獎、兩次主持艾美獎、二〇一五年主持奧斯卡金像獎），還是個魔術師。他在《追愛總動員》當中飾演的巴尼是個超級樂觀積極、愛穿高級西裝到處釣馬子的甘草角色，被視為該劇賣座的最大功臣。

泰德跟羅賓約會後回到公寓。

Marshall: So? Did you kiss her?
Ted: No, the moment wasn't right.
[Marshall and Lily look at Ted in disbelief]
Ted: Look, this woman could actually be my future wife. I want our first kiss to be amazing.
Lily: Aw, Ted, that is so sweet. So, you **chickened out** like a little bitch.

馬修： 怎麼樣？你跟她接吻了沒？
泰德： 沒有，時機不對。
（馬修和莉莉難以置信地看著泰德）
泰德： 唉，這女人可能真的會是我未來的妻子，我希望我們的第一次接吻是驚天動地的。
莉莉： 噢，泰德，你真是太可愛了。所以你就像個小女人一樣退縮了。

 學英文 54

chicken out 逃避退縮
chicken 在口語中有「膽小鬼」的意思，chicken out 表示因恐懼而退縮。

A: Did you go on that skydiving trip?
你有去參加跳傘之旅嗎？
B: No. I chickened out at the last minute.
沒有。我在最後一刻打了退堂鼓。

F·R·I·E·N·D·S
六·人·行

55

Over ten years and ten seasons, *Friends* [1)]**beamed** into living rooms across the U.S. and around the world, becoming one of the most popular sitcoms ever. Fans spent so much time with the characters over the years that they felt like they actually knew them: [2)]**neat freak** [3)]**chef** Monica, geeky [4)]**paleontologist** Ross, [5)]**sarcastic** [6)]**executive** Chandler, [7)]**oddball** [8)]**masseuse** Phoebe, spoiled daddy's girl Rachel and struggling actor and **ladies' man** Joey.

《六人行》在美國和全世界各地的客廳播映的十年十季期間,成為有史以來最受歡迎的情境喜劇之一。影迷們花了許多時間與劇中角色一起度過這十年,感覺自己好像真的認識這些角色:異常潔癖的廚師莫妮卡、書呆子氣的古生物學家羅斯、愛諷刺的高階主管錢德勒、怪裡怪氣的按摩師菲比、被寵壞的嬌嬌女瑞秋,還有演藝事業挫折重重的花花公子喬伊。

© Warner Bros

花花公子相關字彙

ladies' man
其實就是 playboy、player,即所謂「花花公子」。

womanizer
是「追求女性很厲害,並將女子玩弄於股掌之間的男子」。在西方傳說中,義大利的 Casanova(卡沙諾瓦)和西班牙的 Don Juan(唐璜)這兩位大情聖就是典型的 womanizer,所以人們也會拿他們的名字來代稱。

stud 原意為「種馬」,引申為性慾旺盛、性生活活躍的男人。

gigolo 舞男,也指被女性包養的小白臉。

philanderer 是指到處和人發生性關係的男子(尤指已婚男子),philander 則為動詞。

This story about six twentysomething New Yorkers begins at **Central Perk** café, where Monica is discussing her date for the evening with Joey, Phoebe and Chandler. When Ross arrives looking [9)]**miserable**, the group learns that his wife has just left him for her [10)]**lesbian** lover. But before they have time to properly comfort him, Monica's high school friend Rachel walks in wearing a wedding dress. Realizing she doesn't love her fiancé, she's just left him at the [11)]**altar** and has nowhere to go. Later at Monica's apartment, while the gang is watching a Spanish-language soap opera and trying to guess what the story is about, Rachel calls her father to tell him that the marriage is off. When he threatens to stop supporting her, she says she'll be staying with Monica—without asking first.

© Warner Bros

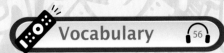

Vocabulary 56

1) **beam** [bim] (v.)（以電磁波）傳送／播送，放射（光束）
The radio program is beamed all over the world.

2) **neat freak** [nit] [frik] (n.) 有潔癖的人
My roommate is a real neat freak.

3) **chef** [ʃɛf] (n.) 主廚
The chef at this restaurant is known for his desserts.

4) **paleontologist** [ˌpelɪənˈtɑlədʒɪst] (n.) 古生物學家
The paleontologist discovered several new species of dinosaur.

5) **sarcastic** [sɑrˈkæstɪk] (a.) 諷刺的
Martha has a sarcastic sense of humor.

6) **executive** [ɪgˈzɛkjətɪv] (n.) 高階主管
Many of the company's executives received large bonuses.

7) **oddball** [ˈɑd͵bɔl] (n./a.)（口）古怪的（人）
My uncle Larry is a bit of an oddball.

8) **masseuse** [məˈsus] (n.) 女按摩師
Danielle is training to be a masseuse.

9) **miserable** [ˈmɪzərəbəl] (a.) 悲慘的，痛苦的
Thomas felt lonely and miserable after his divorce.

10) **lesbian** [ˈlɛzbɪən] (a./n.) 女同性戀（的）
It's now legal for gay and lesbian couples to get married.

11) **altar** [ˈɔltɚ] (n.) 聖壇，祭壇，供桌
The worshippers placed offerings on the altar.

12) **split up** [splɪt] [ʌp] (phr.) 分開，分手
The class split up into groups for the exercise.

13) **apologetic** [əˌpɑləˈdʒɛtɪk] (a.) 認錯的
The waiter was apologetic about bringing the wrong dish.

14) **look up** [lʊk] [ʌp] (phr.) 情況好轉，進步
After all that bad luck, things are finally looking up for me.

　　這個關於六位二十多歲的紐約人的故事在中央振奮咖啡館展開，莫妮卡在和喬伊、錢德勒和菲比討論她今晚的約會對象時，羅斯一副悽慘模樣走進咖啡館，大家於是得知他的妻子剛剛離開他，跟她的同性戀人在一起。但大家正要好好安慰他時，莫妮卡的高中同學瑞秋穿著婚紗走進咖啡館。原來瑞秋發現自己不愛她的未婚夫，剛從婚禮上逃跑，無處可去。稍晚在莫妮卡的公寓裡，大家一邊看著西班牙語肥皂劇，一邊試著猜測劇情在講什麼時，瑞秋打電話給她的父親，告訴他要取消婚約。瑞秋的父親威脅不再資助她時，她說要和莫妮卡一起住——而且事先沒徵求莫妮卡同意。

That evening, the group [12)]**splits up**. Ross, Chandler and Joey go to Ross' place to help him set up his new furniture, Monica goes on her date with Paul the "wine guy," and Rachel stays at the apartment and leaves [13)]**apologetic** messages on her fiancé's answering machine. After sleeping with Paul, Monica finds out the next day that he lied to get her in bed, the first in a long line of bad relationship choices. But things are [14)]**looking up** for Rachel. Deciding it's time to become independent, she cuts up her credit cards—with a little help from the gang—and gets her first job serving coffee at Central Perk. And then Ross asks Rachel if he can ask her out, marking the beginning of one of the most famous on-again, off-again relationships in TV history.

　　那天晚上，大家各自解散。羅斯、錢德勒和喬伊到羅斯的住處，幫他組裝新家具，莫妮卡則去跟她的約會對象「紅酒男」保羅約會，而瑞秋留在公寓裡，在她未婚夫電話的語音信箱裡留言道歉。莫妮卡跟保羅過夜後，隔天發現他是為了上床而欺騙她，這對莫妮卡所選擇的一連串糟糕的關係來說，只是剛開始而已。不過瑞秋的情況有所好轉。瑞秋決定是時候獨立了，首先要剪掉信用卡——在大家的幫忙下——接著在中央振奮咖啡館找到第一份服務生的工作。然後羅斯問瑞秋能不能和她約會，展開了電視史上最有名的分分合合關係之一。

Central Perk 中央振奮咖啡館

劇中 Central Perk café 位於中央公園旁，又與 Central Park 諧音。此外，perk 有動詞「（喝咖啡之類）感到振奮」的意思，而且 perk 當名詞又是 percolated coffee「滲濾式咖啡」的縮寫。

看影集

在中央振奮咖啡館討論莫妮卡的約會對象。

Monica: There's nothing to tell! He's just some guy I work with!

Joey: C'mon, you're going out with the guy! There's gotta be something wrong with him!

Chandler: So does he have a hump? A hump and a hairpiece?

Phoebe: Wait, does he eat chalk? *[the others stare at her]* Just, 'cause, I don't want her to **go through** what I went through with Carl!

Monica: OK, everybody relax. This is not even a date. It's just two people going out to dinner and…not having sex.

Chandler: Sounds like a date to me.

莫妮卡：沒什麼好說的！他只是跟我一起工作的人！

喬　伊：拜託，是妳要跟這人約會！他一定有什麼問題！

錢德勒：那他有駝背嗎？駝背又戴假髮？

菲　比：等等，他吃粉筆嗎？（其他人瞪著她）只是，因為，我不希望她經歷我跟卡爾經歷過的事！

莫妮卡：好了，各位別緊張。這根本不算是約會，只是兩個人一起吃晚餐，而且……不會上床。

錢德勒：對我來說，這就是約會。

看影集

瑞秋身穿濕透的婚紗，在咖啡館坐下來。

Monica: So you wanna tell us now, or are we waiting for four wet bridesmaids?

Rachel: Oh God…well, it started about a half hour before the wedding. I was in the room where we were keeping all the **presents**, and I was looking at this gravy boat, this really gorgeous Limoges gravy boat. When all of a sudden, I realized that I was more turned on by this gravy boat than by Barry! And then I got really freaked out, and that's when it hit me—how much Barry looks like Mr. Potato Head. You know, I mean, he always looked familiar, but…. Anyway, I just had to get out of there, and I started wondering, "Why am I doing this, and who am I doing this for?" So anyway I just didn't know where to go, and I know that you and I have kind of **drifted apart**, but you're the only person I knew who lived here in the city.

Monica: Who wasn't invited to the wedding….

Rachel: Ooh, I was kind of hoping that wouldn't be an issue.

📖 **學英文** 🎧 57

go through 歷經（折磨）

這個詞表示忍受痛苦才熬過來。

A: Ted's been looking terrible lately. Is he OK?
   泰德最近氣色好糟。他還好嗎？

B: No. He's going through a nasty divorce.
   不好。他正被離婚的事搞得焦頭爛額。

bridal registry 結婚禮物清單

在美國，新人會先到百貨公司或家飾大賣場註冊送禮，登記自己喜愛或需要的品項，這張清單就是 bridal registry，新人接著只要拿著條碼掃描器逛賣場，對準想要的商品「嗶一下」，這些東西就會自動列入禮物清單（registry list）。新人只要將商店的註冊碼告訴賓客，客人就能查到尚未被認購的禮物，如此禮物便不會重複了。

各種朋友關係

老是講 friend 太無趣了，可以視情況換些口語的講法，如：
pal、buddy（簡稱 bud）、bro（男性）、man（男性）、sis
（女性）。

homie 老鄉
因住在附近認識的朋友，比如從小一起玩到大的朋友。是
homeboy 或 homegirl 的簡稱，原本是幫派用語，因 rap「饒舌
歌曲」採用而廣為流傳。

BFF 最好的朋友
best friend forever 的頭字語，一般只有年輕女孩使用。

fast crowd 豬朋狗友
fast 有「放蕩」的意思，fast crowd 就是貪玩、不務正業的朋
友。

fair-weather friend 酒肉朋友
fair-weather 是「好天氣」，引申為「順遂的時候」，是指享樂
時才出現，當你有難就跑光光的朋友。

friends with benefits 炮友
有性關係的普通朋友。

brother/sister from another mother 情同兄弟／姐妹
表示兩人感情好到只差不是同一個媽媽生的。

接著補充一些跟朋友有關的說法：

bros before hoes 不會重色輕友
用來表示男性堅不可摧的兄弟情誼，不會受到女性的破壞。

ex 前男／女友
即 ex-boyfriend、ex-girlfriend 的縮寫，也指前夫或前妻。

That's what friends are for. 朋友就是應該要這樣。
做朋友就是要講義氣，

A friend in need is a friend indeed. 困境之中的朋友才是真正的朋友。
也就是「患難見真情」的意思。

莫妮卡：那妳現在想告訴我們了嗎？還是我們在等那四
　　　　個淋濕的伴娘？

瑞　秋：噢，天哪……事情在婚禮前大概半小時開始。
　　　　我在放禮物的房間裡，我看著那個肉汁盅，真
　　　　的是非常華麗的里摩瓷器（編註：有法國景德
　　　　鎮之稱，以陶瓷及琺瑯工藝聞名）肉汁盅。突
　　　　然之間，我發現我看到那個肉汁盅都比看到貝
　　　　瑞還興奮！然後我真的是嚇到了，這時突然有
　　　　個想法浮現在我腦海裡──貝瑞看起來真的很
　　　　像蛋頭先生。你們知道，我是說，他一直看起
　　　　來很眼熟，但是……反正，我就是必須離開那
　　　　裡，我開始懷疑：「我為什麼要這樣做，我這
　　　　是為了誰？」所以，反正我就是不知道要去哪
　　　　裡，我知道妳和我有點疏遠了，但妳是我在城
　　　　裡唯一認識的人。

莫妮卡：而且沒有受邀參加婚禮……。

瑞　秋：噢，我原本有點希望那不會成為問題。

© Nicescene / Shutterstock.com

學英文 🎧 58

drift apart 各奔東西，疏遠
drift 有「漂流」的意思，表示慢慢朝一個方向移動。drift
apart 就是形容昔日好友各自為生活奔忙，導致漸行漸
遠。

A: Are you and Barbara still friends?
　　妳跟芭芭拉還是朋友嗎？

B: Not really. We used to be really close, but we drifted
　apart.
　　不算是了。我們以前很要好，但慢慢就沒聯絡了。

© Warner Bros

© Warner Bros

交往狀態相關英文

既然談到 hit on（主動追求，煞到）及 hit it off（一拍即合），就來多學一點感情關係發展的說法吧！

flirt 調情
跟人眉來眼去，講一些挑逗對方的話，算是交往的最初始狀態之一。

sb. is taken 名花／草有主
也就是那個人已經有對象，你最好死了這條心。

be dating/seeing someone 交往中
是指在成為正式男女朋友之前會有的交往、約會階段，也會說 be going out with someone。

go steady 穩定交往
這是高中、大學生的講法，成年人會說 (be) exclusive（彼此認定）。若是以長期承諾（婚姻）為前提的交往，則是 long-term committed relationship。

open relationship 開放關係
相對於 long-term committed relationship，表示不介意彼此同時跟其他人交往。

break up 分手
跟 split up 意思相同。聽到心儀的人跟另一半分手，當然要趕緊去安慰他：There are plenty of fish in the sea.（天涯何處無芳草。）接著伺機趁虛而入。

dump sb. 甩掉某人
甩掉別人的人是 dumper，被甩的人則是 dumpee。

on a break 分開一陣子
目的是要給彼此一點空間冷靜一下，可別跟 break up 搞混。

be on the rocks 感情觸礁
表示彼此不睦，交往不順利。

on-again, off-again 分分合合，藕斷絲連
這個詞表示斷斷續續，經常用來形容情侶間的關係。

get back together 復合
分手之後發現舊愛還是最美，還是回到彼此身旁。

 看影集

喬伊試著「安慰」瑞秋。

Joey: Hey, you need anything, you can always come to Joey. Me and Chandler live across the hall—and he's away a lot.
MonicA: Joey, stop **hitting on** her! It's her wedding day!
Joey: What, like there's a rule or something?

喬　伊：嘿，妳需要什麼，隨時都可以來找喬伊。我和錢德勒住在對面——而且他大部分時候都不在。
莫妮卡：喬伊，別打她的主意！今天是她結婚的日子！
喬　伊：幹嘛，是有什麼規定嗎？

學英文 🎧 59

hit on 跟 **hit it off** 的差別？
hit on 是一個俚語，表示「主動追求」的意思，通常因過度積極的態度而令人討厭。

A: Before I could even open my mouth, she told me she wasn't interested.
我都還沒開口說話，她就說她對我沒興趣。
B: Ha-ha. I guess guys must hit on her a lot.
哈哈。我猜很多男人都會跑去黏她。

另一個片語 hit it off，則是指兩人相處很融洽，有「一拍即合」的意味，用在兩人剛認識的時候。

A: How was your blind date?
妳的盲目約會如何啊？
B: It was great. Me and Paul really hit it off.
很好。保羅和我真是一拍即合。

看影集

羅斯、喬伊和錢德勒在羅斯的公寓。

Ross: You know what the scariest part is? What if there's only one woman for everybody, you know? I mean, what if you get one woman, and that's it? Unfortunately, in my case, there was only one woman—for her.

Joey: What are you talking about? One woman? That's like saying there's only one flavor of ice cream for you. Let me tell you something, Ross. There's lots of flavors out there. There's Rocky Road, and Cookie Dough, and Cherry Vanilla! You could get them with jimmies, or nuts, or whipped cream! This is the best thing that ever happened to you! You got married, you were, like, what, eight? Welcome back to the world! Grab a spoon!

Ross: I honestly don't know if I'm hungry or horny.

Chandler: **Stay out of** my freezer!

羅　斯：你們知道最可怕的是什麼嗎？假如大家一輩子都只能有一個女人，懂嗎？我是說，假如你交了一個女人，就這樣了？很不幸，以我的例子來說，的確只有一個女人──而且還是別人的。

喬　伊：你在說什麼？一個女人？好像是說冰淇淋只能有一種口味。讓我告訴你，羅斯，世界上有很多種口味，有堅果巧克力、餅乾粒，還有櫻桃香草！你還可以選彩色糖粒，或是果仁，或是鮮奶油！這是你一生中最棒的事！你結婚了又怎樣？你只有八歲左右吧？歡迎回到這個世界！拿根湯匙吧！

羅　斯：我真的不知道自己是飢餓還是飢渴。

錢德勒：離我的冰箱遠一點！

📖 學英文 🎧 60

stay out (of) 遠離（某事物或地方）

stay out of 就等於 stay away from「離……遠一點」。

A: Since your parents are out of town, we should throw a party at your place!
既然你爸媽出遠門了，我們就該到你家開趴！

B: I'd better not. I promised them I'd stay out of trouble.
最好不要。我答應他們不會惹麻煩了。

共同主演《六人行》的六名演員，都因本劇成為世界知名演員，但全劇播畢之後，在演藝圈繼續發展最好的，要算是飾演瑞秋的珍妮佛安妮斯頓（Jennifer Aniston）。她被安潔莉娜裘莉（Angelina Jolie）橫刀奪愛搶走前夫布萊德彼特（Brad Pitt），相關新聞長年佔領娛樂版面，讓她聲勢持續不墜。二〇一五年，她終於再度找到終身伴侶賈斯汀塞洛克斯（Justin Theroux）。

© Helga Esteb / Shutterstock.com

© Featureflash Photo Agency / Shutterstock.com

© HBO

SEX AND THE CITY
慾望城市

Sex and the City, a sitcom about the sex—and romantic—lives of four Manhattan career women, was one of HBO's most successful shows. Over its six season history, Sex and the City was nominated for 54 Emmy Awards, winning seven. It also [1]**spawned** two **feature films**, and can still be seen in [2]**reruns** worldwide.

《慾望城市》是關於曼哈頓四位職場女性的性——和浪漫愛情——生活，是 HBO 最成功的影集之一。共演出六季的《慾望城市》在播放期間獲得五十四項艾美獎提名，贏得七項獎，更衍生出兩部電影，在全世界也仍然可以看到重播。

In the first episode of Sex and the City, which [3]**aired** way back in 1998, we're introduced to Carrie Bradshaw, who writes a sex column for the New York Star. Carrie considers herself a "sexual [4]**anthropologist**," and her best sources are her friends—[5]**PR** executive Samantha Jones, [6]**corporate** lawyer Miranda Hobbes and art dealer Charlotte York. At a birthday dinner for Charlotte, Samantha tells the others that they should forget about relationships and "have sex like a man." While the [7]**cynical** Miranda doesn't think men are really good for either, Carrie and Charlotte aren't ready to give up on the possibility of romance. But when Carrie runs into Kurt, a hot guy who used her for sex before, she decides to give Samantha's [8]**suggestion** a try. While the sex is great, it leaves her feeling empty…and then she bumps into a handsome stranger on the sidewalk, who she nicknames Mr. Big.

© HBO

© HBO

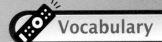

1) **spawn** [spɔn] (v.) 產生，衍生，造成
The award-winning book spawned a hit TV series.

2) **rerun** [ˋriˏrʌn] (n.) 重播（節目）
There's nothing but reruns on TV tonight.

3) **air** [ɛr] (v.) 播送，播放
The classical music show airs every evening at 8 p.m.

4) **anthropologist** [ˏænθrəˋpɑlədʒɪst] (n.) 人類學家
The anthropologist studied the tribe's language and customs.

5) **PR = public relations** [ˋpʌblɪk] [rɪˋleʃəns] (phr.) 公共關係，公關活動
We decided to hire a PR firm to improve our public image.

6) **corporate** [ˋkɔrpərɪt] (a.) 企業的，公司的
Apple's corporate headquarters is in California.

7) **cynical** [ˋsɪnɪkəl] (a.) 憤世嫉俗的，悲觀的
Voters are becoming more and more cynical about politics.

8) **suggestion** [səgˋdʒɛstʃən] (n.) 建議
If anyone has any suggestions, feel free to speak up.

9) **chaos** [ˋkeɑs] (n.) 混亂，雜亂
The country was in chaos after the war.

10) **publishing** [ˋpʌblɪʃɪŋ] (n.) 出版（業）
(v.) publish
Karen works as an editor at a publishing company.

11) **big shot** [bɪg] [ʃɑt] (n.) 大人物
Darren only got into Princeton because his dad is a big shot.

12) **limousine** [ˋlɪməˏzin] (n.) 豪華轎車（簡稱 limo [ˋlɪmo]）
The couple rented a limo for their wedding.

《慾望城市》在一九九八年首播的第一集，先帶觀眾認識凱莉布雷蕭，她為《紐約明星報》寫性愛專欄。凱莉自認為「性人類學家」，她最佳的研究對象是她的朋友們──公關主管莎曼珊瓊斯、企業律師米蘭達霍布斯，以及藝術經銷商夏綠蒂約克。在夏綠蒂的一次慶生晚餐上，莎曼珊告訴大家不要在乎交往關係，「要像男人一樣做愛」。憤世嫉俗的米蘭達認為男人不值得交往或做愛，凱莉和夏綠蒂則無法放棄浪漫愛情的可能性。不過，當凱莉遇到科特後，一個曾經利用她做愛的性感男子，她決定試試莎曼珊的建議。雖然做愛的過程很棒，但卻讓她覺得空虛……於是她在路邊遇到一位英俊的陌生人，並暱稱他為「大人物」。

The next night at a nightclub called ⁹⁾**Chaos**, where Carrie has **set** Miranda **up** with her nice guy friend Skipper, Samantha points out a man that she calls "the next Donald Trump," who turns out to be Mr. Big. Meanwhile, Charlotte is on a date with a ¹⁰⁾**publishing** ¹¹⁾**big shot**, but when she plays hard to get, he heads to Chaos himself and finds a one-night stand—no other than Samantha, who's available after striking out with Mr. Big. When Carrie leaves the club at dawn, Big gives her a ride home in his ¹²⁾**limo**, and she finds out that he's a romantic. As you may guess, this won't be the last time they meet!

隔天晚上，凱莉在混沌夜店想撮合米蘭達和她的男性好友史奇普時，莎曼珊指一個人給她看，說那是「下一個唐納川普」，結果正是大人物。同時，夏綠蒂和一個出版界大亨約會，但在她跟他玩欲擒故縱的遊戲時，他卻自行前往混沌夜店找一夜情──對象正是被大人物拒絕後恢復單身的莎曼珊。當凱莉在凌晨離開夜店時，大人物開他的豪華轎車載她回家，路途中則發現他是個浪漫主義者。正如你所猜的，這不會是他們倆人最後一次見面。

feature film 劇情長片

feature film 通常是指情節虛構的故事性電影，其拍攝目的是為了院線上映，一般長度在一個小時以上，而短於此長度的則稱為「短片」short film。

撮合相關字彙

set up 撮合，製造見面機會
matchmaker 媒人，幫人做媒就是 make a match。
blind date 盲約，相親，跟不認識的對象約會
online dating 網路約會，因為對象摸不到又看不真切，感覺很朦朧，又叫做 nearsighted date（近視約會）。
double date 兩對男女一起約會，以避免尷尬。
matchmaking event 聯誼活動，又稱 mixer。
speed dating 快速約會，一種聯誼活動的形式，透過各種快速更換交談對象的活動設計，增加一場聯誼能認識到的對象。

浪漫情境喜劇

看影集

凱莉正在唸她寫的性愛專欄。

Carrie: Once upon a time, an English journalist came to New York. Elizabeth was attractive and bright, and right away she hooked up with one of the city's typically eligible bachelors. Tim was 42, a well-liked and respected investment banker who made about 2 million a year. They met one evening in typical New York fashion at a gallery opening. It was love at first sight. For two weeks they snuggled, went to romantic restaurants, had wonderful sex, and shared their most intimate secrets. One warm spring day he took her to a townhouse he saw in **Sunday's New York Times**.

Realtor: There are four bedrooms upstairs. Do you have any children?

Tim: Not yet!

Carrie: That day, Tim popped the question.

Tim: How would you like to have dinner with my folks Tuesday night?

Elizabeth: I'd love to!

Carrie: On Tuesday, he called with some bad news.

Tim: My mother's not feeling very well. Could we **take a rain check**?

Elizabeth: Of course. Tell your mom I hope she feels better.

Carrie: When she hadn't heard from him for two weeks, she called.

Elizabeth: Tim, it's Elizabeth. That's an awfully long rain check!

Carrie: He said he was **up to his ears** and that he'd call her the next day.

Elizabeth: He never did call, of course! Bastard!

Carrie: Then I realized no one had told her about the end of love in Manhattan.

凱　　莉：從前有個英國記者來到紐約。伊莉莎白既有魅力又聰明，她立刻和城市裡一位典型的黃金單身漢交往。四十二歲的提姆是受人喜愛和尊敬的投資銀行家，年收入約兩百萬美元。他們兩人是某天晚上在最典型的紐約場合──畫廊開幕典禮──認識。倆人一見鍾情。兩個星期以來，倆人膩在一起、到浪漫餐廳用餐、享受魚水之歡，並分享彼此最私密的秘密。一個溫暖的春日，他帶她到一間在紐約時報週日版上看到的住宅。

房產經紀：樓上有四個房間，你們有小孩嗎？

提　　姆：還沒有！

凱　　莉：那天，提姆提出問題。

提　　姆：星期二晚上妳願意和我家人吃晚餐嗎？

伊莉莎白：我很樂意！

凱　　莉：星期二那天，他打電話來報告了一些壞消息。

提　　姆：我母親身體不太舒服。我們可以延期嗎？

伊莉莎白：沒問題。轉告你母親，願她早日康復。

凱　　莉：等了兩個星期都沒有消息，她打電話給他。

伊莉莎白：提姆，我是伊莉莎白。你延期也拖得太久了！

凱　　莉：他說他在忙，隔天再回電。

伊莉莎白：當然，他沒有再回電了！混蛋！

凱　　莉：然後我明白了，沒有人告訴她在曼哈頓愛情已不復存在了。

The New York Times 週日版

《紐約時報》的訂戶可選每日版，或是單訂週日版，因為忙於工作的週間，許多人根本沒時間讀報，到了星期天，一些紐約客的最大享受，就是找個地方窩著讀一整天《紐約時報》週日版。

《紐約時報》週日版除了當日那一落 The New York Times 的報紙，還有 Sunday Review《週日評論》、The New York Times Book Review《紐約時報書評》、The New York Times Magazine《紐約時報雜誌》，以及 T: The New York Times Style Magazine《T：紐約時報風尚誌》，重量超過兩公斤（一九八七年九月十三日的週日版，甚至重達五點一五公斤！）。至少七、八百頁的週日版當中，食衣住行育樂無所不包，還有滿滿的廣告，是紐約人消費的重要參考。

© HBO

Charlotte: You mean with **dildos**?

Samantha: No. I mean without feeling.

莎曼珊： 聽著，假如妳在這個城市裡是成功的女業務，妳有兩個選擇。費盡心力，試試看能不能找到另一半，或是豁出去，像男人一樣去做愛。

夏綠蒂： 妳是說綁上假陽具嗎？

莎曼珊： 不是，我是說不動感情的。

 學英文 64

bang one's head against the wall 白費力氣

字面上是「用頭撞牆」，表示再怎麼努力也只是浪費時間。也可以說 beat one's head against the wall。

A: I'm trying to get my cat to learn tricks, but it's pretty frustrating.
我在試著教我的貓一點把戲，但很令人氣餒。

B: There's no use banging your head against the wall. You can't train a cat.
你別白費力氣了。貓是不受教的。

性話題相關字彙

dildo 人造陰莖
女用的性玩具（sex toy），經常做成 vibrator「電動按摩棒」。男性陰莖為 penis，女性陰道則為 vagina。

masturbate 自慰
將其視為不潔的人，會稱為 self-abuse「自瀆」。masturbate 這個字男女通用，而表示男性自慰的說法多不勝數：beat off、jack off、jerk off、wack off、wank off（英式英文）、play with oneself、rub one out、slap the salami、spank the monkey、choke the chicken。

orgasm 性高潮
「射精」的動作稱為 ejaculation。造成遺精的「春夢」則是 wet dream。

threesome 3P
人數再多就變成 foursome，依此類推。

pheromone 費洛蒙
讀作 [ˋfɛrəˏmon]，有研究發現性賀爾蒙會刺激分泌費洛蒙，吸引異性。

contraceptive 避孕的藥物和用品
讀作 [ˏkɑntrəˋsɛptɪv]，「避孕」是 birth control。一般常見的有 condom「保險套」、female condom「女性保險套」、birth control pills「口服避孕藥」、birth control shot「施打避孕針」、birth control patch「避孕貼片」、IUD（intrauterine device）「子宮內避孕器」、diaphragm「子宮帽」、spermicide「殺精劑」等等。

sexually transmitted diseases 性病
像是 syphilis「梅毒」、chlamydia「披衣菌感染」、gonorrhea「淋病」、herpes「皰疹」、genital warts「菜花」及 AIDS「愛滋病」等等。

 **學英文** 63

take a rain check 改約下一次

購票入場的活動若因雨延期，會發給購票者 rain check 做為下次入場的憑證，在日常會話中引申為「這次沒辦法，改約下一次。」

A: How would you like to come over for dinner tonight?
你今天晚上想不想來共進晚餐呢？

B: Sorry, I already have plans tonight. Can I take a rain check?
抱歉，我今晚已經有安排。我們可以改約下一次嗎？

be up to one's ears 深陷於……

形容某樣東西多到耳朵的高度，表示「某事或某物多得不得了」。要表示「某事物很多」或「有很多事要做」時可說 up to (one's) ears (in something)，這個片語中的 ears 可用 neck「頸部」來代換。

A: Wanna catch a movie tonight?
今晚要去看電影嗎？

B: I can't. I'm up to my ears in homework.
我不行。我回家有一大堆功課要做。

看影集

四人在米蘭達的慶生晚餐上討論性愛。

Samantha: Look, if you're a successful saleswoman in this city, you have two choices. You can **bang your head against the wall** and try and find a relationship, or you can say screw it, and just go out and have sex like a man

©HBO

在同一場生日派對上。

Samantha: Sweetheart, this is the first time in the history of Manhattan that women have had as much money and power as men, plus the equal luxury of treating men like sex objects.

Miranda: Yeah, except men in this city fail on both counts. I mean, they don't wanna be in a relationship with you but as soon as you only want them for sex they don't like it. All of a sudden they can't perform the way they're supposed to.

Samantha: That's when you dump them!

Carrie: Oh, come on ladies. Are we really that cynical? What about romance?

Charlotte: Yeah!

Samantha: Oh, who needs it?

Miranda: It's like that guy Jeremiah, the poet. I mean, the sex was incredible, but then he wanted to read me his poetry and go out to dinner and the whole chat bit, and I'm like, "let's **not even go there**."

Charlotte: What are you saying? Are you saying that you're just going to give up on love? That's just sick.

Carrie: Oh, no. Believe me, the right guy comes along and you two right here, this whole thing *[whistles]* right **out the window**.

莎曼珊：親愛的，這是曼哈頓有史以來第一次女人和男人一樣有錢有權，外加可以把男人當性對象一樣享樂。

米蘭達：是啊，問題是這個城市裡的男人這兩方面都不如人意。我是說，他們不會想跟人認真交往，但若只想跟他們做愛，他們也不喜歡。他們突然之間連該有的表現都沒了。

莎曼珊：這時候就該甩掉他們！

凱莉：噢，拜託，小姐們，我們要這麼憤世嫉俗嗎？難道沒有浪漫的愛情嗎？

夏綠蒂：對啊！

莎曼珊：噢，誰需要那個？

米蘭達：就像耶利米那傢伙，那個詩人。我是說，我們的性生活很棒，但是他後來還想唸他寫的詩給我聽，一起共進晚餐，聊聊天，我就說：「少來了。」

夏綠蒂：妳在說什麼？妳是說妳要放棄愛情嗎？妳病了。

凱莉：喔，不是，相信我，當對的人出現，妳們兩位（莎曼珊和米蘭達）現在說的一切（口哨）都煙消雲散了。

「慾女」的最愛：鞋子

劇中的凱莉曾經差點流落街頭，因為她都繳不起房租了，還把錢拿去買鞋。看看下面琳瑯滿目的女性鞋款，就知道她為什麼再怎麼買都不嫌多了。

high heels 高跟鞋	**sandals** 涼鞋
stilettos 細跟高跟鞋	**flip-flops** 人字拖
wedges 楔型鞋	**t-straps** Ｔ字繫帶鞋
platform shoes 厚底鞋	**galoshes** 高筒橡膠雨靴
peep-toe shoes 魚口鞋	**moccasins** 鹿皮軟鞋
sling-backs 後跟勾帶鞋	**loafers** 樂福鞋
boots 靴子	
flats 平底鞋	
pumps 淺口無帶鞋	
Mary Janes 扣帶娃娃鞋	
sneakers 布鞋	
slippers 拖鞋	

(not) go there 別提了

通常用否定，意思是「不想談這件事」，表示不願意繼續討論某個話題。

A: Maybe if you treated Mike better, he wouldn't be having an affair.
　或許妳對麥克好一點，他就不會外遇了。

B: You think it's my fault he's cheating on me? Don't even go there!
　你認為他背叛我是我的錯？別說了！

out the window 消失，泡湯了

用來表示事物一去不復返，全部心血都白費了。

A: Did you save the document before your computer crashed?
　電腦當機前，你有儲存文件嗎？

B: No. That's hours of work out the window.
　沒有。辛苦好幾個小時全都白忙了。

📷 看影集

倆人約會後，出版業高層卡波特唐肯替夏綠蒂叫計程車。

Capote: So, what are you doing next Saturday?

Charlotte: I'm having dinner with you. *[kisses him and gets into cab]*

Capote: Hey, wait. You're going to the West Side, right?

Charlotte: Right. *[to driver]* West 4th and Bank, please.

Capote: Hey, scoot over, will you? *[gets into cab]* Two stops—4th and Bank, and West Broadway and Broom.

Charlotte: You're going to Chaos?

Capote: Oh, yeah.

Charlotte: Why?

Capote: Look, I understand **where you're coming from** and I totally respect it, but I really need to have sex tonight!

卡波特：那妳下星期六要做什麼？

夏綠蒂：和你吃晚餐。（親吻他並坐上計程車）

卡波特：嘿，等等。妳要去西區，對吧？

夏綠蒂：對。（轉向司機）請到西四街和銀行街。

卡波特：嘿，妳能坐過去一點嗎？（坐進計程車）兩站——西四街和銀行街口，還有西百老匯街和布倫街口。

夏綠蒂：你要去混沌夜店？

卡波特：噢，對。

夏綠蒂：為什麼？

卡波特：是這樣，我了解妳的立場，也完全尊重妳，但我今晚真的需要做愛！

💬 學英文 🎧 66

where one is coming from 某人的立場、想法

字面上的意思是「一個人的出身背景」，引申為「某人的想法、立場、意思或狀況」。

A: I think all illegal immigrants should be sent home.
　我認為所有非法移民者都該被遣送回國。

B: Well, I don't agree with you, but I understand where you're coming from.
　這個嘛，我不同意你的看法，但我可以理解你的立場。

© Featureflash Photo Agency / Shutterstock.com

飾演凱莉的莎拉潔西卡帕克（Sarah Jessica Parker）從小就接受歌舞訓練，為了栽培她成為童星，父母從俄亥俄州搬到紐約市附近，最後定居曼哈頓。帕克十一歲開始登上百老匯，接著在電視及電影界演了二十年的戲，終於接到凱莉這個讓她成為世界巨星的角色。

影集結束後，她依然非常活躍，除了接不完的服裝代言，兩三年拍一部《慾望城市》的電影續集，還經營自己的女鞋品牌 SJP，繼續她的時尚女神事業。

© HBO

新聞急先鋒
THE NEWSROOM℠

67

Written by Aaron Sorkin of *West Wing* [1)]**fame**, *The Newsroom* provides a behind the scenes look at the team who creates the news at a [2)]**fictional** 24-hour news **channel**, Atlantis Cable News. While ACN may be fictional, the news they report is real. Each [3)]**episode** deals with a real life news event, starting with the 2010 Gulf of Mexico oil spill.

© HBO

《新聞急先鋒》是以《白宮風雲》一劇走紅的艾倫索金所寫的另一部作品，是關於虛構的二十四小時新聞頻道，「亞特蘭蒂斯有線新聞台」新聞製作團隊的幕後故事。亞特蘭蒂斯新聞台雖然是虛構的，但他們報導的新聞卻是真實的。每一集處理的都是真實生活中的新聞事件，從二○一○年的墨西哥灣漏油事件開始。

有線電視、無線電視的差別

cable TV 有線電視
有線電視的「線」，是指利用同軸電纜（coaxial cable）傳送影像，美國電視台是屬於區域性的，所以在加州跟紐約所看到的頻道（channel）並不相同。

broadcast TV 無線電視
無線電視是利用家中天線（antenna）接收電視台發射的電波，頻道數有限，優點是不需額外付費，而這些頻道統稱為聯播網（network），類似台灣的台視、中視、華視等頻道。broadcast 這個字當動詞，是「播放節目」的意思。

satellite TV 衛星電視
衛星電視是利用衛星天線接收衛星發送的訊號，連上衛星機上盒收看節目，頻道數依購買不同方案而有所差異。

The star of the show is news [4)]**anchor** Will McAvoy—played by Jeff Daniels, perhaps best known for his role in *Dumb and Dumber*—who we first meet at a college [5)]**panel** discussion. McAvoy is known as an anchor who never says anything [6)]**offensive**, but this changes in an instant when he's asked about what makes America the greatest country in the world. Pushed by the host for an honest answer, McAvoy loses his temper and responds with a [7]**tirade** about why America isn't the greatest country. Unhappy with the media storm that follows, the **network** sends him away on a long vacation.

這部影集的主角是新聞主播威爾麥艾維，由傑夫丹尼爾飾演──他在《阿呆與阿瓜》裡的角色或許最廣為人知──他在戲中第一次出場是在大學裡的小組討論會上。麥艾維是公認說話從不冒犯他人的主播，但當他被問到美國為什麼是世界上最偉大的國家時，態度突然轉變。在主持人催促要誠實回答下，麥艾維發起脾氣，用激烈的言辭回答美國為什麼不是最偉大的國家。不滿於媒體為此事炒得沸沸揚揚，新聞台要他休長假。

When McAvoy finally returns, he learns that most of his staff are leaving for another show. And that's not the only bad news: his old [8]**executive** producer Don, who found him too difficult to work with, is being replaced by his ex-girlfriend MacKenzie—the last person in the world he wants to see. She's back from a long [9]**assignment** in Afghanistan, and is excited about turning *News Night with Will McAvoy* into a real news show. And while she and Will are having an argument about their past, her [10]**senior** producer Jim discovers just the kind of story she's looking for. A BP oil [11]**rig** has exploded in the [12]**Gulf** of Mexico, and with some quick [13]**research** he finds out that it's not an accident, but a manmade [14]**disaster**. The news team manages to put together a report just in time for **broadcast**, and while the other networks are running stories about flight delays and the latest iPhone, ACN is breaking the biggest story of the year!

當麥艾維終於回到新聞台時，他得知大部分工作人員都要離開，到其他節目。但這不是唯一的壞消息：他以前的執行製作唐恩，認為麥艾維太難共事，要換成他的前女友瑪坎西──這世上他最不想看到的人。她長期被派往阿富汗採訪結束後回來，對於要將《威爾麥艾維晚間新聞》變成真正的新聞節目感到興奮。她和威爾為過去的事爭吵時，她的資深製作人吉姆發現到她一直想要追的新聞。英國石油公司在墨西哥灣的鑽油台發生漏油事件，在快速調查後，他發現這不是意外，而是人為造成的災難。正當其他電台在報導飛機延誤和最新 iPhone 的新聞時，亞特蘭蒂斯新聞台的新聞團隊設法即時整理出一份報導，搶先播報這則年度最勁爆的新聞！

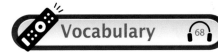

Vocabulary 68

1) **fame** [fem] (n.) 聲望，名聲
The actress moved to Hollywood in search of fame and fortune.

2) **fictional** [ˋfɪkʃənəl] (a.) 虛構的
The events in the novel are real, but the main characters are fictional.

3) **episode** [ˋɛpə.sod] (n.)（影集、電影或廣播節目的）一集
Did you see the lastest episode of *Game of Thrones*?

4) **anchor** [ˋæŋkɚ] (n.) 新聞主播
The station just hired a new evening news anchor.

5) **panel** [ˋpænəl] (n.) 專家小組，討論小組
The report was compiled by a panel of experts.

6) **offensive** [əˋfɛnsɪv] (a.) 冒犯人的
Some women found the politician's remarks offensive.

7) **tirade** [taɪˋred] (n.) 激烈的言語
The boss went into a tirade when he learned of Paul's mistake.

8) **executive** [ɪgˋzɛkjətɪv] (a.) 執行的，主管級的
Roberta works as an executive secretary.

9) **assignment** [əˋsaɪnmənt] (n.) 工作，任務，作業，功課
Her first assignment as a reporter was to cover the election.

10) **senior** [ˋsinjɚ] (a.) 資深的，高級的
I have an appointment with the senior vice president.

11) **rig** [rɪg] (n.) 鑽油台
Working on an oil rig is a dangerous job.

12) **gulf** [gʌlf] (n.) 海灣
Many wars have been fought in the Persian Gulf.

13) **research** [ˋrisɝtʃ / rɪˋsɝtʃ] (n./v.)（學術）研究，調查
A team of scientists is conducting research on the new virus.

14) **disaster** [dɪˋzæstɚ] (n.) 災難，禍害
Taiwan is frequently hit by natural disasters.

© HBO

看影集

在小組討論會上，威爾回答大學生關於美國為什麼是世上最偉大的國家的問題。

Will: Just in case you accidentally wander into a voting booth one day, there are some things you should know, and one of them is there is absolutely no evidence to support the statement that we're the greatest country in the world. We're seventh in literacy, 22nd in science, third in median household income, number four in labor force, and number four in exports. We lead the world in only three categories: number of incarcerated citizens per capita, number of adults who believe angels are real, and defense spending—where we spend more than the next 26 countries combined, 25 of whom are allies. Now, none of this is the fault of a 20-year-old college student, but you nonetheless are without a doubt a member of **the worst, period generation, period ever, period**. So when you ask what makes us the greatest country in the world, I don't know what the fuck you're talking about.

威爾：萬一有天妳不小心晃進了投票所，有幾件事情妳應該要知道，其中一件是，完全沒有證據可以支持我們是世界上最偉大的國家這種說法。我們在識字率上排名第七，科學教育排名第二十二，平均家庭收入排名第三，勞動力排名第四，出口量排名第四。我們只有在三方面排名世界第一：人均監禁率、相信世界上有天使的成年人數和國防支出——花費比排名在後的二十六個國家總和還高，而且其中二十五個是我們的盟友。那麼，對二十歲的大學生來說，這不是妳的錯，不過，毫無疑問地，妳是有史以來最糟糕世代中的一份子。所以，當妳問，我們為什麼是世上最偉大的國家時，我真的不知道妳他媽的在說什麼。

學英文 🎧 69

period 的用法

這句台詞用了三次 period 這個字，是因為 period 當感嘆詞表示斬釘截鐵、不容置疑的態度。the worst period generation period ever period 其實就是 the worst generation ever，而前者帶有「有史以來最糟糕的世代，就這樣」的語氣。

A: If you let me go to the party, I promise I'll come home before midnight.
如果你讓我參加這個派對，我保證會在午夜之前回來。

B: No. You're not going, period!
不行。你不准去，就這樣！

看影集

新聞部總監查理史基納突然公布消息，威爾的同台主播艾略特有了自己的節目，並要帶走威爾的工作人員。

Will: Where's my staff?

Charlie: The answer to that question has several parts. First, we're gonna try Elliot out at 10:00, he's starting in two weeks.

Will: Good. Thank you. With the right **EP**, he'll do great at 10:00.

Charlie: I think so, too, and I know how much he appreciates your lobbying hard for him, he really **looks up to** you.

Will: What's this got to do with my staff?

新聞工作人員

journalist 新聞從業人員
從事新聞業（journalism）所有工作人員的統稱。

reporter 記者
透過彙整資訊（research）、採訪（interview）之後進行報導（report），所做的「報導」稱做 story。

correspondent 通訊員，特派記者
駐外地甚至戰地，為報紙或雜誌撰寫新聞稿的記者。

photojournalist 攝影記者
提供新聞現場照片的記者。而專門偷拍名人私生活照片，再高價賣給雜誌或報社，以謀取暴利的攝影師，則被稱作 paparazzi（狗仔隊）。

editor 編譯
彙整外電資訊，整理記者所提供的文字及圖片報導。

columnist 專欄作家
在報紙、期刊經常或定期發表個人評論的作家。寫 editorial「社論」的則為 editorialist「社論作家」。

anchor 主播
在電視台內播報新聞，負責掌握節目進度，並安排最新消息插播。經常會有一、兩位 co-anchor「副主播」一起播報。

© ChameleonsEye / Shutterstock.com

field reporter 採訪記者
在新聞發生現場或記者會（press conference）上收集資訊，透過連線報導，並回答主播的問題。在連線新聞中的「受訪專家（或民眾）」稱為 guest。

weather anchor 氣象主播
提供氣象預報（weather forecast），如果是由「氣象學者」擔任主播，則稱之為 meteorologist，以強調其專業。

executive producer 執行製作
簡稱 EP。電視新聞節目的 EP 除了要負責新聞內容的製播，還要負責成本控管等行政管理工作，是帶領整個新聞團隊的靈魂人物。

Charlie: He's taking your staff.
Will: What are you talking about?
Charlie: Well, strictly speaking, he's taking your EP, and your EP's taking your staff.

威爾：我的工作人員呢？
查理：這問題的答案要分好幾部分說明。首先，我們要試試看讓艾略特在十點播新聞，兩週後開始。
威爾：很好，謝謝你。只要有適合的執行製作，他的十點節目會做得很棒。
查理：我也這麼認為，而且我知道他很感激你幫他強力遊說，他真的很尊敬你。
威爾：這跟我的工作人員有什麼關係？

查理：他要帶走你的工作人員。
威爾：你在說什麼？
查理：嗯，嚴格來說，他要帶走你的執行製作，而你的執行製作要帶走你的工作人員。

🔊 **學英文** 70

look up to sb.　尊敬某人
中文用「仰之彌高」來形容對某人的敬佩之情。look up 正有向上看的意思，look up to sb. 就表示對人的敬佩。

A: Do you think Rob would make a good team captain?
　你覺得羅伯會是個好隊長嗎？
B: Yes. All the other players look up to him.
　會。隊上每個球員都很敬佩他。

 看影集

吉姆和電子媒體專家尼爾桑帕特在討論漏油事件。

Neal: They may have bigger problems than the missing crew.

Jim: Why?

Neal: I checked out **BP Deepwater Horizon**. That rig is drilling at 18,000 feet below sea level. There are only a couple of things that could have failed. And if it was the wrong one….

Jim: Pressure.

Neal: It would be like trying to toss a hat on a fire hose.

Don: What the hell are you two talking about?

Jim: It's more than 11 missing guys. There might be a massive oil spill 50 miles off the coast of Louisiana.

尼爾：他們可能還有比船員失蹤更嚴重的問題。

吉姆：為什麼？

尼爾：我調查了英國石油公司的深水地平線鑽油台，那個鑽油台在海平面下方一萬八千英尺鑽探石油。故障的原因沒幾個，但假如真的是其中一個的話……。

吉姆：壓力。

尼爾：那就像是想用帽子蓋住消防水管。

唐恩：你們兩個到底在說什麼？

吉姆：情況遠比十一人失蹤嚴重。距離路易斯安那州外海五十英里處可能有大量石油外洩。

墨西哥灣漏油事件

這起英國石油公司深水地平線（BP Deepwater Horizon）鑽油井原油外洩事件（一般稱作 BP oil spill）發生於二〇一〇年四月二十日，直到九月十九日才封住油井，死亡的十一人至今未尋獲，漏出的量約有七十八萬立方公尺，污染的海域廣達兩千五百平方公里，對鄰近路易斯安那州、密西西比州、阿拉巴馬州漁業造成災難性的影響。英國石油公司於二〇一五年與美國政府和解，賠償金額達一百八十七億美元。

 看影集

威爾和瑪坎西在爭論新聞該如何報導。

Will: This isn't nonprofit theater. It's advertiser-supported television. You know that, right?

Mackenzie: I'd rather do a good show for 100 people than a bad one for a million, if that's what you're saying.

Will: What is it you're talking to me about right now?

Mackenzie: I've come here to produce a news broadcast that more closely resembles the one we did before you got popular by not bothering anyone, **Leno**.

Will: I think **Jay** and I would rather be employed, if it's all the same to you.

Mackenzie: It's not all the same to me, you punk. I've come here to take your IQ and your talent and **put it to** some patriotic fucking **use**. And where does it say that a good news show can't be popular?

Will: **Nielsen ratings**.

威　爾：這不是非營利劇院。是廣告商贊助的電視。妳知道這點，對吧？

瑪坎西：我寧可為一百人做好節目，也不願為一百萬人做爛節目，假如這是你想表達的。

威　爾：妳到底想說什麼？

瑪坎西：我來這裡是為了製作我們以前做過的新聞節目，在你還沒變成受歡迎、不得罪人的雷諾主播之前。

威　爾：我想傑跟我一樣，寧可保住工作，除非妳很介意。

瑪坎西：我當然介意，你這笨蛋。我來這裡是要用你的智商和才華來做點對國家有用的事。而且誰說好的新聞節目不能大受歡迎？

威　爾：尼爾森收視率。

Jay Leno 傑雷諾

脫口秀《今夜秀》（The Tonight Show）的主持人，他以幽默但不尖酸刻薄、從不冒犯受訪者聞名。

© Featureflash Photo Agency / Shutterstock.com

put something to (good) use 善加利用

把一樣東西用在對的地方。若是形容人，則表示好好運用一個人的能力或技巧。

A: Why do you donate to that charity?
你為什麼捐錢給那個慈善機構？

B: Because they put the money to good use.
因為他們會善用捐款。

看影集

成功報導漏油事件後，威爾和查理在談論瑪坎西。

Will: You didn't bring her in to **right the ship**. You brought her in to build a new one. You knew Don would go with Elliot. You orchestrated the whole thing.

Charlie: Yeah. For a long time now, I badly wanted to watch the news on my TV at night. Then it occurred to me—I run a news division.

Will: She's indifferent to ratings, competition, corporate concerns, and, generally speaking, consequences.

Charlie: Good, 'cause you just described my job.

Nielsen ratings 尼爾森收視率調查

這家公司的創辦人亞瑟尼爾森（Arthur Nielsen）是一位市場分析師，一九二〇年代開始分析品牌廣告效果，逐漸轉而廣播節目市場分析，一九三〇年代開始提出具有公信力的「尼爾森廣播收聽率調查」。一九五〇年代，該公司將廣播收聽率調查方法運用於電視，現已成為全球電視產業最主要的收視群眾分析資料。

威爾：你不是帶她來幫這艘船導回正軌，而是帶她來打造新船的。你知道唐恩會跟著艾略特離開。整件事是你一手策劃的。

查理：沒錯。長久以來，我一直很想在晚上看電視新聞。然後我想到──我有個新聞部門。

威爾：她不關心收視率、競爭對手、企業事務，總而言之，就是不計後果。

查理：很好，因為你剛剛說的都是我的工作。

right the ship 導向正途

這句海事用語常用於表示新官上任，right 在這裡是動詞，意指要把出錯的地方改正，或是挽回頹勢。

A: Our profits are really down this quarter.
我們的這季的獲利真的很差。

B: Don't worry. I'm sure we'll be able to right the ship next quarter.
別擔心。我想下一季一定能挽回頹勢。

飾演麥艾維（Will McAvoy）的傑夫丹尼爾斯（Jeff Daniels）長得就是居家好男人的樣子，適合演爸爸、主播、高階軍官、高階主管。他和《ID4 星際終結者》（*Independence Day*）當中的比爾普曼（Bill Pullman）（右），是不是長得很相似呢？

© Tinseltown / Shutterstock.com

© DFree / Shutterstock.com

紙牌屋
HOUSE of CARDS

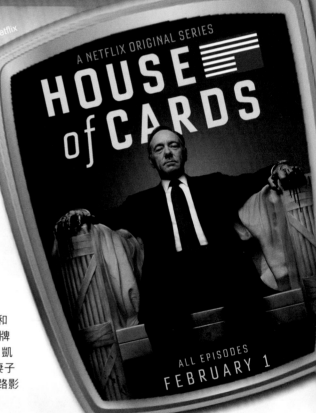

© Netflix

Adapted from a BBC series of the same name, *House of Cards* is a political drama about the rise of Washington power couple Frank and Claire Underwood. Unlike most TV series, *House of Cards* is released on the web by **Netflix** one full season at a time, making it perfect for **binge-watching**. The show has been the first web-only series to receive major award [1]**nominations**, with Kevin Spacey and Robin Wright both winning Golden Globes for their [2]**portrayals** of the ruthless Frank Underwood and his equally ruthless wife Claire.

改編自 BBC 同名影集的《紙牌屋》是關於華府一對權力夫妻，法蘭克和克萊爾安德伍德崛起過程的政治戲劇。與大部分電視影集不同的是，《紙牌屋》是由 Netflix 在網路上一次發布完整一季的影集，非常適合追劇的觀眾。凱文史貝西和羅蘋萊特分別飾演鐵石心腸的法蘭克安德伍德與他同樣無情的妻子克萊爾，兩人都藉此劇獲得金球獎，這也是第一部獲得重要獎項提名的網路影集。

Watch Instantly 的 Netflix

成立於一九九七年的 Netflix 原本經營郵寄出租影片光碟服務，2007 年推出 Watch Instantly，只要付一筆定額的月租費，就可以無限次收看串流影片（streaming video）。《紙牌屋》是 Netflix 為拓展串流服務業務所籌劃的第一部自製作品，這部大受好評的影集一開始僅限訂閱戶才看得到，二〇一三年第一季推出就替 Netflix 增加了三百萬新訂戶。

binge-watching 追劇

binge 是「大吃大喝」的意思，因此 binge-watching 表示「一口氣看多集電視影集」，在短短幾天內把整季、甚至好幾季影集全部看完的行為，也叫 marathon viewing。

In the show's opening scene, no time is wasted [3]**acquainting** the audience with the character of Democratic South Carolina [4]**Congressman** Frank Underwood. Hearing his neighbor's dog get hit by a car, he rushes outside to comfort the fatally wounded animal. "Moments like this require someone who will act, who will do the [5]**unpleasant** thing, the necessary thing," he says as he [6]**strangles** the dog to death. What does a man like this do when Garrett Walker, the guy he

© Netflix

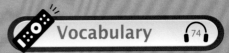
helped elect president, doesn't keep his promise to [7]**appoint** him secretary of state? By [8]**hatching** a [9]**plot** that would make Machiavelli proud, of course.

這部影集一開場就不浪費時間，讓觀眾認識南卡羅來納州民主黨籍國會議員法蘭克安德伍德這個角色。法蘭克聽說鄰居的狗被車撞到時，急忙衝到屋外安撫重傷命危的狗。「像這種時刻需要有人採取行動，雖然令人不愉快，卻是必要的，」他一面說著，一面將狗勒死。像這樣的人，在幫助加勒特沃克選上總統後，對方卻沒信守承諾任命他為國務卿時，他會怎麼做？當然，就是策劃一椿連馬基維利（編註：義大利文藝時期政治家，為達政治目的可不擇手段的代名詞）都與有榮焉的陰謀。

In his quest for a [10]**cabinet** position, Frank starts a relationship with an [11]**ambitious** young female reporter, who agrees to print damaging stories about his political [12]**rivals**. At the same time, he [13]**manipulates** a troubled congressman from Philadelphia, Peter Russo, into helping him make Walker's new secretary of state look bad so he can replace her with his [14]**ally**, [15]**Senator** Catherine Durant. But wait—isn't that the position Frank wanted for himself? When he starts plotting to have the new vice president, former Pennsylvania governor Jim Matthews, return to his old job, we know that Frank has higher ambitions. Just how high? Time for some binge-watching!

為了尋求內閣職務，法蘭克與一位年輕、野心勃勃的女記者交往。這位女記者同意報導對他的政治對手不利的新聞。同時，他操縱一位惹上麻煩的國會議員，來自賓州的彼得羅素，好幫助他讓沃克的新國務卿名聲敗壞，這樣沃克就可以換掉原本的國務卿人選，改任命他的同盟，參議員凱薩琳杜蘭特。不過，慢著——法蘭克不是自己想要這個職位嗎？當他開始密謀讓副總統，前賓州州長吉姆馬修斯回到他原本的職位時，我們就知道法蘭克還有更大的野心。到底有多大？追劇就知道了！

◎ 看影集

法蘭克對著鏡頭講話，介紹政治人物。

Frank: **President-elect** Garrett Walker. Do I like him? No. Do I believe in him? That's beside the point. Any politician that gets 70 million votes has **tapped into** something larger than himself, larger than even me, as much as I hate to admit it. Look at that winning smile, those trusting eyes. I **latched onto** him early on and made myself vital. After 22 years in Congress, I can smell which way the wind is blowing. Jim Matthews, his vice president, former governor of Pennsylvania. He did his duty in delivering the Keystone State. Now they're about to **put him out to pasture**. But he looks happy enough, doesn't he? For some, it's simply the size of the chair. Linda Vasquez, Walker's chief of staff. I got her hired. She's a woman, check. And a Latina, check. But more important than that, she's tough as a two-dollar steak. Check, check, check. When it comes to the White House, you not only need the keys in your back pocket, you need the gatekeeper.

法蘭克：當選總統的加勒特沃克，我喜歡他嗎？不。我信任他嗎？這不重要。任何獲得七千萬票的政治人物，背後支持他的力量遠大於他個人，甚至超越我，雖然我不想承認。看看他迷人的笑容，他無邪的眼神。我早就鎖定他，讓我自己扮演重要角色。在國會中二十二年，我能聞到風向。他的副總統吉姆馬修斯，前賓州州長，盡責地拿下磐石之州（編註：賓州的暱稱）。現在他們要讓他沒事做。但他看起來很開心，是吧？對某些人來說，這只是位子的大小而已。沃克的幕僚長琳達瓦斯奎茲，是我讓她獲得聘用。她是女性，符合條件。是拉丁裔，符合條件。但更重要的是，她就像廉價牛排一樣韌，樣樣都符合。說到進軍白宮，你口袋裡需要的不只是鑰匙，還需要守門人。

選舉相關字彙

candidate 候選人

「必贏的候選人」是 shoo-in，這個說法源自賽馬場，表示可以輕鬆贏得比賽的馬。後來延伸到政治選舉上，表示內定、穩贏的候選人。而 a dream ticket 「（政治）夢幻組合」是指兩個政治人物合作能相互加分，使選舉的贏面大增。

campaign 競選活動

run for office「參選公職」的候選人都要在競選活動上提出 platform「政見」，爭取支持。

canvass 遊說拉票

「助選員」就是 canvasser。

voter turnout 投票率

election day 「投票日」當天出席投票 voter 「選民」的比例。「中間選民」為 swing voter，「選票」是 vote / ballot，「票匭」是 ballot box，「不記名投票」為 secret ballot。

landslide victory 壓倒性的勝利

landslide 是「土石滑落、坍方」，但在政治用語中，則表示某人或某個陣營在選舉中獲得大量民意支持，也可以直接說 landslide（當名詞用）。勝選之後，就等著參加 inauguration 「就職典禮」了。

政黨相關字彙

· ruling party 執政黨

· opposition party 反對黨

· majority party 多數黨

· minority party 少數黨

· partisan 死忠黨員

· bipartisan 涉及兩黨的（通常是指執政黨和反對黨）

tap into 借助，利用

tap 就是「水龍頭」，接好水管插上水龍頭，水就能源源不絕流出，引申為從某件事上得到好處。

A: Why do you think that candidate is winning so many votes?
你覺得那位候選人為何能贏得高票？

B: I think it's his ability to tap into voters' frustration with the political system.
我想是因為他善於利用選民對政治制度的不滿。

latch onto sb./sth. 纏著某人，緊抓不放

latch 是指把門「閂上」，或用鎖頭「鎖上」的動作，引申為緊緊把握，如果對象是人，就表示儘管討人厭，還是緊抓不放。

A: Where did that stray dog come from?
那條流浪狗是哪兒來的？

B: We were taking a walk, and he just latched onto us and followed us home.
我們去散步，牠一路跟著我們，就跟回家了。

put sb. out to pasture 強迫退休

pasture 是放牛羊吃草的「牧草地」，原指把幫忙務農多年的老牛馬放到草地上安養天年，引申為嫌一個人太老，強迫他退休。對白中的副總統原本是位高權重的州長，法蘭克是在嘲諷他變成沒有實權的副總統，並不是說他退休。

A: Are you looking forward to your retirement?
你很期待退休嗎？

B: No. I wanted to keep working, but they put me out to pasture.
不。我想要繼續工作，但他們要我卸甲歸田。

trickle-down economics
涓滴經濟學

供給面經濟學（supply-side economics）認為高稅率會影響工作意願，不利總體稅收，應降稅才能促進生產。美國前總統雷根（Ronald Reagan）採納之後，成就美國經濟最強盛的時代，因而出現 Reaganomics「雷根經濟學」一詞。但反對者將其戲稱為 trickle-down economics，表示供給面經濟學說穿了，就是把錢都給上層社會的有錢人，讓他們有錢可花，然後期待下層的窮人能夠利益均沾。

這裡法蘭克只是要嘴皮，他主張外交以某些國家為重點，影響力就會擴散他國，因此借用 trickle-down 一詞。

看影集

法蘭克抵達會議討論他的職位，只有幕僚長琳達瓦斯奎茲在現場

Frank: Is the President-elect running late?

Linda: No. He couldn't make it. I'll brief him, though.

Frank: OK. This is the memo I drafted on our Middle East policy we've been developing. Now, I want to borrow from Reagan. I'd like to **coin the phrase** "**trickle-down** diplomacy."

Linda: Frank, I'm going to stop you there. We're not nominating you for Secretary of State. I know he made you a promise, but circumstances have changed.

Frank: The nature of promises, Linda, is that they remain immune to changing circumstances.

Linda: Garrett has thought long and hard about this, and he's decided we need you to stay in Congress.

法蘭克： 總統當選人遲到了嗎？

琳　達： 不，他沒辦法來了。不過我會向他做個簡報。

法蘭克： 好。這是我起草的備忘錄，是我們在研究的中東政策。那麼，我想借用雷根的說法創造新詞，「涓滴外交」。

琳　達： 法蘭克，我要打斷你一下。我們不會提名你為國務卿。我知道他承諾過你，但情況有變。

法蘭克： 琳達，承諾的意思是，就算情況有變也不會改變。

琳　達： 加勒特想了很久才做出這個艱難的決定，他決定我們需要你留在國會。

學英文 🎧 76

coin a phrase 造新詞

是指為了引起他人的興趣而玩文字遊戲，創造一種新的說法。也可以說 coin a new term 或 new word。

A: Do you know who coined the phrase "the buck stops here"?
你知道「責任推託，到此為止」這句話是誰第一個說的嗎？

B: Yeah. It was President Harry Truman.
知道啊。是杜魯門總統。

政治劇情

法蘭克與幕僚長道格斯坦普一起密謀報復總統。

Doug: Retribution?

Frank: No. It's more than that. Take a step back. Look at the bigger picture.

Doug: I think I see what you're getting at. Kern first?

Frank: That's how you devour a whale, Doug. One bite at a time.

Doug: Who would you want for Secretary of State?

Frank: Give me a list of choices. And however we do this, we'll also need a buffer.

Doug: You mean an errand boy?

Ffank: Yes. Somebody we control completely.

Doug: I'll **keep my ear to the ground**.

道　格：報復？

法蘭克：不，不只如此。退一步，考量更大的局面。

道　格：我想我知道你在想什麼了。先拿科恩開刀？

法蘭克：這就是吞掉鯨魚的方法，道格。一次一口。

道　格：你想讓誰做國務卿？

法蘭克：給我一份名單。不論怎麼做，我們還需要個擋箭牌。

道　格：你是說一個供我們差遣的人？

法蘭克：是，一個我們可以完全控制的人。

道　格：我會留意的。

 學英文 77

keep/have one's ear to the ground 留意

美洲原住民會趴在地上聽，看看有沒有大批人馬或動物接近，引申為密切注意新的訊息或動向，掌握事情的發展。

A: There's a rumor that the company may be laying off employees.
據說公司可能要裁員了。

B: So I hear. I guess we'd better keep our ears to the ground.
我有這麼聽說。我看我們最好多加留意。

法蘭克與凱薩琳杜蘭特見面，看她是否對國務卿職位有興趣

Catherine: Walker just nominated Kern.

Frank: It's a long road to confirmation.

Catherine: Kern is a **boy scout**.

Frank: Nobody's a boy scout. Not even Boy Scouts.

Catherine: What do you have?

Frank: Absolutely nothing.

Catherine: [laughs] Then what are we talking about?

Frank: Just asking a simple question, does the job interest you?

Catherine: Why would you want Michael gone?

Frank: Cathy, you and I came up together. The Foreign Affairs Committee needs a secretary we can work with. Someone who isn't afraid to stand up to Walker when he's wrong.

凱薩琳：沃克才剛提名科恩。

法蘭克：確認還需要一段時間。

凱薩琳：科恩就像童子軍一樣身家清白。

法蘭克：沒有人是清白的，就算真正的童子軍也一樣。

凱薩琳：你握有他什麼把柄？

法蘭克：什麼都沒有。

凱薩琳：（笑）那我們還有什麼好談的？

負面選舉字彙

smear 抹黑
一種 negative campaign「負面選戰」，常用的手段是透過媒體放話，甚至買廣告攻擊競選對手。

push poll 引導式民調
透過設計過的 poll「民調」影響民眾選擇對己方有利的選項，再公佈民調，以利用媒體影響選情。

intimidation 逼退對手
透過各種脅迫手段讓對手棄選。

vote-buying 買票
以金錢或贈品收買選民投票支持。

flip-flop 政策、立場搖擺不定
flip-flop 多用於美國，u-turn 通常用於英國，而 backflip 多用於紐澳地區。這三個字都是用來形容政策導向常常變來變去，只為討好所有的人民。

political contribution 政治獻金
指某些個人或財團捐獻給支持政黨的金錢。合法的政治獻金並無不妥。

法蘭克：我只問妳一個簡單的問題，妳對這職位有興趣嗎？

凱薩琳：你為什麼要弄走麥可？

法蘭克：凱西，你我並肩作戰多年。外交事務委員會需要一個我們可以合作的國務卿，一個在沃克出錯時，不怕挺身而出的人。

📖 學英文 🎧 78

boy scout 正人君子

© catwalker / Shutterstock.com

boy scout 即「童子軍」，被視為智仁勇的象徵，美國人要表示自己講話絕無欺瞞，都還要學童子軍敬禮。說一個人是 boy scout，表示他人格毫無瑕疵，有時有嘲諷意味。

A: Do you think the corruption accusations against the mayor are true?
你覺得關於市長貪污的指控是真的嗎？

B: I wouldn't be surprised. He's no boy scout.
我不會意外。他可不是正人君子。

📷 看影集

道格斯坦普與警察局長巴尼胡爾見面，說服他放過因為酒駕和載妓女而被逮捕的彼得羅素。

Doug: You've been police commissioner for what, almost a decade now?

Barney: We're here to talk about my résumé?

Doug: Mayor of D.C. would look good on that résumé, wouldn't it? We know that you've been angling to run for some time. Experience is your **strong suit**. Endorsement and fundraising are not. We can help with that.

道格：你當警察局長多久了，快十年了吧？

巴尼：我們見面是為了討論我的履歷嗎？

道格：履歷上有華盛頓市長應該會好看一點，不是嗎？我知道你一直在醞釀競選。經歷才是你的王牌，背書和募款都不是。這點我們可以幫你。

📖 學英文 🎧 79

strong suit 強項

撲克牌有四個花色（suit），在橋牌等遊戲中，手上某種花色的牌越多、點數越大就越有利，而手上最強最多的那種花色，就是他的 strong suit（也叫 long suit）。因此 strong suit 就是一個人的專長、特殊技能，也就是最擅長的事。

A: Dylan sure loses his temper easily.
迪蘭還真容易發脾氣。

B: Yeah. Patience isn't his strong siut.
對啊。耐性不是他的強項。

© Featureflash / Shutterstock.com

《紙牌屋》被戲稱為「白宮甄嬛傳」，連美國前總統柯林頓都曾說這部戲「百分之九十九的劇情都是真的」。而飾演法蘭克（Frank Underwood）的凱文史貝西（Kevin Spacey）不但私底下認識柯林頓，長年贊助美國民主黨，連他跟羅蘋萊特（Robin Wright）這對螢幕政壇夫妻，都常被與柯林頓夫婦聯想在一起，希拉蕊柯林頓宣布參選時，許多人都期待《紙牌屋》第四季內容能有相關轉折。

SCANDAL 醜聞風暴

ABC's [1] *Scandal* is a political [2] **thriller** about Olivia Pope, a Washington "fixer" based on the [3] **real-life** Judy Smith, a former White House press [4] **aide** who started her own crisis management firm. In *Scandal*, Judy's fictional [5] **version** served in the [6] **administration** of President Fitzgerald Grant before leaving to start Olivia Pope & [7] **Associates**, which [8] **specializes** in protecting the public images of the rich and powerful.

© ABC

美國廣播公司製作的《醜聞風暴》，是關於華府「危機處理專家」奧利維亞波普的政治驚悚影集，是根據前白宮新聞助理茱蒂史密斯的真實生活改編，她後來自己成立危機管理公司。在《醜聞風暴》中，茱蒂的虛構版在費茲傑羅格蘭特總統的政府中任職，後來離職，成立奧利維亞波普事務所，專門為有錢有勢的公眾人物維護形象。

come out of the closet 出櫃

同性戀者常用 in the closet「在衣櫃裡」來比喻同性戀或雙性戀向親友、社會隱藏其性傾向（sexual orientation）的說法。因此，當同志向他人表明同志身分時，稱為 come out of the closet「走出衣櫃」，簡稱「出櫃」，又叫 come out「現身」。

Scandal begins with a young lawyer named Quinn Perkins showing up for a blind date with Harrison Wright, who's really there to offer her a job. And how could she refuse? He works for Olivia Pope, Washington's top fixer. Back at the office, Quinn gets to meet her new boss, who, along with associate Stephen Finch, has just successfully [9] **negotiated** with Ukrainian [10] **gangsters** for the return of an ambassador's baby boy. After meeting the rest of the team— investigator Abbey Whelan and ex-CIA tech expert Huck—Quinn is immediately put to work when a man walks in with blood on his shirt. Sully St. James, a war hero and [11]**conservative** public speaker, tells them his girlfriend Paige has been murdered, but that he didn't do it.

《醜聞風暴》故事一開始，年輕律師昆恩帕金斯出席與哈瑞森萊特的盲目約會，而哈瑞森其實是來提供昆恩一份工作。而她又如何能拒絕？哈瑞森的老闆是華盛頓的頂尖危機處理專家奧利維亞波普。場景回到辦公室，昆恩與她的新老闆見面，還有同事史蒂芬奇。奧利維亞和史蒂芬剛剛成功與烏克蘭歹徒談判，要求他們釋放大使的男嬰。見過團隊的其他同事後——像是調查員艾比威爾蘭和前中情局科技專家哈克——一位襯衫沾著血跡的男子走進來，昆恩便立刻開始工作。他是戰爭英雄和保守派演說家蘇利詹姆士，他說他的女友佩琪被殺害，而兇手不是他。

Olivia persuades U.S. [12]**Attorney** David Rosen to wait 24 hours before arresting Sully, and the team starts investigating. Meanwhile, White House [13]**Chief of Staff** Cyrus Beene comes to her with another case—White House aide Amanda Tanner claims she had an affair with the president, and Cyrus wants her silenced. Olivia locates Amanda and threatens to destroy her career, which seems to work—until she shows up at a hospital after a suicide attempt. The team later finds [14]**evidence** that Sully wasn't at the scene of the crime—a tape showing him kissing his gay lover outside a bar—and persuades him to **come out of the closet** and prove his [15]**innocence**. Finally, Olivia begins to believe Amanda's story when she says the president called her "Sweet Baby"—which is what he used to call Olivia. Yes, her relationship with the president was more than [16]**professional**!

奧利維亞說服聯邦檢察官大衛羅森在逮捕蘇利前，再等二十四小時，而她的團隊也開始調查此案。同時，白宮幕僚長賽瑞斯畢恩為了另一件案子來找奧利維亞——白宮助理亞曼達坦納自稱與總統有婚外情，而賽瑞斯要她保持緘默。奧利維亞找到亞曼達，威脅會毀掉她的生涯，這招看似奏效——但她卻因自殺未遂而出現在醫院裡。奧利維亞的團隊後來找到蘇利不在犯罪現場的證據——一段錄影顯示他在酒吧外親吻他的同性戀人——並說服他出櫃以證明自己清白。最後奧利維亞開始相信亞曼達的說法，因為亞曼達說總統叫她「甜心寶貝」——這是他以前對奧利維亞的稱呼。沒錯，她和總統的關係超越了職場範圍！

© ABC

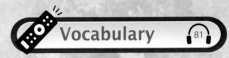

Vocabulary

1) **scandal** [ˋskændəl] (n.) 醜聞
   The scandal ruined the politician's reputation.

2) **thriller** [ˋθrɪlɚ] (n.) 驚悚片（小說）
   Jenny likes to read thrillers and mystery novels.

3) **real-life** [ˋriəlˏlaɪf] (a.) 真實的，現實的
   Jamie Foxx became a real-life hero when he rescued a man from a burning car.

4) **aide** [ed] (n.) 助理
   The man serves as a senior aide to the president.

5) **version** [ˋvɝʒən] (n.) 版本
   Which version of Windows do you have on your computer?

6) **administration** [ədˏmɪnəˋstreʃən] (n.) （美國）某總統的政府、任期
   Hillary Clinton served as Secretary of state in the Obama administration.

7) **associate** [əˋsoʃɪət] (n.) （生意上的）夥伴，合夥人
   I'd like to introduce you to my associate.

8) **specialize (in)** [ˋspɛʃəˏlaɪz] (v.) 專門從事，專攻
   The travel agency specializes in adventure travel.

9) **negotiate** [nɪˋgoʃɪˏet] (v.) 協商，談判
   The government refuses to negotiate with terrorists.

10) **gangster** [ˋgæŋstɚ] (n.) 幫派份子
    Many of the nightclubs in the city are owned by gangsters.

11) **conservative** [kənˋsɝvətɪv] (a.) 保守（派）的，傳統的
    Saudi Arabia is a very conservative country.

12) **attorney** [əˋtɝnɪ] (n.) 律師，檢察官
    If you can't afford an attorney, the court will provide one.

13) **chief of staff** (phr.) 幕僚長，參謀長
    The governor was caught having an affair with his chief of staff.

14) **evidence** [ˋɛvədəns] (n.) 證據，跡象
    There's no evidence that the suspect committed the crime.

15) **innocence** [ˋɪnəsəns] (n.) 無罪，清白
    The murder suspect claimed innocence.

16) **professional** [prəˋfɛʃənəl] (a.) 專業的，職業的
    Cynthia wants to be a professional musician.

© ABC

看影集

昆恩在酒吧與哈瑞森見面赴「盲約」。

Quinn: Harrison Wright?

Harrison: Quinn Perkins.

Quinn: I can't stay.

Harrison: What are you drinking?

Quinn: I can't stay. I'm sorry. I only came because Lori wouldn't give me your number so I could cancel, and I didn't want you to be waiting here, because **getting stood up** in this particular bar is like falling face down on a runway. And even though I don't know you, Lori's got this annoying habit of meddling, so it seemed only decent to....

Harrison: What are you drinking?

Quinn: I can't stay is what I'm saying. I don't do blind dates.

Harrison: My parents met on a blind date. They've been inseparable ever since.

Quinn: I'm happy for your parents and for you, because it means you exist, but I don't do blind dates.

Harrison: This isn't a blind date.

Quinn: What?

Harrison: It's a job interview. What are you drinking?

Quinn: **Dirty martini**. What do you mean this is a job interview?

昆　恩：哈瑞森萊特？

哈瑞森：昆恩帕金斯？

昆　恩：我不能留下。

哈瑞森：妳要喝什麼？

昆　恩：我不能留下，抱歉。我來這裡只是因為蘿莉不給我你的電話號碼，所以我無法取消，我也不想讓你在這裡等，因為在這種酒吧被放鴿子，就像在時裝伸展台上摔得狗吃屎。雖然我不認識你，蘿莉又有愛管閒事的壞習慣，所以似乎只能這樣做才比較禮貌⋯⋯。

哈瑞森：妳要喝什麼？

昆　恩：我說我不能留下。我不盲約的。

哈瑞森：我父母就是盲約認識的。他們從來沒分開過。

昆　恩：我為你的父母和你高興，因為這樣才有了你，但我不盲約的。

哈瑞森：這不是盲約。

昆　恩：什麼？

哈瑞森：這是工作面試。妳要喝什麼？

昆　恩：油漬馬丁尼。工作面試是什麼意思？

學英文 82

get stood up 被放鴿子

你在跟人約定的時間，站在約定的地點等不到人，就像被罰站一樣活受罪。經常的用法是 stand sb. up 或 stand up sb.。

A: What are you doing here all by yourself?
　你一個人在這邊幹嘛？

B: I got stood up.
　我被放鴿子了。

看影集

奧利維亞正與烏克蘭歹徒談判，要他們釋放大使的男嬰。

Oskar: You got the money?

Olivia: Of course, all three million.

Oskar: We said six.

Olivia: I have three.

Oskar: That's a problem.

Olivia: Well, it's all the ambassador had **on** such **short notice**, so you're just gonna have to take it.

Oskar: You leave the three. When you come back with the rest, we have a deal.

Olivia: That's not gonna happen, Oskar.

Oskar: No?

Olivia: Nyet. What's going to happen is you and Vlad are gonna take the three million and leave right now for Dulles to make your flight to the motherland. The reason you're gonna want to go right now, beside the fact that it's just good travel sense to give yourself enough time for international check-in, is in exactly four hours and 15 minutes, both of your names are gonna suddenly "pop up" on Homeland Security's no-fly list. Lucky for you, you're booked on a flight that leaves in two and a half hours. So if it were me, I'd much rather spend three million dollars in Kiev than here in Georgetown—way more **bang for your buck**. In fact, it may even feel like six once you're there.

奧利維亞：沒錯。你和弗拉德必須接受這三百萬，然後立刻離開，到杜勒斯搭機回母國。你們最好馬上出發，因為你們要給自己足夠的時間辦理國際航班的登機手續，而且再過四小時十五分鐘整，你們的名字會「出現」在國土安全部的禁飛名單上。幸運的是，你們的班機已經訂好了，起飛時間是在兩個半小時後。所以，假如我是你們的話，我寧可回基輔花這三百萬，也不會留在喬治城——這對你們來說更划算。事實上，三百萬在那裡就跟六百萬一樣。

奧 斯 卡：妳帶錢來了嗎？
奧利維亞：當然，總共三百萬。
奧 斯 卡：我們說好六百萬。
奧利維亞：我只有三百萬。
奧 斯 卡：那就有問題了。
奧利維亞：嗯，大使在短時間內只能湊到這些，你只能接受了。
奧 斯 卡：留下三百萬，等妳把剩下的數目拿回來，我們就交貨。
奧利維亞：不可能的，奧斯卡。
奧 斯 卡：不可能？

學英文 83

on/at short notice 臨時通知

notice 在這邊是名詞「通知，預先告知」的意思，short 是指時間很短。

A: Do you think you can get someone to fill in for you at work?
你有辦法找到人來代你的班嗎？

B: I don't know. It may be hard to find somebody on such short notice.
不知道耶。這麼臨時通知，可能很難找到人。

bang for the buck 物超所值

buck 在英文口語指的是「一塊錢」。這句話是源自美軍向國防部爭取貴重軍火和戰機，表示「用同樣的預算買到殺傷力最大的武器」，現在則指「得到的超過付出的。」bang 前面可加上 more 或 lots of 強調非常物超所值。

A: I'm thinking of buying a German sports car.
我在考慮買一輛德國跑車。

B: German cars are nice, but a Japanese car will give you more bang for the buck.
德國車是不錯，但是日本車更是物超所值。

martini 雞尾酒之王

martini 是酒吧裡最常被點的雞尾酒之一，最基本的配方是琴酒（gin）、苦艾酒（vermouth），加橄欖或檸檬皮絲裝飾，其他變化調法超過二百種，以下是其中一些：

dry martini 採用不甜苦艾酒（dry vermouth）調成。

dirty martini 在馬丁尼中加入少許醃漬橄欖的滷汁。

vodka martini、**gin martini** 以伏特加取代苦艾酒，或是純以琴酒調成的馬丁尼。

wet martini 採用甜苦艾酒（wet vermouth）調成。

perfect martini 甜苦艾酒、不甜苦艾酒各佔一半調成。

lemon drop martini 檸檬糖果馬丁尼是以伏特加酒、糖、檸檬汁、柑橘調味酒（orange liqueur）加冰塊搖製而成，甜味及檸檬味很足，能掩蓋酒精氣味，是適合女性飲用的調酒（girly drink）。

© ABC

看影集

奧利維亞的團隊在辦公室討論是否該接下蘇利的案子。

Abby: Lieutenant Colonel Sullivan "Sully" St. James, age 32, did two tours in Iraq, was injured saving the lives of his entire unit, a war hero.

Stephen: And not just any war hero—the first living Marine awarded the Medal of Honor for action in any war since Vietnam.

Abby: A famous war hero, working class, patriotic, comes from a long line of soldiers. Here he is with the president. Also Sexiest Man Alive 2010.

OliviA: **Poster boy** for the military.

Abby: And for the conservative right. That's how he makes his living. He gives expensive speeches, makes a fortune. He's **anti-choice**, pro-gun, hates the gays, and likes it when kids pray in school.

Stephen: Abby.

Abby: I'm just saying he sickens me politically. I'm not saying we shouldn't help him.

---

anti-choice 反墮胎
認為在胚胎（fetus）形成時，就已算是一個「人」，具有生存的權利，因此這派的主張又稱為 pro-life。

pro-choice 支持墮胎
認為女性對其身體有自主權，應有選擇墮胎的權力（abortion rights）。

艾　　比：蘇利文「蘇利」聖詹姆士中校，三十二歲，在伊拉克服役過兩次，因為拯救整個部隊而負傷，是戰爭英雄。

史蒂芬：而且不是一般的戰爭英雄——自越戰以來首次因行動獲得榮譽勳章，而且還在世的海軍陸戰隊隊員。

艾　　比：有名的戰爭英雄、勞工階級、愛國、出身軍人世家。這是他和總統的合照，也曾被選為二〇一〇年最性感男人。

奧利維亞：軍隊的活招牌。

艾　　比：也是保守黨右派的活招牌，這也是他的飯碗。他的演說收費昂貴，靠這個賺大錢。他反墮胎、支持擁槍、反同性戀，支持學童在學校裡禱告。

史蒂芬：艾比。

艾　　比：我只是說，從政治的角度來說他讓我厭煩。我沒說我們不該幫他。

學英文 🎧 84

poster boy 代表人物，典範
poster 是「海報」，poster boy 就是被用來做宣傳的典範人物，或是最能象徵所希望達成目標、所標榜特質的代表。若為女性人物，要說 poster girl，若為兒童，則是 poster child。

A: Why do so many people support Donald Trump?
為什麼那麼多人支持唐納川普？

B: Because he's a poster boy for business success.
因為他是事業成功的典範。

看影集

奧利維亞和艾比拿著蘇利親吻男人的錄影帶與他對質。

Sully: You can't show that tape to anyone.

Olivia: I need the name of the man you were kissing.

Sully: You can't show that tape, and you can't have a name.

Olivia: It's your alibi.

Sully: No. I'm…you cannot tell people that I am gay. I am a hero.

Abby: The police have a warrant for your arrest. **All due respect,** people finding out you're gay is no big deal compared to that.

Sully: No. I am a hero. I honor the uniform.
Olivia: Sully….
Sully: I honor the uniform!
Olivia: Sully, look at me. The rules have changed. **Don't ask, don't tell** is over.
Sully: That is talk! I am a conservative Republican! I am publicly anti-gay! I am the deacon in my church. They're talking about me running for Congress one day. I am Lieutenant Colonel Sullivan St. James. I'm a hero. I can't be gay.

with all due respect 恕我直言
擔心接下來所講的話會冒犯對方，就先講這一句，字面上的意思是「我懷著無比的敬意（說）」。

A: If we want to increase sales, we should lower the commissions given to our sales reps.
　　如果想要提高業績，我們應該降低給業務員的佣金。

B: With all due respect, I don't think that's a good way to improve our sales figures.
　　恕我直言，我不認為那是提升業績數字的好方法。

飾演奧利維亞（Olivia Pope）的凱莉華盛頓（Kerry Washington）原本就已參與多部電影的演出，但都是某某人的另一半，如《雷之心靈傳奇》雷查爾斯的妻子、《最後的蘇格蘭王》伊迪阿敏的妻子、《驚奇四超人》石頭人的女朋友、《決殺令》姜戈的妻子，終於在接演《醜聞風暴》後闖出自己的一片天。

蘇　　利：你們不能把錄影帶拿給別人看。
奧利維亞：我要知道你親吻的人是誰。
蘇　　利：你們不能公開錄影帶，我也不會讓你們知道他是誰。
奧利維亞：這是你的不在場證明。
蘇　　利：不，我……你不能告訴別人我是同性戀。我是英雄。
艾　　比：警方有你的逮捕令。恕我直言，跟這件事相比，讓大家知道你是同性戀沒什麼大不了。
蘇　　利：不行，我是英雄，我要維護軍人的榮耀。
奧利維亞：蘇利……。
蘇　　利：我要維護軍人的榮耀！
奧利維亞：蘇利，看著我。規則已經改了。不問不說已經是過去式了。
蘇　　利：那些都是空話！我是保守派的共和黨人！我是公開反對同性戀的！我是教會的執事。他們都在說我有一天要競選國會議員。我是蘇利文聖詹姆士中校。我是英雄，我不能是同性戀。

© Helga Esteb / Shutterstock.com

Don't ask, don't tell 不問，不說
簡稱 DADT，是美軍一九九四至二〇一〇年間對待軍隊內同志的政策，也就是禁止軍隊騷擾未出櫃同志，但也要同志不要公開自己的性向。這樣的政策並未能保障已出櫃同志，基本上還是反同志，因此已於二〇一一年廢止。美國的同性戀者現在可以公開服役。

政治驚悚

反恐危機
HOMELAND

*H*omeland, which is loosely based on the Israeli series *Prisoners of War*, is an American political drama starring Claire Danes as Carrie Mathison, a [1]**dedicated** CIA officer who struggles with [2]**bipolar** [3]**disorder**. Originally a field agent in Baghdad, Carrie is [4]**reassigned** to a desk job at CIA headquarters after she's caught meeting with an [5]**informant** inside an Iraqi prison. Just before the guards drag her away, the informant whispers in her ear, "An American prisoner of war has been turned."

《反恐危機》是一部美國政治戲劇，大致上以以色列影集《戰俘》為基礎，由克萊兒丹妮絲飾演患有躁鬱症的美國中情局情報員，凱莉麥迪遜。凱莉原本在巴格達做特工，在伊拉克監獄和一位線人會面時被抓到後，被調回情報局總部擔任文書工作。在守衛把她拖走前，那位線人在她耳邊低聲說：「有位美國戰俘已經叛變。」

Things get [6]**complicated** for Carrie when she learns at a CIA [7]**briefing** by her boss, David Estes, that U.S. Marine [8]**Sergeant** Nicholas Brody, who was reported missing in action eight years ago, has been [9]**rescued** in a **Delta Force** [10]**raid** on the base of Al-Qaeda [11]**terrorist** Abu Nazir. While Carrie believes that Brody is the prisoner her informant was talking about, the U.S. government and her superiors at the CIA consider him a war hero. When her [12]**mentor**, Middle East Division Chief Saul Berenson, tells her there's no chance of the CIA investigating Brody, Carrie decides to set up [13]**surveillance** at his house on her own.

Homeland Security 國土安全部

全名為 Department of Homeland Security，這個新聞名詞通常伴隨著美國的恐怖攻擊（terrorist attack）事件、救災行動等；Homeland Security 成立於 911 恐怖攻擊事件後，作為積極加強維護國土安全的一個組織，匯集了二十二個不同聯邦機構，成為第三大聯邦部門。其核心任務主要為防止恐怖主義（terrorism）、維護邊界安全、管理移民法（immigration law）、維護網路空間（cyberspace）、救災抗災行動等。

Delta Force 三角洲部隊

專司反恐及人質救援的美國陸軍特種部隊，其相關資訊及行動都被列為最高機密。一般認為這支部隊的成員除了體能及心智極強，均須精通外語或具備特殊作戰技能。

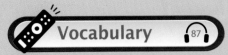

在一次中情局的匯報上，凱莉從主管大衛伊斯特那裡得知，八年前在行動中失蹤的海軍陸戰隊中士尼可拉斯布羅迪，在三角洲部隊突擊蓋達恐怖分子阿布納吉爾的基地時獲救，此後凱莉的情況就變得複雜了。凱莉相信布羅迪就是她的線人口中的戰俘，但美國政府和她在中情局的上司都認為他是戰爭英雄。她的導師，中東地區部門主管索爾貝倫遜告訴她，中情局不可能調查布羅迪，於是凱莉決定自行在他家中裝設監視器。

Meanwhile, Sergeant Brody is having problems of his own. Carrie doesn't find any evidence that he's an enemy agent, but she does discover that his wife is having an affair with his best friend, and that his son and daughter treat him like a stranger. But Saul soon finds out about Carrie's illegal surveillance, and decides to report her to the [14]**authorities**. Luckily, she discovers an important clue that makes Saul change his mind. Whenever Brody appears on TV, the fingers on his right hand tap against his palm in a regular pattern. Is he just [15]**shaky** after being held [16]**captive** by terrorists for so long, or is he a terrorist himself, sending messages to Al-Qaeda? Why not join Carrie on her investigation?

同時，布羅迪中士也有自己的問題。凱莉找不到任何證據證明布羅迪是敵方的特務，但她發現他妻子與他的好友有婚外情，而他的兒子和女兒待他就像陌生人。但索爾很快發現凱莉非法架設監視器，並決定向當局舉報。幸好她發現了重要線索，讓索爾改變主意。只要布羅迪出現在電視上，他的右手手指就會以固定模式敲打手掌。他是因為被恐怖分子關押太久留下顫抖的後遺症？還是他本來就是恐怖分子，並且用此方法向蓋達組織傳遞訊息？想知道的話，何不跟凱莉一起來調查？

Vocabulary

1) **dedicated** [ˋdɛdəˌketɪd] (a.) 專注的，投入的
John is a dedicated and diligent student.

2) **bipolar** [baɪˋpolə] (a.) 躁鬱的，有兩極的
A new drug has been developed to treat bipolar patients.

3) **disorder** [dɪsˋɔrdə] (n.) 疾病，（生理或心理）失調
Many young women suffer from eating disorders.

4) **reassign** [ˌriəˋsaɪn] (v.) 重新分配，調動
(v.) assign 分配，分派
Did you hear that Donald is being reassigned to the Paris office?

5) **informant** [ɪnˋfɔrmənt] (n.) 告密者，線民
The police learned about the plot from an informant.

6) **complicated** [ˋkɑmpləˌketɪd] (a.) 複雜的，難懂的
The instructions were too complicated for me to understand.

7) **briefing** [ˋbrifɪŋ] (n.) 簡報
Dozens of reporters attended the press briefing.

8) **sergeant** [ˋsɑrdʒənt] (n.)（陸軍、海軍陸戰隊）中士
The sergeant led his men on a ten-mile hike.

9) **rescue** [ˋrɛskju] (v./n.) 營救，解圍
The fireman rescued the girl from the burning building.

10) **raid** [red] (n./v.) 突襲
The soldiers carried out a daring raid on the enemy base

11) **terrorist** [ˋtɛrərɪst] (n.) 恐怖分子，恐怖主義者
The terrorists responsible for the bombing were never caught.

12) **mentor** [ˋmɛntə] (n.) 精神導師，師父
You should find a mentor to advise you on your career.

13) **surveillance** [sɜˋveləns] (n.) 監視
The police have the suspect under surveillance.

14) **authority** [əˋθɔrətɪ] (n.)（多為複數）當局，警方，管理機關，專家
Local authorities are investigating the crime.

15) **shaky** [ˋʃeki] (a.) 顫抖的，緊張不安的
Drinking too much coffee makes me shaky.

16) **captive** [ˋkæptɪv] (a./n.) 被俘虜的，被監禁的；俘虜，囚徒
The captive soldiers were rescued during the battle.

© Showtime

政治驚悚

© Showtime

看影集

凱莉和索爾在討論線人提供給她的情報。

Saul: You're suggesting that Abu Nazir planted intelligence in his own safe house just so we could recover Sergeant Brody?

Carrie: I realize it sounds like a reach.

Saul: **To say the least**. Why not just drop him near a checkpoint and make it look like he escaped? Why would you sacrifice 13 trained fighters?

Carrie: Because Abu Nazir is **playing the long game**. This way, no one suspects a thing.

Saul: Except you.

Carrie: Yeah, except me.

索爾： 妳在暗示阿布納吉爾故意洩漏自己的藏身之處，好讓我們能發現布羅迪中士？

凱莉： 我知道這聽起來有點牽強。

索爾： 就是說啊。為什麼不把他丟到哨站附近，讓他看起來像是自己逃出來的？為什麼要犧牲十三個訓練有素的戰士？

凱莉： 因為阿布納吉爾要打持久戰。這樣就沒有人會懷疑。

索爾： 除了妳。

凱莉： 對，除了我。

學英文

to say the least 就是說啊

the least 是「最少」，這句話表示完全同意對方的說法，也可以表示「這樣說已經很客氣了」。

A: The professor's lecture today was so boring.
那位教授今天的課好無聊。

B: To say the least!
就是說啊！

play the long game 放長線釣大魚

表示佈局很久，等待最後一口氣大豐收。

A: If prices are falling, why don't you sell your stocks before you lose even more money?
如果價格持續下跌，你為何不在賠更多錢之前賣掉股票？

B: The market will recover eventually. I'm playing the long game.
股市最終還是會回檔。我做的是長線佈局。

看影集

同一場對話。

Carrie: Sergeant Brody's due home from Germany tomorrow morning, which gives us just under 22 hours.

Saul: To do what?

Carrie: To authorize a surveillance package. To **tap** his phones, **wire** his house, **follow** him wherever he goes.

Saul: David will never **sign off on** that and you know it.

Carrie: Of course he won't. The White House needs a poster boy for the war, and David just served him up on a platter. That's why I'm coming to you.

Saul: I'm not **going over his head**, not on a hunch.

凱莉： 布羅迪中士明天早上要從德國回家了，我們還剩下不到二十二小時。

索爾： 做什麼？

凱莉： 批准一套監視設備，監聽他的電話，在他房子裡安裝竊聽器，隨時隨地跟蹤他。

索爾： 大衛不會批准的，妳也知道。

凱莉： 他當然不會。白宮需要有人替這場戰爭宣傳，而大衛想把他推上台去。所以我來找你。

索爾： 我不能越權，不能只憑直覺行事。

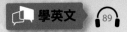

sign off on 簽核，批准

報告完成會需要上級審核確認，提出計畫會需要上級批准通過，兩種情況主管都要在上面簽下大名，這個動作就是 sign off on。

A: What do you think about my proposal?
你對我的提案有什麼想法？

B: It's a good idea, but I don't think the boss will sign off on it.
點子不錯，但我不認為老闆會批准。

go over sb.'s head 越級報告，越級行事

字面上是「從一個人頭上跨過去」，比喻「越級」，直接去找某人的上司討論事情。

A: What do you do when customer service won't help you?
客服人員不幫你的話，你會怎麼做？

B: I go over their heads and complain to management.
我會跳過他們，去跟主管抱怨。

看影集

凱莉來到布羅迪的家，她以前在中情局的朋友維吉爾和他弟弟準備裝設監視器。

Carrie: I got 30 minutes.

Virgil: And good to see you too, Carrie.

Carrie: Who the fuck is he?!

Virgil: Relax, it's all good. It's my brother Max.
Max, say hi to the client.

Max: Hi.

Carrie: What happened to Nick and Eddie?

Virgil: Out of your price range. I told you, for a grand a day, it's gonna be **bare bones**. Hey, you got a bad feeling about this? You want to roll this thing up before we get started, you just say the word.

Carrie: Eyes and ears in every room. Then it's back to my place to set up the monitors.

凱　莉：我只有三十分鐘。

維吉爾：很高興看到妳，凱莉。

凱　莉：他是誰？！

維吉爾：放心，沒事。他是我弟弟麥克思。麥克思，跟客戶打招呼。

麥克思：嗨。

凱　莉：尼克和艾迪呢？

維吉爾：價錢超出妳的預算，我告訴過妳，一天一千元，只能給你陽春型的。嘿，妳有不好的預感嗎？在我們動手前，你想收手的話就說吧。

凱　莉：每個房間都要裝監視器和竊聽器。然後回到我住處架設監控螢幕。

bare bones 基本款，簡明版

字面上就是去掉皮和肉，只剩骨架子，引申為沒有任何花俏功能的基本款式，或是最簡明的內容。

A: How many cable channels do you get?
你裝了幾個有線電視頻道？

B: Only 20 channels. We got the bare bones package.
只有二十台。我們選最陽春的方案。

跟監竊聽相關英文

tap 監聽
即 wiretap，截斷電話線，或攔截電話、網路訊號進行監聽錄音。這兩個字也都可以當名詞，指「竊聽器」。

bug 監聽
用法跟 tap 一樣，也同時能當名詞，指「竊聽器」。

wire 裝麥克風竊聽
這個字原本是在房屋裡「安裝線路」，引申為在房子、汽車、身上安裝隱藏式麥克風，這個字也可以當名詞，指「隱藏式麥克風」。

eavesdrop 攔截監聽
除了監聽電話，也攔截往返電子郵件。這個字也指一般拉長耳朵偷聽別人說話。

tail 跟踪
即「尾隨」。可以當動詞，也可以當名詞。

hack 駭入
運用強大的電子工程技能進入電腦資料庫、智慧手機等竊取資料。

tracking device 跟監裝置
安裝在汽車、人員等追蹤目標上，透過 GPS 進行跟監。

spy camera 針孔攝影機
隱藏在手錶等配戴裝置上，或安裝在房屋當中偷拍的微型攝影器材。

政治驚悚

© Showtime

看影集

凱莉參加布羅迪的中情局任務報告。

Carrie: Sergeant Brody, my name is Carrie Mathison. I served as a case officer in Iraq. Your picture was on our **MIA** wall. I saw it every day for five years. It's good to meet you in person.

Brody: Thank you, ma'am.

Carrie: I'm sorry we were unable to find you sooner.

Brody: I appreciate that.

Carrie: I'd like to start with the first few days of your captivity if you don't mind.

Brody: Not at all.

Carrie: How soon after you were taken did the interrogations begin?

Brody: Pretty much right away.

Carrie: What did they want to know?

Brody: Anything I could tell them about U.S. ground operations, supply routes, communication codes, rules of engagement.

Carrie: When you were debriefed in Germany, you said you gave up no such information.

Brody: My **SERE training** was excellent.

凱　莉：布羅迪中士，我叫凱莉麥迪遜。我在伊拉克擔任專案官員。你的照片掛在我們的行動失蹤人員牆上。五年來每天都會看到，現在很高興親自見到你。

布羅迪：謝謝妳，女士。

凱　莉：抱歉我們沒有盡快找到你。

布羅迪：謝謝妳這麼說。

凱　莉：你若不介意的話，我想從你剛被捕的頭幾天開始問起。

布羅迪：一點也不。

凱　莉：你被捕後過了多久開始審訊？

布羅迪：幾乎是立刻就開始。

凱　莉：他們想知道什麼？

布羅迪：任何關於美國地面行動、補給路線、通訊密碼、交戰規則的事。

凱　莉：你在德國做任務報告時，你說你沒有透露這類情報。

布羅迪：我接受了非常優秀的生存訓練。

學英文　91

MIA 任務中失蹤

missing in action 的縮寫，是指軍事人員在戰鬥行動當中失蹤，可能是在戰爭中死亡、被俘、叛逃。

A: What's the second *Rambo* movie about?
《藍波》第二集是在演什麼？

B: Rambo goes to Vietnam looking for soldiers who went MIA during the war.
藍波去越南尋找越戰時任務中失蹤的士兵。

這個字有時被用來開玩笑，指有人搞失蹤，或沒請假、沒告知又找不到人。另一個常見的說法是 go AWOL [`ewol]（absent without leave，未請假而缺勤）。

A: Do you know where John is? I can't find him anywhere.
你知道約翰在哪嗎？我到處都找不到他。

B: No. I haven't seen him since this morning—must have gone MIA.
不知道。我從早上就沒看到他──一定是蹺班了。

SERE 特種訓練

SERE 是美國空軍在韓戰之後研發的訓練，內容涵蓋 survival, evasion, resistance, escape：

survival 生存，包括各種野外生存技能

evasion 躲避，例如在受傷情況下隱匿並避免被捕

resistance 抵抗，例如對審問虐待的耐受能力

escape 逃脫，例如了解軍中相關作業程序，以有效求助、安全逃脫

美國軍方非常重視 SERE，所有特種部隊隊員都必須接受這項訓練，特勤人員（special operations personnel）及戰鬥機組人員（military aircrew）更必須完成高階課程訓練，因為他們最容易身陷敵營。

恐攻相關字彙

no-fly list 禁飛名單
這份名單是由 Terrorist Screening Center「美國恐怖分子篩濾中心」（簡稱 TSC，FBI 的分支機構）整理發布，與美國簽署「恐怖分子篩濾資訊交換協議」的國家也會收到。當一個人登上 no-fly list，表示不只被限制出境，連在境內搭機都不行。no-fly list 上不只有人，也有禁止出入境的飛機名單。

Osama bin Laden 賓拉登
蓋達組織（al-Qaeda）首領，該組織被認為是全球性的恐怖組織，被美國政府指為一九九八年美國大使館爆炸案和二〇〇一年釀成兩千九百九十八人死亡的 911 恐怖攻擊（September 11 attacks）幕後領導人，或至少是主要策劃者之一。二〇一一年五月二日，美國總統歐巴馬宣布賓拉登在巴基斯坦被美軍海豹部隊（Navy SEALs，全名為 U.S. Navy Sea, Air and Land）第六分隊突襲擊斃，遺體於次日海葬於北阿拉伯海。

Taliban 塔利班
波斯語「學生」的意思，也被譯為「神學士」，屬於伊斯蘭教遜尼派，以暴力手段執行伊斯蘭律法，因協助隱匿賓拉登，一直被視為恐怖分子同路人。

ISIS 伊斯蘭國
Islamic State of Iraq and Syria 的簡稱，或稱為 ISIL（Islamic State of Iraq and the Levant），奉行極端恐怖主義（terrorism），活躍於伊拉克及敘利亞地區。該組織已承認犯下俄羅斯 Metrojet 客機爆炸案、巴黎恐怖攻擊、布魯塞爾機場爆炸案。

© Featureflash Photo Agency / Shutterstock.com

🎬 看影集

索爾走進凱莉的公寓，發現她在操作監視器。

Saul: You think for one minute you **get away with** this?

Carrie: I thought that once I had some proof....

Saul: Do you have any? Anything? Even suggesting that Sergeant Brody's what you think he is?

Carrie: No.

Saul: Then get a lawyer. 'Cause you're gonna need one when you report to the **IG** first thing in the morning.

索爾：妳以為妳能逃得過嗎？
凱莉：我以為找到一些證據之後……。
索爾：找到了嗎？有任何證據嗎？可以證明布羅迪就是妳所想的那種人？
凱莉：沒有。
索爾：那就請個律師吧，因為明天我早上妳向檢察長報告時會需要的。

> **IG 檢察長**
> 是 inspector general 的縮寫。

📖 學英文

get away with sth. 躲過懲罰，得逞
get away 是「逃離」的意思，get away with sth. 就是「帶著……逃跑」，表示做事不想承擔後果，還想逃跑。

A: I'm thinking of cheating on the test tomorrow.
我明天考試想要作弊。

B: Don't. You won't get away with it.
別這樣。你不會得逞的。

> 飾演本劇女主角凱莉的克萊兒丹妮斯（Claire Danes）出道極早，十四歲時就靠電視影集《我所謂的生活》得到人生中第一座金球獎，十六歲與李奧納多狄卡皮歐（Leonardo DiCaprio）合演《羅密歐與茱麗葉》，第一次主演電影就令人印象深刻。

GREY'S ANATOMY

實習醫生

93

One of television's most successful and longest running medical dramas, *Grey's* [1)]**Anatomy** follows the ups and downs, both personal and professional, of a group of young [2)]**surgical** interns at a fictional Seattle Hospital. The show, whose title is a play on the famous medical text *Gray's Anatomy* and the name of the lead character, Meredith Grey, has won [3)]**numerous** awards over its 12-season history, including four Emmys and two Golden Globes.

《實習醫生》是電視史上最成功、也是播映時間最久的醫療戲劇之一，是關於一群年輕外科實習醫生在虛構的西雅圖醫院中，面對人生和職場的起起伏伏。這部影集的名稱採用一部有名的醫學著作，《格雷氏解剖學》，也是主角的名字，梅莉迪絲格蕾，在播映十二季期間，獲得無數獎項，包括四座艾美獎和兩座金球獎。

As the show opens, Meredith wakes up to find a naked man next to her. But she has no time to make [4)]**small talk** with her one-night stand. It's her first day as an intern at Seattle [5)]**Mercy** Hospital, and she's running late. At the hospital, she meets her fellow interns—the super [6)]**competitive** Christina Yang, [7)]**insecure** George O'Malley, ex-underwear model Izzie Stevens and arrogant Alex Karev. They've all been [8)]**assigned** to train under resident Miranda Bailey, nicknamed "The Nazi." After giving her [9)]**terrifying** "new intern speech," Bailey rushes them up to the roof where a new patient—a young beauty [10)]**contestant** with [11)]**seizures**—has just arrived by [12)]**helicopter**.

本劇一開場是梅莉迪絲醒來，發現身邊躺著一位裸男。但她沒時間和她的一夜情對象閒聊，因為今天是她第一天到西雅圖仁愛醫院當實習醫生的日子，而且她快遲到了。在醫院裡，她認識了幾位實習同事——超級好強的克莉絲汀娜楊、沒自信的喬治歐麥利、前內衣模特兒伊茲史帝芬，和自負的艾力克斯卡瑞。他們都被派到綽號「納粹」的住院醫師米蘭達貝莉手下訓練。貝莉在發表了嚇人的「新實習生訓話」後，催促他們到屋頂去接一位剛剛被直升機送來的新病患——患有癲癇的年輕選美參賽者。

醫療教學相關英文

intern 實習醫師

醫學院高年級生。擔任臨床助理，協助醫師及護理工作，如：為住病患做病史詢問、送病患去檢驗或開刀，幫忙抽血、打點滴、送檢等等，但不能開處方。

resident 住院醫師

醫學院畢業，考取醫師執照，已分科的正式醫師。住院病人主要都由住院醫師照顧，遇到醫療狀況要靠他們當場解決。住院醫師期限一般為四到五年，資深的住院醫師也會負責教學、行政工作。

attending 主治醫師

已考取專科醫師執照，醫生要到這個時候才能開始看門診，收住院患。除了看診、巡病房、擬定治療計劃，還要負責教學、行政管理及學術論文發表。

After assigning the patient to Meredith, Bailey introduces her to the new attending in charge of the case, Dr. Derek Shepherd, who turns out to be the naked man from that morning! And things get even more [13]**awkward**. When Shepherd asks Meredith to assist him on the patient's [2]**surgery**, Christina is [14]**furious**, thinking she was chosen because she slept with her boss. But in spite of this bad start, Meridith and Christina end up becoming best buddies.

貝莉將病患交給梅莉迪絲後，將她介紹給這個病例的新主治醫師德瑞克雪普，原來他就是今天早上的裸男！之後情況變得更尷尬了。當雪普要求梅莉迪絲擔任病患的手術助理時，克莉絲汀娜以為梅莉迪絲之所以獲選，是因為跟上司上床，因此非常憤怒。不過，儘管一開始的情況是如此糟糕，梅莉迪絲和克莉絲汀娜最後仍變成死黨。

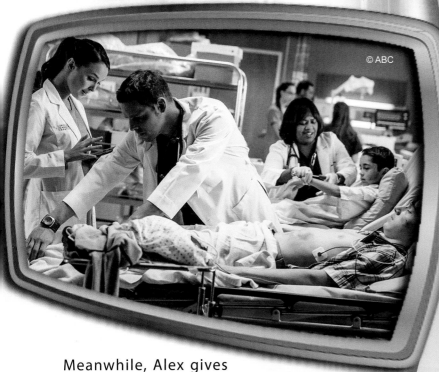

© ABC

Meanwhile, Alex gives George the nickname "007"—[15]**licensed** to kill—after his patient dies on the [16]**operating** table. Derek and Meridith's brain surgery, on the other hand, is a complete success. Her mother, who was once a famous [2]**surgeon**, would be so proud. Unfortunately, she'll never know—she has [17]**Alzheimer's**, which we learn when she visits her at a nursing home later that night.

同時，喬治的病患在手術台上過世後，艾力克斯給喬治取了個綽號叫007──殺人執照。德瑞克和梅莉迪絲的腦科手術卻完全成功。梅莉迪絲的母親一定會為她感到驕傲，因為她母親以前是知名的外科醫師。不幸的是，她不會知道了，當觀眾看到梅莉迪絲在當天晚上到一家養老院探望她時，就知道她患有阿茲海默症。

Vocabulary 94

1) **anatomy** [əˋnætəmɪ] (n.) 解剖結構，解剖學
   The professor teaches a course in plant anatomy.

2) **surgical** [ˋsɝdʒɪkəl] (a.) 外科的 (n.) surgery 外科，外科手術 (n.) surgeon 外科醫生
   The doctor asked the nurse to prepare the surgical instruments.

3) **numerous** [ˋnjumərəs] (a.) 為數眾多的
   The snowstorm caused numerous traffic accidents.

4) **small talk** [smɔl] [tɔk] (phr.) 閒話家常
   Carol is good at making small talk with strangers.

5) **mercy** [ˋmɝsɪ] (n.) 仁慈，善行
   The prisoner got on his knees and begged for mercy.

6) **competitive** [kəmˋpɛtətɪv] (a.) 好競爭的，好強的
   The players on that team are very competitive.

7) **insecure** [ˏɪnsəˋkjʊr] (a.) 缺乏安全感的，沒有自信的
   Michelle is very insecure about her looks.

8) **assign** [əˋsaɪn] (v.) 分配，分派，指定
   Two police detectives were assigned to the murder case.

9) **terrifying** [ˋtɛrəˏfaɪɪŋ] (a.) 可怕的，恐怖的
   Getting attacked by a shark was a terrifying experience.

10) **contestant** [kənˋtɛstənt] (n.) 參賽者
    The contestants on the show are all so talented.

11) **seizure** [ˋsiʒɚ] (n.)（癲癇等）病發，痙攣
    The patient had a seizure when he was given the wrong medicine.

12) **helicopter** [ˋhɛlɪˏkɑptɚ] (n.) 直升機
    The injured climbers were rescued by helicopter.

13) **awkward** [ˋɔkwɚd] (a.) 尷尬的，難為情的
    There was an awkward silence at the dinner table.

14) **furious** [ˋfjʊrɪəs] (a.) 狂怒的，兇猛的，猛烈的
    My parents were furious when they saw my report card.

15) **licensed** [ˋlaɪsənst] (a.) 得到許可的，有執照的
    The movie star is also a licensed pilot.

16) **operating** [ˋɑpəˏretɪŋ] (a.) 外科手術的
    The patient was wheeled into the operating room for surgery.

17) **Alzheimer's** [ˋɑlzˏhaɪmɚz] (n.) 阿茲海默症，即 Alzheimer's disease
    There is currently no cure for Alzheimer's.

看影集

梅莉迪絲在沙發上醒來，發現一個裸男躺在地上。她叫醒他，他從地上撿起她的胸罩。

Man:　　　This is…?

Meredith:　Humiliating on so many levels. You have to go.

Man:　　　Why don't you just come back down here and we'll **pick up where we left off**?

Meredith:　No, seriously. You have to go, I'm late. Which isn't what you want to be on your first day of work, so….

男　　子：這是……？

梅莉迪絲：真是丟臉到極點。你該走了。

男　　子：妳何不回來，繼續我們沒做完的事？

梅莉迪絲：不行，我是說真的。你該走了，我要遲到了。沒人想在第一天上班遲到，所以……。

🗣 學英文　95

pick up where one left off　繼續未完成的事

pick up 有很多意思，在這裡作「繼續」解釋。leave off 有「停止，中斷」的意思，整句就是「從中斷的地方繼續做下去」。

A: Adam wants to get back together with you?
　 亞當想跟妳復合？

B: Yeah. He seems to think we can just pick up where we left off.
　 嗯。他似乎以為我們能就這麼繼續下去，跟從未分手一樣。

© ABC

看影集

貝莉給新實習生訓話。

Bailey: Rule number one, don't bother **sucking up**. I already hate you, that's not gonna change. **Trauma protocol**, phone lists, pagers. Nurses will page you, you answer every page at a run. A run, that's rule number two. Your first shift starts now and lasts 48 hours. You're interns, grunts, nobodies, bottom of the surgical food chain, you run labs, write orders, work every second night till you drop and don't complain! On call rooms. Attendings hog them—sleep when you can, where you can, which brings me to rule number three. If I'm sleeping, don't wake me, unless your patient is actually dying. Rule number four, the dying patient better not be dead when I get there. Not only would you have killed someone, you would have also woke me for no good reason. We clear?

貝莉：第一條規則，別想巴結我，我本來就討厭你們，這點不會變的。外傷規則、電話名單、呼叫器。護士會呼叫你們，每次被呼叫都要用跑的。用跑的，這是第二條。你們的第一輪值班從現在開始，連續四十八小時。你們是實習生、無名小卒、小人物，外科食物鏈中的最底層，你們要送檢體、下訂單、每隔一天通宵值班，直到倒下為止，而且不要抱怨！值班室，都被主治醫師佔去了，可以睡覺時，有適合的地方就睡，這是第三條。假如我在睡覺，別叫醒我，除非你的病人真的快死了。第四條，快死掉的病人在我到之前最好不要死掉，因為這不只代表你殺了人，你還白白叫醒我。明白了嗎？

protocol 標準流程
trauma protocol 是一套完備的外傷急救流程，讓醫療人員在緊迫的情況下，有條不紊地彼此配合進行救治。

suck up (to sb.) 拍馬屁

suck up 是描述在他人跟前巴結諂媚的模樣。

A: Why did Martin get a promotion?
馬丁為什麼能夠升官？

B: Probably because he's always sucking up to the boss.
大概是因為他都會巴結老闆吧。

看影集

癲癇病人抵達醫院頂樓後，外科醫生普瑞斯頓柏克過來評估病情。

Burke: So I heard we got a wet fish on dry land?

Bailey: Absolutely, Dr. Burke.

Burke: Dr. Bailey, I'm gonna **shotgun** her.

Bailey: That means every test in the book—**CT, CBC, Chem-7**, a **tox screen**. Cristina, you're on labs; George, patient **workups**; Meredith, get Katie for a CT. She's your responsibility now.

Izzie: Wait, what about me?

Bailey: You—honey, you get to do **rectal exams**.

Trauma 外傷相關字彙

- penetrating trauma 穿刺傷
- internal bleeding 內出血
- blunt trauma 鈍器所傷
- bullet wound 槍傷
- knife wound 刀傷
- hemorrhage 出血
- hematoma 血腫
- abrasion 擦傷
- cut 割傷
- bruise 瘀傷
- sprain 扭傷
- strain 拉傷
- burn 燒燙傷
- frostbite 凍傷
- fracture 骨折
- contusion 挫傷
- dislocation 脫臼
- laceration 撕裂傷
- ruptured organ 內臟破裂

柏克： 我聽說來了一個癲癇發作的病人？

貝莉： 沒錯，柏克醫師。

柏克： 貝莉醫師，我先幫她整個掃過一遍。

貝莉： 這表示每一樣檢查都要做——電腦斷層、血液常規、生化七項、毒物篩檢。克莉絲汀娜，妳負責跑檢驗室；喬治，備齊病例資料；梅莉迪絲，帶凱蒂做電腦斷層。她現在由妳負責。

伊茲： 等等，那我呢？

貝莉： 妳，親愛的，妳做直腸檢查。

©ABC

shotgun 霰彈槍
彈殼內裝彈丸，發射時彈殼爆裂，會分散打到很多地方。借用來表示為不管有用沒用，先把全部的檢驗都做一遍，以收集完整資訊。

醫療檢驗英文

CT scan 電腦斷層
發音為 [kæt] [skæn]（因此有時也會寫做 CAT scan），即 computerized tomography，以全方位的 X 光掃描建立 3D 影像，進行診斷。

CBC 血液常規
即 complete blood count，病人血液中各種血球（blood cells）如紅血球（red blood cells）、白血球（white blood cells）、血小板（platelets）數量、蛋白質濃度、空物質濃度的報告。

Chem-7 生化七項
所有健康檢查必備，檢查新陳代謝（metabolic）七個基本項目，包括 sodium「鈉」、potassium「鉀」、chloride「氯化物」、carbon dioxide「二氧化碳」、glucose「葡萄糖」、creatinine「肌酸酐」、blood urea nitrogen「血清尿素氮」含量。

tox screen 毒物篩檢
toxicology screen 的簡稱，為一系列血液檢查（blood test），以確定是否有藥物（drug）或乙醇（ethanol，即酒精）反應。

rectal exam 直腸檢查
將探測儀伸入直腸（recum）檢查是否有腫塊。

workup 徹底檢驗，收集病人醫療資料
這個字可指某方面的檢驗，如 blood workup「血液化驗」。對白中則是指收集病人所有醫療相關數據及背景，除了就醫及牙科紀錄（medical and dental records）、家族及個人病史（family and personal medical history）、社會背景及職業（social and occupational history），還要將入院後所有化驗報告（lab report）、X 光檢查（x-ray exam）、診斷手術紀錄納入。

© ABC

Izzie: Talk about parental pressure.

Cristina: God I would kill to have Ellis Grey as a mother. I'd kill to be Ellis Grey. All I need is one good case.

Meredith: *[sitting down and complaining about patient]* Katie Bryce is a **pain in the ass**. If I hadn't taken the **Hippocratic Oath**, I'd **Kevorkian** her with my bare hands.

看影集

實習生們坐在餐廳桌子旁，談論梅莉迪絲的知名母親。

Cristina: Her mother is Ellis Grey.

Izzie: Shut up. *The* Ellis Grey?

George: Who's Ellis Grey?

Cristina: The Grey method? Where'd you go to med school, Mexico?

Izzie: She was one the first big chick surgeons and she practically invented the abdominal laparotomy.

Cristina: She's a living legend. She won the Harper Avery. Twice!

George: So I didn't know *one* thing.

克莉絲汀娜： 她的母親是艾莉絲格蕾。

伊茲： 騙人，那個艾莉絲格蕾？

喬治： 誰是艾莉絲格蕾？

克莉絲汀娜： 沒聽過格蕾療法？你在哪裡念醫學院的？墨西哥嗎？

伊茲： 她是最早的大師級女外科醫師之一，剖腹手術可說是她發明的。

克莉絲汀娜： 她是活生生的傳奇人物。她得過哈帕艾佛瑞獎，還得了兩次！

喬治： 我只是不知道這麼一件事。

伊茲： 媽媽給她的壓力肯定很大。

克莉絲汀娜： 天哪，我真希望我母親是艾莉絲格蕾。我真希望自己是艾莉絲格蕾。我只想要一個好病例。

梅莉迪絲： （坐下抱怨病人）凱蒂布萊斯真是討厭。假如我沒發過希波克拉底誓言，我會親手讓她安樂死。

Hippocratic Oath 希波克拉底誓詞

古希臘人希波克拉底（Hippocrates，生卒於約西元前 460-370）被視為西方醫學之父，其所訂立的醫師誓言 Hippocratic Oath 至今仍為醫學論理的規範，其中明定不得為人施行墮胎及安樂死，而現代版的 Hippocratic Oath 大多已調整這部分，改為秉持醫德、協助預防疾病、盡力救治病人，並加入保護病人隱私等符合現代潮流的內容。

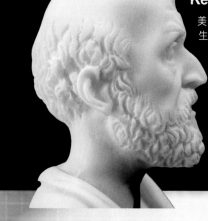

Kevorkian 凱沃基安醫師

美國病理學家 Jack Kevorkian（1928-2011）被稱為「死亡醫生」，他協助自願的重症者安樂死（euthanasia），捍衛病人有選擇結束病痛折磨，安詳死去的權利，前後為超過一百五十位病人結束生命。儘管被以二級謀殺判刑坐牢八年獲得假釋，條件是不准他再以任何形式從事或宣傳安樂死，但他的尋求安樂死合法化的勇氣，已獲得世人普遍認同。上面的對白是在開玩笑，將 Kevorkian 變成動詞，表示「執行安樂死」。

© Helga Esteb / Shutterstock.com

Dr. Jack Kevorkian

pain in the ass 討厭的人事物

這是用讓人屁股痛形容討厭的事物。比較文雅的說法有 pain in the rear 或 pain in the neck。

A: You don't think I should take English with Mr. Herman?
你不建議我去上赫曼老師的英文課？

B: No. He's a real pain in the ass.
不建議。他有夠討厭的。

看影集

艾力克斯和護士討論病人起了爭執後，遇到梅莉迪絲。

Alex: God, I hate nurses. I'm Alex. I'm with Jeremy. You're with the Nazi right?

Meredith: She may not have pneumonia, you know? She could be splinting or have a PE.

Alex: Like I said, I hate nurses.

Meredith: What did you just say? Did you just call me a nurse?

Alex: Uh, **if the** white **cap fits**.

艾力克斯：天啊，我討厭護士。我是艾力克斯。我是傑瑞米那組。妳是納粹那組，對吧？

梅莉迪絲：她可能不是肺炎，你知道吧？她可能是呼吸肌強直或肺栓塞。

艾力克斯：就像我說的，我討厭護士。

梅莉迪絲：你剛剛說什麼？你剛剛叫我護士？

艾力克斯：呃，妳也對號入座啊。

 學英文 🎧 98

if the cap/shoe fits, (wear it) 自己承認吧，對號入座

更常聽到的說法是 if the shoe fits, (wear it)，可在指出別人的錯誤之後，說這句話要犯錯的人自己承認或檢討。另一種狀況是你指桑罵槐，但被罵的人聽出來了，這時你就可以說 if the cap/shoe fits, wear it 表示「是你自己要對號入座」。對話中的white cap是指白色的護士帽。

A: Everyone keeps telling me I'm lazy.
大家都說我懶惰。

B: If the shoe fits, wear it.
如果大家這麼說，那應該有道理。

© Everett Collection / Shutterstock.com

《實習醫生》一播十二年，伴隨目前三十到四十歲的美國人一起成長，劇中從第一集開始接演超過十季的人物，對劇迷來說簡直像是認識十年的老朋友。其中由韓裔加拿大女星吳珊卓（Sandra Oh）飾演的克莉絲汀娜楊在第十季時編劇讓她遠赴歐洲執業，由派區克丹普西（Patrick Dempsey）飾演的德瑞克雪普在第十一季時車禍身亡，都讓電視機前的許多人掉下眼淚。

© CBS

© CBS

thegoodwife
法庭女王

Partly inspired by the Eliot Spitzer [1]**prostitution** scandal, *The Good Wife* is a legal drama starring Juliana Margulies as Alicia Florrick, wife of State's Attorney Peter Florrick. Once a successful litigator, for the past 13 years Alicia has been the "good wife," raising her kids and supporting her husband in his career. But when her husband is jailed following a sex scandal—a video of him with a [2]**call girl** is leaked to the [3]**press**—Alicia returns to her former [4]**profession** to support her family.

《法庭女王》是部分以艾略特史畢哲召妓醜聞（編註：他於二〇〇六年當選紐約州州長，二〇〇八年因召妓案下台，他當時的妻子擁有哈佛法學院文憑）為藍本的法律劇作，由茱莉安娜瑪格麗絲飾演州檢察官彼得佛里克的妻子亞莉莎佛里克。亞莉莎曾經是名成功的訴訟律師，十三年來一直是個「賢妻」，養育孩子，輔佐丈夫的事業。但當她丈夫因為性醜聞而入獄時——他和應召女郎的影片被洩漏給媒體——亞莉莎為了家計而重操舊業。

Six months after the scandal breaks, Alicia's Georgetown classmate Will Gardner gets her a position as a junior litigator at Chicago law firm Stern, Lockhart and Gardner, where he's a senior partner. As the firm's top litigators are busy on a class action suit, Alicia is assigned a pro bono case, which senior partner Diane Lockhart **briefs her on**.

法律相關字彙

class action 集體訴訟
由一群原告代表所有受害者提起告訴，常見的例子是消費團體代表消費者向廠商求償，也稱作 class suit。

pro bono 公益服務
pro bono 是拉丁文 pro bono publico（for the public good，為公眾利益服務）的簡稱，指專業人士免費為窮人或慈善團體服務，與一般志工服務不同。美國律師協會（American Bar Association，簡稱 ABA）期望會員每年能提供至少五十小時的公益法律服務。

deadlocked jury 僵局陪審團
也稱 hung jury。由於陪審團必須對有罪或無罪做出決定，其中只要有一人不同意，就會使案件陷入僵局。

法律劇情

Second-grade teacher Jennifer Lewis was [5]**accused** of murdering her ex-husband, Michael, but the trial ended in a **deadlocked jury**. Alicia is assigned to defend Jennifer in the retrial, and Diane tells her to use her strategy from the first trial. But Alicia soon finds out the case isn't what it seems. All of the [6]**jurors** but one—a cat lady who ignored the evidence—thought Jennifer was [7]**guilty**, and when she visits Peter in prison, he tells her that other evidence was buried.

醜聞爆發後六個月，亞莉莎在喬治城大學的同學威爾嘉納，替她在芝加哥的史洛嘉法律事務所安排一個初級訴訟律師的職位，嘉納是那家事務所的資深合夥人。正當事務所的高級訴訟律師在忙著打一場集體訴訟案時，亞莉莎被分配到一件無償服務的案子，由另一位資深合夥人黛安洛克哈替她解說案情。案子是關於小學二年級老師珍妮佛路易斯被指控謀殺前夫麥可，但審理此案的陪審團陷入僵局。亞莉莎被指派為珍妮佛的重審辯護，而黛安告訴她要用第一次審案時的策略。但亞莉莎隨即發現，案情不如表面上所看到的那樣。所有陪審員都認為珍妮佛有罪，除了一位無視於證據的養貓怪女子。而且，她到監獄裡探望彼得時，他告訴她，有其他證據被隱藏。

Alicia realizes she needs a new suspect, so with help from [8]**in-house** investigator Kalinda Sharma, she takes a second look at the original evidence. The [9]**prosecution** used a security video to prove that the red truck Jennifer said the killer drove was never at the scene of the crime, but Alicia discovers that the video wasn't from the night of the murder—a security guard had been copying earlier tapes to hide the fact that he was sleeping on the job. Then she uses the buried evidence—dog hair covered with a [10]**lotion** used on racing dogs—to link the crime to the brother of Michael's new wife. Now that there's a new suspect for the prosecution to focus on, Jennifer is [11]**acquitted**!

亞莉莎意識到她需要新嫌犯，在內部調查員卡琳達夏瑪的幫助下，她再次查看原本的證據。檢方用一段監視器影片證明珍妮佛所說嫌犯開的紅色卡車從沒在犯罪現場出現，但亞莉莎發現那段影片不是案發當晚的——是一位保全複製了以前的影片，以隱瞞他在值班時睡覺的事實。然後她利用被隱藏的證據——沾有賽狗用乳液的狗毛——將兇殺案與麥可新任妻子的弟弟連結起來。於是檢方將重點放在新嫌犯身上，珍妮佛無罪獲釋！

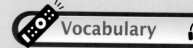
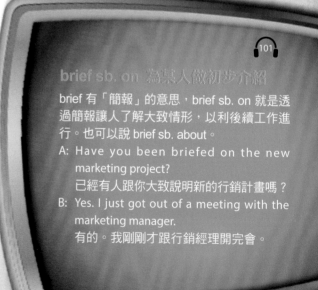

🎧101

brief sb. on 為某人做初步介紹

brief 有「簡報」的意思，brief sb. on 就是透過簡報讓人了解大致情形，以利後續工作進行。也可以說 brief sb. about。

A: Have you been briefed on the new marketing project?
   已經有人跟你大致說明新的行銷計畫嗎？

B: Yes. I just got out of a meeting with the marketing manager.
   有的。我剛剛才跟行銷經理開完會。

© CBS

看影集

亞莉莎第一天上班，進入會議室時，會議已經差不多要結束了。

Will: This is a major class action—a case that could propel us to the top rank of full service firms. And I don't think I need to remind you what that will do to your year-end bonuses. Anyway, Sheffrin-Marks fired their last firm because they **took their eye off the ball**. So, until further notice, your personal lives have been cancelled.

Diane: So, we'll need some of you to help with the lower profile client work to free up our top **litigators**.

Will: Ed, you take the **witness prep** on highway redistribution. Don, you take the Brighton criminal, and Alicia will take the pro bono. Everyone else, your task is to show Sheffrin-Marks **our A game**, OK? Let's do this!

 學英文 🎧 102

take one's eye off the ball 有所鬆懈

眼睛必須緊盯著球，才能隨時掌握球的去向，keep one's eye on the ball 就是「隨時保持機警」。

A: I hear Professor Lee's history class is really hard.
我聽說李教授的歷史課很不輕鬆。
B: Yeah. You have to keep your eye on the ball if you want a good grade.
對啊。想要好成績，就不能有所鬆懈。

因此一個人放鬆警戒，就是 take one's eye off the ball。

A: Being a manager must be a challenging job.
擔任經理一定是很有挑戰性的工作。
B: Yes, it is. You can't afford to take your eye off the ball for a minute.
對，沒錯。一刻都不能放鬆。

威爾：這是場重要的集體訴訟，這個案子能讓我們成為頂尖的全能服務事務所。而且我應該不用提醒你們，這關係到你們的年終獎金。不論如何，薛夫林馬克斯公司解僱之前的事務所，是因為他們不夠專心。所以，除非有進一步通知，否則你們的私人行程都要取消。

黛安：那麼，我們需要一些人處理較不重要的案子，好讓高級訴訟律師能處理集體訴訟案。

威爾：艾德，你處理公路重新分配案的證人準備。唐恩，你處理布萊頓刑事案，亞莉莎處理無償案。其他人，你們的任務是要讓薛夫林馬克斯公司見識我們的能力，好嗎？開工！

檢察官、律師相關字彙

district attorney 地區檢察長

簡稱 DA，是美國各州司法體系的最高執法者，即 state prosecutor / attorney（州檢察官，公訴人）。

assistant district attorney 助理地區檢察官

簡稱 ADA，與 DA 同為 state prosecutor，受 DA 指派偵辦案件，決定是否起訴犯罪嫌疑人。若決定起訴，就要代表全州人民上法庭，讓嫌犯被定罪。

attorney 律師

在美國，這個字跟 lawyer 意思相同，都是取得執照的法律工作者，可以提供法務諮詢，並代表原告及被告上法庭。在英國，barrister 專指「出庭律師」，從事非訴訟業務的「事務律師」為 solicitor。

litigator 訴訟律師

專門打民事訴訟（civil lawsuit）的律師，因此又稱 civil litigation attorney。由於民事法庭的法律程序非常繁瑣，案件涵蓋領域又廣，從中止合約（breach of contract）到醫療疏失（medical malpractice）都有可能，有些訴訟律師會上專攻特定領域；在大型事務所內的律師分工更細，甚至只負責審判前某環節的準備工作，如對白中的 **witness prep**（witness preparation，協助關鍵證人準備上法庭），而專門上法庭的「出庭律師，辯護律師」可稱為 trial lawyer。

one's A game　個人最佳表現

A game 原本是指運動員在比賽場上的最佳表現，可延伸運用於任何場合。最常見的用法是 bring one's A game。

A: Are you prepared for the sales presentation tomorrow?
　　明天的業務報告你準備好了嗎？
B: Yep. I'm ready to bring my A game.
　　好了。我準備要拿出看家本領了。

看影集

會議後，威爾將亞莉莎交給黛安。

Diane:　So, Will **speaks highly of** you. He says you graduated top of your class at Georgetown. When was this?

Alicia:　Fifteen years ago.

Diane:　Uh-huh…and you spent 2 years at?

Alicia:　Crozier, Abrams & Abbott.

Diane:　Good firm. Will says you clocked the highest billable hours there. Why did you leave?

Alicia:　Well, the kids and Peter's career.

Diane:　Hm. I want you to think of me as a mentor, Alicia. It's the closest thing we have to an **old boys' network** in this town. Women helping women, OK?

Alicia:　OK.

Diane:　When I was starting out, I got one great piece of advice. Men can be lazy, women can't. And I think **that goes double for** you. Not only are you coming back to the workplace fairly late, but you have some very prominent baggage. But, hey. *[points to photo of herself with Hillary Clinton]* She can do it, so can you!

黛　安：嗯，威爾對妳的評價很高。他說妳在喬治城大學時，在班上是第一名畢業的。那是什麼時候？

亞莉莎：十五年前。

黛　安：呃……妳有兩年的時間在哪裡？

亞莉莎：克艾雅律師事務所。

黛　安：那是不錯的事務所。威爾說，妳在那裡累積的計費工時是最多的。妳為什麼離開？

亞莉莎：嗯，為了孩子和彼得的事業。

黛　安：嗯，我希望妳把我當導師，亞莉莎。這樣的關係最能與男性人脈網絡相匹敵。女人也要互相幫助，好嗎？

亞莉莎：好。

黛　安：我剛開始工作時，聽到一句很棒的忠告。男人可以偷懶，女人不行。我覺得這對妳來說更是如此，不僅是因為妳很晚才回到職場，也因為妳身上背的包袱太沉重。不過，嘿（指著自己和希拉蕊的合照）她可以做到，妳也可以！

學英文　

speak highly of…　誇讚

speak highly 意思是「評價很高」，也就是對某人、事、物大加讚美的意思。

A: Thanks for offering me the position.
　　謝謝你給我這個職位。
B: Certainly. I'm sure we've made the right decision. Your former employer speaks highly of you.
　　這是應該的。我很確定我們做了正確的決定。你過去的雇主對你讚譽有加。

that goes double for　更是如此

go 有「適用，恰當」的意思，go double for 字面上是「兩倍適用於」，表示強調語氣「絕對是這樣」。

A: I always assume that lawyers are lying.
　　我總是認定律師在撒謊。
B: Ha-ha. And that goes double for politicians.
　　哈哈。政治人物更是如此。

---

old boys' network　男性同窗人脈

old boys' network 也稱作 old boy network、old boys' club，是以男性就讀名校時所結識的死黨為中心，擴散出來的人際網路。這群人畢業之後，多直接透過父執輩的 old boys' network 進入大企業工作，快速位居要職。這種現象在保守的法律、金融等行業中很常見，network（關係網）以外的人很難有平等機會，若身為女性，處境更是雪上加霜。

© CBS

看影集

黛安向亞莉莎解說無償案件。

Diane: Like many law firms, we donate 5% of billable hours to pro bono. Sadly, I'm long past my quota on this one—Jennifer Lewis, 26 years old, taught second grade, accused of killing her ex-husband. Prosecution thought it was a **slam dunk**, 45 years, but the jury came back last week deadlocked. Six jurors voted to **convict**, six not. I'm not even sure why the State Attorney is retrying except he wants…Justice! *[Her dog Justice is licking Alicia's hand]* He wants to prove himself. So, stick with my strategy from the first trial. The police focused on Jennifer so early in the investigation, they never even looked for the carjacker. Deadlock a jury a second time, they'll never retry a third, OK? OK, our investigator can get you **up to speed** for the **bail hearing** at three.

Alicia: The hearing's today?

Diane: Well, we could delay, but that would leave Jennifer incarcerated for another month. Don't worry, you'll be fine!

黛　安： 就和許多法律事務所一樣，我們會把百分之五的計費工時捐給無償服務的案件。可惜的是，我的配額已經超過了——珍妮佛路易斯，二十六歲，小學二年級老師，被指控謀殺前夫。檢方以為這個案子可以輕鬆勝訴，要關四十五年，結果陪審團上星期陷入僵局。六名陪審員投有罪，六人投無罪。我也不知道州檢察官為什麼要重審，除非他想要……正義！（她的狗「正義」正在舔亞莉莎的手）他想要證明自己的能力。所以，就要用我第一次開庭的策略。警方一開始調查時就將重點放在珍妮佛，從來沒去找過劫車犯。陪審團若是第二次陷入僵局，他們絕不會開第三次庭，瞭解嗎？好了，我們的調查員給妳三點鐘保釋庭所需的資料。

亞莉莎： 今天有保釋庭？

黛　安： 嗯，我們可以延期，但這樣會讓珍妮佛多監禁一個月。別擔心，妳做得到的。

學英文 104

slam dunk 必然之事
原本是籃球的「灌籃」動作，球直接從籃框上方塞進去，哪有不得分的道理，因此引申為一定會發生的事。
A: You think Donald Trump is going to win the election?
　你覺得唐納川普會贏得選舉？
B: Yeah. I think he's a slam dunk.
　對。我覺得他一定會成功。

up to speed 掌握最新資料
字面上是「跟上速度」，bring/get (sb.) up to speed 表示讓人跟上資料更新、情況發展的速度，也就是「讓人掌握最新資料、狀況」。
A: Did you hear about the problem we've having with that client?
　你有聽說我們跟那個客戶之間的問題嗎？
B: Yeah. Roger just brought me up to speed.
　有。羅傑剛剛跟我說了最新情況。

法律相關字彙

convict 宣判有罪
在法庭戲上，聽到陪審團宣布 we find the defendant guilty「我們認為被告有罪」，法官敲下法槌這一刻，即是 convict。這個字當名詞，就是「已獲判決的犯人」或「（服刑中的）囚犯」。

acquit 宣告無罪
如果陪審團說的是 we find the defendant not guilty「我們認為被告無罪」，即是 acquit，被告即可當庭釋放。

hearing 聽審，聽證
舉辦 hearing 是要確保可能被依法剝奪權利（生命、自由或財產）者，有表達意見的機會，結束之後由法官作出裁決。除了司法機關，立法及行政機關在新法令、政策會影響特定人士時，也會舉辦聽證會。在 bail hearing 上，被拘留嫌犯可爭取較低 bail「保釋金」，甚至免保釋金 release on own recognizance「具結釋放」，簡稱 OR。

Innocence Project 清白專案

這個非營利的冤獄平反組織是在一九九二年由 Barry Scheck 及 Peter Neufeld 共同建立，他們利用基因鑑定技術證明遭誤判者的清白，並以公布調查結果、宣傳冤獄成因來推動司法改革，以杜絕冤獄發生。Innocence Project 已成功幫助數百名重刑犯（平均都已被關押超過十三年）及死刑犯平反。

看影集

亞莉莎遇到另一位新律師凱瑞，她還不知道凱瑞也在競爭同一個職缺。

Cary:　I'm Cary, the other new associate.

Alicia:　Oh, right. Alicia.

Cary:　Yeah, look. I know we should **be at each other's throats**, but I just want to say I really respect what you're doing here—raising a family and then jumping right back into this. My mom, she's thinking of doing the same thing.

Alicia:　Great.

Cary:　Yeah. So you're on the pro bono, right?

Alicia:　Mm-hm.

Cary:　Yeah, that's great! I interned last summer at the **Innocence Project**. My dad's best friend is **Barry Scheck**, and it was just amazing—helping people. Here, they got me on the Sheffrin-Marks. I'm sure it'll be challenging, but at the end of the day, what have you really done? Saved a corporation a few billion dollars?

Alicia:　You wanna trade?

Cary:　I would, but I guess they have other plans, so….

凱　瑞：我是凱瑞，另一位新加入的律師。

亞莉莎：喔，對，我是亞莉莎。

凱　瑞：妳好，聽著，我知道我們應該是死敵，但我只是想說，我真的很佩服妳——要照顧家庭，又要回到職場。我媽媽，她也在考慮這麼做。

亞莉莎：很好。

凱　瑞：是啊，那妳現在是在處理無償案件，對吧？

亞莉莎：嗯。

凱　瑞：太好了！我去年暑假在「清白專案」實習。我爸爸最好的朋友就是巴里夏克，幫助別人的感覺真的很棒。在這裡，他們安排我處理薛夫林馬克斯公司的案子。我相信這挑戰性很高，但到頭來，真有什麼作為？幫一家公司省下幾十億元？

亞莉莎：你想交換嗎？

凱　瑞：我想，但我猜他們自己有安排，所以……。

學英文　🎧105

be at each other's throats 激烈對立

字面上是「互掐脖子」的意思，也就是激烈的爭執、競爭。

A:　Did you hear that Michael and Stephanie got divorced?
　　你聽說麥可和史蒂芬妮離婚了嗎？

B:　I'm not surprised. They were always at each other's throats.
　　我不意外。他們之前老是在大吵大鬧。

© Tinseltown / Shutterstock.com

飾演本片女主角亞莉莎的茱莉安娜瑪格麗絲（Juliana Margulies）在電視圈成名甚早，一九九四年參與演出長壽醫療影集《急診室的春天》，飾演英俊醫生道格羅斯（喬治庫隆尼飾演）的護理師女朋友，隔年就獲得黃金時段艾美獎劇情類最佳女配角獎，之後諸多獎項提名、得獎不斷，近期又以《法庭女王》獲得兩座黃金時段艾美獎劇情類最佳女主角獎（二〇一一及二〇一四年）。

她的丈夫是哈佛法學院畢業的律師，外形俊美，也成為紅毯上的焦點。

謀殺入門課

Produced by the same team that created hit shows like *Grey's Anatomy* and *Scandal*, *How to Get Away with Murder* is a legal thriller starring Viola Davis as Annalise Keating, a [1]**prominent** [2]**defense** attorney and law [3]**professor** at Middleton University in Philadelphia. For her portrayal of Annalise, Davis has won not only [4]**critical** acclaim, but also an Emmy for [5]**Outstanding** Lead Actress in a Drama Series—the first ever for an African-American woman.

---

it's only fitting (that) 理所當然……

fitting 是「適當的，相稱的」，這句話表示「……是再適合不過的方式」。

A: The boss wants me to tell Jessica that she's being fired.
老闆要我通知潔西卡，說她被炒魷魚了

B: Well, you're the one who hired her, so it's only fitting that you tell her.
呃，她是你聘雇的，由你通知她是理所當然。

《謀殺入門課》是推出《實習醫生》和《醜聞風暴》等熱門影集的製作團隊所製作的法律驚悚劇，由薇拉戴維絲飾演安娜莉絲基廷，她是傑出的辯護律師，也是費城米德頓大學的法律學教授。戴維絲不但因為飾演安娜莉絲而大獲好評，更獲得艾美獎劇集類最佳女主角獎，是有史以來第一位非裔美國女性拿下這項獎。

Considering the show's title, **it's only fitting** that it begins with a murder. In the opening scene, four students are standing in the woods arguing about how to [6]**dispose of** a dead body. To understand who they are and how they got to this point, we need to go back in time. Three months earlier, students are filling up Professor Keating's [7]**lecture** hall for the first day of Criminal Law 100, or, as she prefers to call it, How to Get Away with Murder.

這部影集都叫這個名字了，以一樁兇殺案展開故事當然再適合不過。在開場中，四位學生在樹林裡爭吵如何處置一具屍體。想了解他們為什麼會到這種地步，要將時間往回推。三個月前，「刑法學 100」第一天開課時，學生們陸續走進基廷教授的課堂，擠滿整間教室，而基廷更喜歡稱這堂課為「謀殺入門課」（直譯為「殺人後如何逍遙法外」）。

When Annalise presents her students with a [8]**case study**—Gina Sadowski, the "Aspirin [9]**Assassin**," has been accused of trying to murder her boss by switching his blood-

© ABC

© ABC

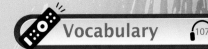

pressure medicine for aspirin, which he is ¹⁰⁾**allergic** to—they soon realize it's a current case of hers. Annalise tells the students they'll be assisting in the defense, and that the four best performers will be given ¹¹⁾**internships** at her law office. ¹²⁾**Studious** Michaela Pratt, ¹³⁾**charming** Connor Walsh and ¹⁴⁾**observant** Laurel Castillo all succeed in finding information helpful to the defense. And when ¹⁵⁾**naïve** Wes Gibbons visits Annalise's office to run an idea by her, he walks in on her having sex with a man…who isn't her husband!

當安娜莉絲向學生介紹一項個案研究時——「阿斯匹靈刺客」吉娜薩多斯基被指控謀殺未遂，將老闆的血壓藥換成會讓他過敏的阿斯匹靈——學生隨即明白這是安娜莉絲現在接的案子。安娜莉絲要學生協助她替被告辯護，表現最好的四名學生可以到她的法律事務所實習。勤奮好學的米凱拉普拉特、迷人的康納沃許，和觀察敏銳的蘿瑞爾卡斯提奧成功替辯方找到有利的線索。當天真單純的衛斯吉賓斯到安娜莉絲的事務所提出他的意見，想請教她的看法時，撞見她正和一名男子做愛，但那名男子不是她丈夫！

But Annalise's husband Sam, a psychology professor who sometimes helps her on cases, may not be so innocent himself. When a female student of his ¹⁶⁾**turns up** dead—yes, another murder—he seems unusually disturbed. You may have guessed that Michaela, Connor, Laurel and Wes are the students chosen by Annalise for internships, but they're also the same four from the woods that night. But the identity of the body—and the killer—is even more shocking. Wouldn't you like to know who they are?

安娜莉絲的丈夫山姆是心理學教授，有時也會協助她處理案子，但他本身也未必單純。他的一位女學生被發現死亡——沒錯，另一樁兇殺案——他看起來異常不安。你可能已經猜到，米凱拉、康納、蘿瑞爾和衛斯會被安娜莉絲選為實習生，但這四人也是那天晚上在樹林的四位學生。不過死者——還有兇手——的身份更是令人震驚。難道你不想知道是誰嗎？

1) **prominent** [ˋprɑmənənt] (a.) 卓越的，著名的
The conference was attended by many prominent scholars.

2) **defense** [dɪˋfɛns] (n.) 辯護，被告及其辯護律師
If you've been charged with a crime, you should hire a good defense lawyer.

3) **professor** [prəˋfɛsɚ] (n.) 教授
The professor gave a lecture on Russian literature.

4) **critical** [ˋkrɪtɪkəl] (a.) 評論的，批評的 (n.) critic 評論家，批評家
The band's first album was a financial and critical success.

5) **outstanding** [aʊtˋstændɪŋ] (a.) 傑出的
The actress received an award for her outstanding performance in the film.

6) **dispose of** [dɪˋspoz] [əv] (phr.) 處理（掉），扔掉
Toxic waste must be disposed of properly.

7) **lecture** [ˋlɛktʃɚ] (n./v.) 演講，講課
Did you attend the lecture on modern art yesterday?

8) **case study** [kes] [ˋstʌdi] (n.) 個案研究
The professor often uses case studies in his teaching.

9) **assassin** [əˋsæsɪn] (n.) 暗殺者，刺客 (v.) assassinate 暗殺，行刺
The assassin was caught before he could kill the president.

10) **allergic** [əˋlɝdʒɪk] (a.) 過敏的
Jason is allergic to cats.

11) **internship** [ˋɪntɝnˌʃɪp] (n.) 工作實習
An internship will look good on your college application.

12) **studious** [ˋstudiəs] (a.) 勤奮好學的
You should be more studious if you want to go to college.

13) **charming** [ˋtʃɑrmɪŋ] (a.) 迷人的，有魅力的
Stephanie likes guys who are charming and handsome.

14) **observant** [əbˋzɝvənt] (a.) 觀察力敏銳的
The thief was caught by an observant neighbor.

15) **naïve** [nɑˋiv] (a.) 天真的
It's naïve to believe that all people are good.

16) **turn up** [tɝn] [ʌp] (phr.) （失去後）被發現或找到，出現
Don't worry—I'm sure your missing keys will turn up eventually.

© ABC

看影集

衛斯帶著凶器到樹林裡和其他人見面，凶器是一座正義女神小型銅像。

Wes: Hey, sorry I took so long. I went back for this. *[holds up trophy]*

Michaela: You take that back right now!

Laurel: No. It's smart. **Commonwealth vs. Deloatche**, a case the prosecution should've won but lost because there was no murder weapon.

Connor: So what are you saying?

Laurel: We clean it and we put it back. Hide it in plain sight—after we bury the body.

Michaela: No. Absolutely not.

Connor: Yeah. I'm with Michaela.

Laurel: No, Connor, think.

Connor: The trophy we need, yes. But the body stays where it is.

Laurel: No, the body is what gets us caught.

Michaela: You are **not thinking straight**.

Laurel: What do you suggest?

Michaela: Something that doesn't involve carrying a body across campus on the busiest night of the year!

衛　斯：嘿，抱歉我來晚了，我回去拿這個。（舉起銅像）

米凱拉：馬上把那個放回去！

蘿瑞爾：不，這很聰明。賓州對抗德洛奇一案，檢方本來會贏的案子，最後輸了，因為找不到凶器。

康　納：所以妳的意思是？

蘿瑞爾：我們把它擦乾淨後放回去，在眾目睽睽下隱藏好——等我們把屍體埋了之後。

米凱拉：不行，絕對不行。

康　納：嗯，我贊同米凱拉。

蘿瑞爾：不對，康納，動動腦。

康　納：我們要處理銅像沒錯，屍體就留在原處。

蘿瑞爾：不行，屍體會害我們被抓。

米凱拉：妳沒想清楚。

蘿瑞爾：那妳想怎麼做？

米凱拉：反正就是不能在一年當中最熱鬧的夜晚扛著屍體穿過校園。

學英文 109

(not) think straight （未）考慮清楚

這個片語都用在否定句，not think straight 表示「沒有好好考慮，沒想清楚」。

A: Why did you go home with such an ugly girl?
你怎麼會跟那麼醜的妞回家？

B: I had a lot to drink. I must not have been thinking straight.
我喝多了。我一定是腦袋壞掉。

看影集

學生在上課第一天走進安娜莉絲的課堂。

Wes: *[sits down]* I'm not usually a first-row kind of guy, but I promised myself I wouldn't hide in the back of the class.

Michaela: *[showing her ring]* I'm engaged.

Wes: Oh. Oh, no. I wasn't hitting on you.

Michaela: Seats are assigned. There's a chart over there.

Connor: **Nice try**, player.

Wes: No. I wasn't trying anything.

Connor: You should find your seat. You don't want to be a **sitting duck** when the shooter gets here.

Wes: What?

Connor: Oh my God. You have no idea what you just walked into.

衛　斯：（坐下）我通常不坐第一排，但我向自己保
　　　　證，不要躲在教室後面。

米凱拉：（秀出她的戒指）我訂婚了。

衛　斯：噢，不是這樣，我不是在跟妳搭訕。

米凱拉：座位已經分配好了，座位表在那邊。

康　納：你想得美啊，花心大少爺。

衛　斯：沒有，我沒有那個意思。

康　納：你應該去找你的位置，你可不想在槍手來時變
　　　　成目標。

衛　斯：什麼？

康　納：天哪，你真是搞不清楚狀況。

學英文 🎧110

Nice try.　想得美

字面上是「很不錯的嘗試」，但實際上卻是不成功的嘗
試，因為說這句話的人真正的意思是「我知道你想做什
麼，但我不會上你的當」，也就是「你想得美」。

A: It's late. I think I'm gonna turn in.
　 好晚了。我要去睡了。

B: Nice try. You said you'd do the dishes tonight.
　 想得美。你說過今天晚上你會洗碗。

sitting duck　待宰羔羊

對獵人來說，鴨子在水面上悠游，當然比在天上飛容易
打到，因此 sitting duck 引申為「容易被攻擊的對象」。

A: It's amazing how many tourists get their wallets stolen
　 here.
　 有那麼多遊客在這裡被偷皮夾真是匪夷所思。

B: Yeah. Tourists are sitting ducks for the local pickpockets.
　 對啊。對當地扒手來說，遊客根本是待宰羔羊。

法律相關英文

Commonwealth vs. XXXX

跟法律相關的劇情中，經常聽到援引判例時說 Name of State vs.
XXXX「某州對抗某甲」，而這裡的 Commonwealth 就是「州」的
意思（首字母要大寫）。

美國有四個州稱作 Commonwealth，包括肯塔基州（Kentucky）、
麻州（Massachusetts）、賓州（Pennsylvania）以及維吉尼
亞州（Virginia）。由於本劇的背景設於賓州的費城，這裡的
Commonwealth 就是指賓州。

法律類型

criminal law 刑法
定義各種犯罪及相對應刑罰的法律。

civil law 民法
調停自然人、法人這些平等主體間的財產及人身關係的糾紛。

international law 國際法
又稱「國際公法」，是主權國家之間的法律，儘管目前各國多願意
承認國際法，但仍缺乏有效制裁違法國家的手段。

📺 看影集

衛斯被鄰居的大聲音樂吵到無法唸書，跑去敲門。

Wes:　　 Hi. Wes. I just moved in next door.

Rebecca: What do you want?

Wes:　　 Uh, your music—I normally wouldn't
　　　　 ask you to turn it down, but today
　　　　 was my first day of law school and I
　　　　 have this….

Rebecca: No.

Wes:　　 What?

Rebecca: The last guy who lived in your
　　　　 apartment was a law student. I **put
　　　　 up with** his crazy loud rabbit sex, his
　　　　 nervous breakdown. You can deal
　　　　 with this.

衛　斯：嗨，我是衛斯。我剛搬來隔壁。

瑞貝卡：你要幹嘛？

衛　斯：呃，妳的音樂——一般來說我不會請妳關小聲
　　　　點，但今天是我法學院入學第一天，我得要
　　　　……。

瑞貝卡：不要。

衛　斯：什麼？

瑞貝卡：上一個住你那間的也是法學院學生。我得忍受
　　　　他驚天動地、沒日沒夜跟人打砲，還有他的精
　　　　神崩潰。你自己看著辦吧。

學英文 🎧111

put up with sth./sb.　容忍

put up with是「忍受」的意思，既然得忍受，當然不會
是好事，因此 put up with 這個片語都用在負面狀況。

A: I don't know why Becky puts up with Tom. He's such a
　 jerk.
　 我真不懂貝琪為什麼要容忍湯姆。他真是個混帳。

B: He may be a jerk, but he's a rich jerk.
　 他或許是混帳，但是個有錢的混帳。

其他法律領域還有：
- maritime law 海事法
- corporate law 公司法
- bankruptcy law 破產法
- environmental law 環境保護法
- immigration law 移民法
- intellectual property law 智慧財產保護法

看影集

學生在課堂上為阿斯匹靈刺客案提出辯護意見。

Michaela: We should offer the **jury** another **suspect** altogether—Mr. Kaufman's wife, Agnes. She was angry about the affair, had access to his office, and knew what aspirin looked like his blood-pressure pill. So what better way to get revenge than to kill your cheating husband and **pin it on** his mistress? [timer rings] Thank you.

Annalise: Take a seat, Miss Pratt. You've moved on to the next round. Mr. Gibbins?

Wes: Right. So, the way I see it is…we say it was self-defense. [laughter] And we do that because, well, Gina was suffering from **Stockholm syndrome**, which is actually quite common in assistants with demanding bosses. The affair was just one example of how far Mr. Kaufman's brainwashing of Gina went. He made her fall in love with him. So, in this way, her poisoning him was an act of self-defense.

米凱拉：我們應該向陪審團提出另一位嫌犯——考夫曼先生的妻子，艾妮絲。她對外遇一事很憤怒，能進出他的辦公室，也知道哪種阿斯匹靈跟他的血壓藥長得很像。有什麼報復手段比殺掉出軌的丈夫然後嫁禍給他情婦更好？（計時器鈴響）謝謝。

安娜莉絲：請坐，普拉特小姐。你可以進入下一輪。吉賓斯先生？

衛　斯：好。我的看法是……我們可以主張自我防衛。（笑聲）這是因為，吉娜患有斯德哥爾摩症候群，這在嚴厲老闆的助理當中其實是很常見的，外遇只是其中一個例子，證明考夫曼先生對吉娜的洗腦有多嚴重。他讓她愛上他，如此一來，她毒殺他就是一種自衛行為。

Stockholm syndrome 人質情結
又稱「人質症候群」，是一種心理學現象，指被害者對加害者心生同情。

 學英文 112

pin sth. on sb. 將……怪罪於某人

pin 當動詞是「用別針別上，用圖釘釘上」，在口語中可以用來表示「把過錯強加在某人頭上」，也就是「怪罪，栽贓」的意思。

A: Do you think the defendant is guilty?
你認為被告有罪嗎？
B: No. I think somebody's trying to pin the murder on him.
不。我覺得有人想要把謀殺的罪名栽贓給他。

法律相關字彙

suspect 嫌疑犯
涉嫌犯罪而遭到刑事追訴者，在檢察機關正式向法院對其提起公訴之前的稱謂。嫌疑犯和罪犯不同，依無罪推定的原則，除非經審判證明有犯罪事實，不然該嫌疑人仍視同無罪。

apprehend 逮捕，拘押
警方採取法律程序，依法將犯人緝捕歸案。類似的字彙還有 arrest 和 capture。

manhunt 搜捕
警方有組織的追蹤緝捕逃犯，「發動大規模搜捕行動」即 launch a massive manhunt。

indict 起訴，告發
唸作 [ɪnˋdaɪt] 指 court「法庭」或 grand jury「大陪審團」以某罪名告發某人。

count 罪名
被起訴或控告的罪項。

arraignment 傳訊
把被告犯下某罪行的 defendant「被告」，傳喚至法庭提問。

grand jury 大陪審團
由十六至二十三名公民組成，負責聽取由檢察官提出的證據，並判定是否有充分的理由相信某人已犯下罪行、應該起訴。

bail 保釋金
為確保在裁定交保後，被告會依時出庭 trial「審判」的一筆保證金。

plead 答辯
plead 是指被告方對起訴的回應。plead guilty 就是「認罪」，而 plead not guilty 則為「不認罪」。

sentence 判刑
sentence 是法律用語，當動詞是「判刑」，當名詞是「刑罰」，即 judge「法官」對嫌犯做出的處罰。

appeal 上訴
是指法官結案後，不滿宣判結果所採取的下一個動作。

injunction 禁制令
經由法院宣判，強制當事人須遵從某事，違背禁制令的任何一方則會牽涉到民事或刑事上的刑罰。

跟白人有關的歧視字眼

white trash

光看字面意思「白人垃圾」就知道是不好聽的話。trash、white trash 都是指社經地位低下的白種人。

trailer trash

字面上是「住在拖車停車場的窮人，跟 white trash 一樣，都指窮困的白人。trailer park 是用來停放旅行車後掛拖車（trailer）及可移動房屋（mobile home）的地方，租金低廉，被視為窮人聚居的地方。

redneck

農夫下田工作時，脖子後面會被太陽曬得通紅，redneck 因此表示「南方種田的窮鄉巴佬」，現在則泛指「美國南方食古不化的貧困白人」。

cracker

原指喬治亞州、佛州的鄉下窮困白人，如今泛指美國南方鄉下的貧困白人的通稱。

hillbilly

阿帕拉契山區（Appalachia）的窮困白人。

honky

也拼做 honkie 或 honkey。是黑人對白人的蔑稱。

📺 **看影集**

在法庭上，老闆的第一助理琳達坦納作證指控吉娜薩多斯基。

Linda: I was his first assistant for 21 years, so to see him on his office floor like that, it was so awful. He wasn't breathing, and his skin kept getting more and more blue. *[to boss' wife]* I'm sorry, Agnes. I tried everything.

Prosecutor: You did everything you could, Ms. Tanner.

Annalise: You don't like Gina, do you? You would yell at her, calling her incompetent, stupid, **podunk trailer trash**?

Linda: No. That's a….

podunk 窮鄉僻壤（的），小地方（的）

這個字源自北美原住民語，原意為「泥沼地」及「住在泥沼地的人」，引申為「偏僻地方」。Podunk（P 大寫）則當名詞「窮鄉僻壤」、「無名小鎮」。

琳　達：我擔任他的第一助理二十一年了，所以看到他躺在辦公室地板上的那個樣子，太恐怖了。他沒了呼吸，臉色越來越發青。（轉向老闆的妻子）我很抱歉，艾妮絲，我盡力了。

檢察官：妳已經盡力了，坦納女士。

安娜莉絲：妳不喜歡吉娜，對吧？妳會對她大吼，罵她無能、笨蛋、窮鄉僻壤來的拖車垃圾？

琳　達：不是，那是……

飾演安娜莉絲的薇拉戴維絲（Viola Davis）出身非常窮困，中學時期迷上戲劇，優異的表現讓她獲得大學獎學金。大學畢業之後，她活躍於舞台劇表演界，偶爾在電視、電影上軋一角。二〇〇八年，在舞台劇改編的電影《誘‧惑》當中，她飾演被猥褻男童的母親。跟劇中另外三位演員：梅莉史翠普、艾美亞當斯、菲利浦西摩霍夫曼比起來，她的戲份雖少，但表現卻十分搶眼，還因此獲得奧斯卡及金球獎最佳女配角提名。

© Ts.ramli

Hannibal
雙面人魔

(113)

Based on the Thomas Harris novel *Red Dragon*, *Hannibal* is a series about the early "career" of Dr. Hannibal Lecter, the brilliant [1]**serial** killer best known to audiences from *The Silence of the Lambs*. But the real star of the show is Will Graham, a criminal profiler who teaches at the FBI Academy in Quantico. Because of Will's [2]**unique** ability to get inside the mind of killers, Special Agent Jack Crawford [3]**convinces** him to return to the [4]**field** to help with an unsolved case: over the past eight months, eight girls have disappeared from Minnesota college campuses

and are [5]**presumed** dead. When Will and Jack visit the home of the most recent victim, they make a [6]**disturbing** discovery—her body has been returned by the killer and is lying on her bed.

《雙面人魔》是根據湯瑪斯哈里斯的小說《紅龍》改編的影集，是關於漢尼拔萊克特醫師早期的「職涯」，對觀眾來說，這位聰明的連續殺人犯在《沉默的羔羊》中最為人熟悉。但這部影集真正的主角是犯罪剖析師威爾葛蘭姆，他在匡提科（編註：位於維吉尼亞州，是美國軍事重鎮）的聯邦調查局學院授課。由於威爾對於瞭解兇手的內心層面有獨特的能力，因此探員傑克科勞佛說服他回到外勤工作幫助解決一件懸案：在過去八個月中，有八位女孩從明尼蘇達州的大學校園失蹤，而且推測已經死亡。威爾和傑克前往最新案件的受害者家中時，發現一件令人不安的事——受害者的屍體已被兇手送回，正躺在受害者的床上。

Using his gift, Will determines that the killer returned the girl because he regretted killing her. And when [7]**investigators** tell him her liver was removed and then put back in, and that she had liver cancer, he realizes the killer is eating his victims. But Will's gift is starting to affect his mental health, so Jack decides to bring in an outside

美國特勤單位

FBI 聯邦調查局
美國聯邦調查局（Federal Bureau of Investigation）隸屬於美國司法部之下，具有跨州調察犯罪事件的權力，當案件涉及全國或影響重大，就會由 FBI 介入。

CIA 中央情報局
美國中情局（Central Intelligence Agency）是政府部門中的一個獨立機構，中央情報局的局長須回報資訊給國家情報總監，再由情報總監直接提供情報給美國總統，並負責國土安全會議上擔任諮詢的角色。
兩者的差別在於 CIA 著眼於國際層面，FBI 則以國內為主。

expert to work on the case: Dr. Hannibal Lecter. Always the helpful [8]**psychopath**, Hannibal [9]**commits** a [10]**copycat** murder that provides the hints Will needs to [11]**identify** the killer, as well as a fresh pair of lungs for a [12]**gourmet** meal. But Hannibal calls to warn the killer, and they arrive at his house just in time to see him kill his wife and [13]**slit** his daughter's throat, before Will shoots and kills him.

威爾運用自己的天賦,判斷兇手送回受害人是因為後悔殺了她。當調查員告訴他,受害者的肝臟被摘除後又被放回,她又患有肝癌時,他便明白兇手在吃受害人。但威爾的精神狀況開始受到自己特殊能力的干擾,於是傑克決定讓一位外部專家參與這件案子:漢尼拔萊克特醫師。漢尼拔一如往昔,一直是個樂意協助的精神變態者,他模仿案情,犯下一樁一模一樣的兇殺案,為威爾提供指認兇手所需的線索,也為自己提供一對新鮮的肺臟當美味佳餚。但漢尼拔打電話提醒兇手,他們即時趕到兇手家中,目睹兇手殺害妻子,割女兒的喉嚨,最後兇手被威爾槍斃。

Working with Will provides Hannibal with the perfect [14]**cover** for his own copycat killing, but what if Will finds out he's a serial killer? He just might have to [15]**frame** Will for his own murders and have him [16]**locked away**.

漢尼拔因為與威爾合作而得以完美掩蓋自己模仿兇殺案的罪行,但假如威爾發現他是連續殺人犯時會怎麼樣?漢尼拔可能要陷害威爾,為自己的兇殺案頂罪,將他送進監獄。

© NBC

 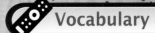

© NBC

看影集

傑克來到威爾的教室，想招攬他參與案件。

Jack: I see you've **hitched your horse to** a teaching post, and I also understand it's difficult for you to be social.

Will: Well, I'm just talking at them. I'm not listening to them. It's not social.

Jack: I see. May I? Where do you fall on the spectrum?

Will: **My horse is hitched to** a post that is closer to Asperger's and autistics than narcissists and sociopaths.

Jack: But you can empathize with narcissists—and sociopaths.

Will: I can empathize with anybody. It's less to do with a personality disorder than an active imagination.

Jack: Um, can I borrow your imagination?

傑克：我知道你內心抓住了教職這根浮木，但我也瞭解你不擅長社交。

威爾：嗯，我只是對他們說話，不用聽他們說話，這不算社交。

傑克：原來如此。我可以問問你嗎？你是屬於哪一種精神狀態？

威爾：我比較接近亞斯伯格症和自閉症，不是自戀或反社會。

傑克：但你對自戀者有同理心，還有反社會者。

威爾：我對任何人都可以有同理心。這靠的是豐富的想像力，跟人格障礙沒什麼關係。

傑克：嗯，那我可以借用一下你的想像力嗎？

學英文 🎧 115

hitch sb./sth (up) (to sth.) 攀附

hitch 是用繩圈拴住或套在一起。這個片語常見的說法是 hitch your wagon to sb./sth.、hitch your wagon to a star，表示為了少奮鬥三十年而「攀龍附鳳」，或是「把握成功的機會」。對白中 Jack 和 Will 是在玩雙關語，因為 post 代表「工作，職位」，也是拴馬的「柱子，木樁」。

A: How did that politician become so powerful?
那個政治人物為什麼變得這麼有權勢？

B: By hitching his wagon to even more powerful politicians.
靠著攀附更有權勢的政治人物囉。

精神疾病及人格障礙

autism 自閉症

一種腦部發展障礙引發神經系統失調的疾病，患者不善與人溝通交際，常不斷重複一些動作。由於與自閉症相同症狀與成因的發展障礙很多，很難與自閉症區分，因此將這些障礙統稱為自閉症光譜（autistic spectrum）。

Asperger's syndrome 亞斯伯格症候群

簡稱 AS，患者智力正常，有社交困難，非常專注於單一興趣，常不斷重複一些動作，語言及認知發展優於自閉症患者。由於跟自閉症無法做有效的區別，美國精神醫學會已取消這個病名，將其納入自閉症譜系障礙。

narcissism 自戀

是自我陶醉的性格，這種人傾向自滿、自私，言行浮誇，無視他人鄙夷的眼光，雖然不是精神疾病，但對社交有不良影響。

sociopath 反社會者

是指對社會有敵意，行事無視道德及良知，被視為一種人格障礙。

傑克帶漢尼拔到匡提科諮詢案件，漢尼拔第一次見到威爾。

Hannibal: Not fond of eye contact, are you?

Will: Eyes are distracting—you see too much, you don't see enough. And it's hard to focus when you're thinking, um, "Oh, those whites are really white," or, "He must have hepatitis," or, "Oh, is that a burst vein?" So, yeah, I try to avoid eyes whenever possible. Jack?

Jack: Yes?

Hannibal: I imagine what you see and learn touches everything else in your mind. Your values and decency are present yet shocked at your associations, appalled at your dreams.

Will: Whose **profile** are you working on? *[to Jack]* Whose profile is he working on?

Hannibal: I'm sorry, Will. Observing is what we do. I can't shut mine off any more than you can shut yours off.

Will: Please, don't **psychoanalyze** me. You won't like me when I'm psychoanalyzed.

心理分析相關字彙

profiler 犯罪心理輪廓分析專家
協助刑事人員分析未知嫌犯的背景、特徵及犯案模式，或推斷未來可能被害者。

psychoanalyst 心理分析學家
一般是為了治療目的，為 mental disorder「精神狀況不佳」的患者進行分析。而 psycologist「心理學家」是研究心理學，而非心理分析。

psychology 心理學，心理
形容詞 psychological「心理（學）上的」也拼做 psychologic。

psychiatric 精神病學的
「精神病院」為 psychiatric hospital / mental hospital。這種「精神科醫生」稱為 psychotherapist。

漢尼拔：你不喜歡眼神交會，對吧？

威　爾：眼睛會分散注意力——不是看得太多，就是看得太少。當你在想，嗯，「他的眼白真的很白」，或是「他一定有肝炎」，或是「喔，那是爆青筋嗎？」就很難集中。所以，沒錯，可能的話我會盡量避免四目交接。傑克？

傑　克：什麼事？

漢尼拔：我猜想你所看到和學到的事會影響你內心所有想法。你的價值觀和道德標準依然存在，不過被自己的聯想所震驚，被自己的夢魘嚇壞。

威　爾：你是在做誰的精神分析？（轉向傑克）他是在做誰的精神分析？

漢尼拔：抱歉，威爾。觀察是我們的天賦。我沒辦法停止觀察，就跟你無法停止觀察一樣。

威　爾：拜託，不要分析我的心理。你不會喜歡被分析後的我。

© NBC

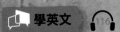

看影集

在匡提科，傑克和威爾討論案情。

Jack: Eight girls abducted from eight different Minnesota campuses, all in the last eight months.

Will: I thought there were seven.

Jack: There were.

Will: When did you **tag** the eighth?

Jack: About three minutes before I walked into your lecture hall.

Will: You're calling them abductions because you don't have any bodies?

Jack: No bodies, no parts of bodies, nothing that comes out of bodies. Nothing.

Will: Then those girls weren't taken from where you think they were taken.

Jack: Then where were they taken from?

Will: I don't know. Someplace else.

傑克：在過去八個月裡，有八個女孩在八處不同的明尼蘇達校園被綁架。

威爾：我以為有七人。

傑克：本來是七人。

威爾：你什麼時候確定有第八人的？

傑克：在走進你的課堂前約三分鐘。

威爾：你說這是綁架，是因為你沒發現屍體？

傑克：沒有屍體、也沒有遺骸，也沒有屍體的分泌物。什麼都沒有。

威爾：那麼那些女孩被帶走的地方就不是你所想的那些地方。

傑克：那她們是在哪裡被帶走的？

威爾：不知道。別的地方。

學英文 🎧

tag 確認死亡

警方在兇殺案現場找到死者之後，會在死者腳趾上套上一個身份標籤（tag），然後將遺體放入屍袋（body bag）。引申為找到屍體或確定死亡，也可以說 bag and tag。

A: Have the police found the body yet?
警方到屍體了嗎？

B: Yeah. It was bagged and tagged last month.
找到了。上個月已經找到並確認死者身份。

看影集

威爾、傑克和布萊恩（另一位調查員）在現場調查遭到模仿殺人犯（萊克特）用鹿角刺死的受害者，威爾發現兇手不是他們一直在尋找的人。

Will: Whoever **tucked** Elise Nichols **into** bed didn't paint this picture.

Brian: He took her lungs. I'm pretty sure she was alive when he cut them out.

Will: Our cannibal loves women. He doesn't want to destroy them. He wants to consume them, to keep some part of them inside. This girl's killer thought that she was a pig.

Jack: You think this was a copycat?

Will: The cannibal who killed Elise Nichols had a place to do it and no interest in field **kabuki**. So, he has a house or a cabin— something with an antler room. He has a daughter—the same age as the other girls. She's an only child. She's leaving home. He can't stand the thought of losing her.

Jack: What about the copycat?

Will: You know, an intelligent psychopath, particularly a **sadist**, is very hard to catch. There's no traceable motive, there'll be no patterns. Have Dr. Lecter draw up a psychological profile.

kabuki 歌舞伎
日本傳統戲劇，以舞台精緻，演員服飾華麗著稱，演員全部為男性。

© NBC

施虐、受虐狂相關字彙

sadist 施虐狂
能從折磨他人或虐待動物獲取快感者。

masochism 受虐狂
能從被他人折磨當中獲取快感者。另外「自我挫敗人格障礙」（masochistic personality disorder）則是一種自找麻煩，故意讓自己受苦的人格障礙。

sadomasochism 施虐與受虐
一種以鞭打（身體痛苦）、羞辱（精神痛苦）互相折磨，從疼痛當中獲致性快感的性活動，簡稱 SM，也稱作 BDSM。

BDSM 皮繩愉虐
一種人類性行為模式。BD 是指 bondage「束縛」及 discipline「調教」，也是 dominance「支配」與 submission「臣服」的意思。SM即上述的施虐及受虐。BDSM 是以雙方知情同意為原則，與 sexual abuse「性虐待」不同。

abuse 虐待
以言語或暴力折磨人，對人造成心理及身體的傷害，是一種犯罪行為。

威　爾：把艾莉絲尼可放回床上的人不是兇手。

布萊恩：他拿走了她的肺臟。我相當確定他割掉肺臟時她還活著。

威　爾：我們找的那個食人魔喜歡女人。他不想毀掉她們。他想吃掉她們，想把她們的一部分保留在體內。但殺這個女孩的兇手把她當成一隻豬。

傑　克：你覺得這是一樁模仿案件嗎？

威　爾：殺了艾莉絲尼可的食人魔有作案的地方，他對戶外演出沒興趣。所以，他有房子或是小木屋，裡頭有鹿角房間。他有女兒，跟其他受害人一樣年紀。她是獨生女，要離開家了。他無法忍受失去她的痛苦。

傑　克：那麼那個模仿犯呢？

威　爾：你知道，聰明的精神變態，尤其是虐待狂，是很難抓到的。動機不明，沒有模式可循。讓萊克特醫師做一份罪犯心理分析。

🗨 **學英文** 🎧 117

tuck into 送進（被窩）
爸媽哄小孩上床睡覺會把棉被蓋好，為了避免孩子踢被，有些還會把被子邊緣拉緊（tuck）壓到床墊下，所以 tuck into bed 或 tuck in 就是把人送進被窩。

A: Where are you going?
　你要去哪？
B: I'm going upstairs to tuck the kids in.
　我要上樓去把孩子送進被窩。

tuck in 的另一個意思是「大口吃」、「狼吞虎嚥」。

A: The food looks delicious.
　這些食物看起還好好吃。
B: Thanks. Tuck in before it gets cold!
　謝啦。趁涼掉之前快大口吃吧！

在《雙面人魔》當中飾演漢尼拔的麥斯密克森（Mads Mikkelsen）是丹麥巨星，在飾演這個恐怖食人魔之前，他在二〇〇六年的《007 首部曲：皇家夜總會》飾演全球頭腦超好的大反派契夫軻（Le Chiffre），從此打開全球知名度。

不過史上最令人害怕的漢尼拔，要算是《沉默的羔羊》當中安東尼霍普金斯（Anthony Hopkins）所詮釋的版本，二〇〇三年，該角色甚至被美國電影學會評為銀幕惡人第二名。

© NBC

© NBC

THE 陰屍路 WALKING DEAD

Considering the [1]**popularity** of [2]**zombies** in American [3]**pop culture**, it's no [4]**coincidence** that *The Walking Dead* is the most watched show in the history of cable TV. Based on the [5]**comic book** series of the same name, *The Walking Dead* is a tale of human survival **in the face of** a zombie [6]**apocalypse**. When small town [7]**sheriff** Rick Grimes awakes from a [8]**coma** after being shot by a fleeing criminal, the world as he knew it is gone. The [9]**abandoned** hospital he finds himself in is covered with blood and bullet holes, and outside he [10]**encounters** hundreds of dead bodies wrapped in sheets.

And when Rick picks up a bicycle in a nearby park, he's shocked to see a woman with no legs— or lips—reaching toward him. Rushing home on the bicycle to look for his wife and son, he finds his house empty. Then, while sitting on his [11]**porch**, a little boy comes up behind him and knocks him out with a shovel.

© Frank Ockenfels 3/AMC

© Gene Page/AMC

　　就殭屍在美國流行文化的普及程度來說，《陰屍路》能在有線電視史上成為收視率最高的節目也就並非巧合了。《陰屍路》是根據同名漫畫系列改編，是關於一群人類在殭屍佔領的世界末日中求生的故事。小鎮警長瑞克格萊姆斯遭到一名逃犯槍擊後昏迷，醒來後發現世界全變了，自己則是躺在一家荒廢的醫院，到處都是血跡和彈孔。他走出醫院，看到好幾百具裹著床單的屍體。瑞克在附近的公園撿到一輛自行車，此時看到一個沒有雙腿也沒有嘴唇的女子向他伸出手，他嚇得驚慌失措，連忙騎上自行車趕回家找他的妻兒，卻發現家中空無一人。然後，他坐在門廊上時，一個小男孩走到他後面用鏟子將他打暈。

villains 恐怖片中的壞蛋

《陰屍路》的殭屍、《噬血真愛》的吸血鬼是很可怕，但前面《雙面人魔》
當中的變態殺人魔是人不是鬼，卻比鬼更恐怖啊！

- **zombie** 殭屍
- **vampire** 吸血鬼，經典人物為德古拉公爵（Dracula）。
- **psycho killer** 變態殺人魔
- **werewolf** 狼人
- **mummy** 木乃伊，因魔咒死而復生的埃及死屍。
- **witch/warlock** 女巫／巫師
- **Frankenstein** 科學怪人，以人為力量使其死而復生的屍體。
- **the Devil** 撒旦（Satan），也就是魔王（Lucifer）。
- **demon** 惡魔、惡鬼，也稱做邪靈（evil spirit）。
- **Death** 死神，有時也稱為死亡天使（Angel of Death），
  常以穿黑袍手持大鐮刀的形象出現。

Rick wakes up tied to a bed, but the boy's father, Morgan, unties him when he tells him his wound was caused by a gunshot and not a bite. Rick learns from him that the country has been [12]**overrun** by "walkers," and that there is a [13]**refugee** center in Atlanta. Thinking his family may be there, he [14]**sets off** for Atlanta in his police car, which he trades for a horse when he runs out of gas. But instead of a refugee center he finds nothing but walkers, and when they start eating his horse, he crawls into an army tank for protection. Luckily, he's rescued by a survivor named Glenn, who leads him, along with several other survivors, to a camp outside the city, where Rick is finally united with his wife and son. But this is just the beginning of their struggle for survival in a new world where humans sometimes prove even more dangerous than the zombies who eat them.

瑞克醒來後發現自己被綁在床上，但在他解釋傷口是槍傷而不是咬傷之後，男孩的父親摩根將他鬆綁。瑞克從他那裡得知整個國家已經被「喪屍」佔領，而亞特蘭大有一座避難中心。瑞克心想他的家人可能在那裡，於是開著自己的警車出發前往亞特蘭大，汽油用完後，他就騎馬繼續前進。但他不但沒找到避難中心，反而遇到一群喪屍。那些喪屍開始吃他的馬時，他為了自保爬進了一輛軍用坦克車。幸好他被一位名叫葛倫的生還者所救，葛倫帶著他和其他幾位生還者到城外的營地，瑞克在那裡終於與他的妻兒團聚。但故事才剛剛開始而已，他們要在新的世界奮力求生，而且有時候人類甚至比會吃人的喪屍還危險。

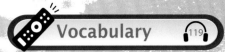

Vocabulary ♫119

1) **popularity** [ˌpɑpjəˈlærətɪ] (n.) 普及，流行，廣受歡迎
The popularity of video games continues to grow.

2) **zombie** [ˈzɑmbɪ] (n.) 殭屍，木訥呆板的人
I had a nightmare about being eaten alive by zombies.

3) **pop culture** [pɑp] [ˈkʌltʃə] (phr.) 流行文化，即 popular culture
The Beatles had a huge influence on pop culture.

4) **coincidence** [koˈɪnsɪdəns] (n.) 巧合
Meeting you here in Tokyo is such a coincidence!

5) **comic book** [ˈkɑmɪk] [bʊk] (phr.) 漫畫書
Malcolm collected comic books when he was a kid.

6) **apocalypse** [əˈpɑkəˌlɪps] (n.) 世界末日，大災難
Scientists fear that global warming may lead to an environmental apocalypse.

7) **sheriff** [ˈʃɛrɪf] (n.) 警長
The town has elected its first female sheriff.

8) **coma** [ˈkomə] (n.) 昏迷，不省人事
The man has been in a coma since the accident.

9) **abandon** [əˈbændən] (v.) 丟棄，遺棄
It is illegal to abandon or abuse a pet.

10) **encounter** [ɪnˈkaʊntə] (v./n.)（意外、偶然）遇到，面對
Laura was surprised when she encountered her ex-boyfriend at the mall.

11) **porch** [portʃ] (n.) 門廊
I think I hear footsteps on the front porch.

12) **overrun** [ˌovəˈrʌn] (v.) 橫行，竄犯
The poor parts of the city are overrun by crime.

13) **refugee** [ˌrɛfjʊˈdʒi] (n.) 難民
Thousands of refugees fled across the border.

14) **set off** [sɛt] [ɔf] (phr.) 出發
We set off on our trip early in the morning.

120

in the face of sth. 面臨威脅

表示跟人正面交鋒，或是不利的情勢就擺在眼前。

A: Why did the soldier receive a medal?
那個士兵為何獲頒獎章？

B: For showing courage in the face of danger.
因為他臨危不懼的表現。

看影集

瑞克在摩根和他兒子杜安的住處醒來。

Morgan: Got that bandage changed now. It was pretty rank. What was the wound?

Rick: Gunshot.

Morgan: Gunshot? What else? Anything?

Rick: Gunshot **ain't** enough?

Morgan: Look, I ask and you answer. That's **common courtesy**, right? Did you get bit?

Rick: Bit?

Morgan: Bit, chewed, maybe scratched— anything like that?

Rick: No, I got shot. Just shot as far as I know.

摩根：你的繃帶換好了。已經發出惡臭了。那是什麼傷口？

瑞克：是槍傷。

摩根：槍傷？還有其他的傷口嗎？

瑞克：槍傷還不夠嗎？

摩根：聽著，我問了你就要回答。這是一般禮節，對吧？你有被咬嗎？

瑞克：被咬？

摩根：咬，咀嚼，也可能被抓，有任何類似傷口嗎？

瑞克：沒有，我被開了一槍，就我所知只有槍傷。

看影集

在晚餐桌上，瑞克指責摩根在他房子外槍殺一名男子，是在他被杜安用鏟子打昏前看到的。

Rick: You shot that man today.

Morgan: Man?

Duane: It **weren't no** man.

Morgan: What the hell was that out of your mouth just now?

Duane: It *wasn't* a man.

Rick: You shot him in the street out front, a man.

Morgan: Friend, you need glasses. It was a walker. Come on, sit down before you fall down.

瑞克：你今天槍殺了那個人。

摩根：人？

杜安：那不是人。

摩根：你剛才說什麼？

杜安：那不是人。

瑞克：你在前面的街頭槍殺了一個人。

摩根：朋友，你要戴眼鏡了。那是喪屍。拜託，在你倒下前還是先坐下吧。

學英文 121

ain't 的用法

ain't 就等於 am not、are not、is not、have not、has not 等等所有助動詞的否定，以前算是俚語，但現在已經充斥在美國人的口語當中，尤其是在美國南方。而 ain't no 是常見的雙重否定語法，但和一般雙重否定不同，這裡的雙重否定是強調否定的意思。

A: You better not tell anybody what I did.
你最好別跟其他人說是我做的。

B: Hey, I ain't no snitch.
嘿，我可不是告密者。

對白中杜安說 It weren't no man. 應該是 It wasn't no man. 也就是 It wasn't a man. 的意思。只是他單複數用錯又雙重否定，因此被爸爸摩根責備。

稍後摩根和瑞克在晚餐上談話。

Morgan: Hey, mister. You even know what's going on?

Rick: I woke up today in the hospital, came home, and that's all I know.

Morgan: But you know about the dead people, right?

Rick: Yeah, I saw a lot of that—out on the loading dock, piled in trucks.

Morgan: No, not the ones they **put down**, the ones they didn't—the walkers, like the one I shot today. 'Cause he'd have ripped into you, tried to eat you, taken some flesh at least. Well, I guess if this is the first you're hearing it, I know how it must sound.

Rick: They're out there now? In the street?

Morgan: Yeah. They get more active after dark sometimes. Maybe it's the cool air or hell, maybe it's just me firing that gun today. But we'll be fine as long as we stay quiet. Probably wander off by morning. But listen, one thing I do know—don't you get bit. I saw your bandage and that's what we were afraid of. Bites kill you. The fever burns you out. But then after a while…you come back.

© AMC

禮儀相關字彙

courtesy 謙恭有禮的言行
common courtesy 即「一般禮節」。

etiquette 禮儀
可指一般社會認可的行為規範，也可專指特定領域的服裝儀容、儀式、座次、說話方式等典章制度，如 court etiquette「法庭禮儀」、work etiquette「職場禮儀」。

politeness 禮貌
指一般應對進退風度優雅、言談不冒犯人的舉止。

manners 舉止態度
good manners 是「有禮貌」，bad manners 就是「沒禮貌」，用餐時的規矩就是 table manners。

social norms 社會規範
包括一般禮節及正式的規定。

code of conduct 行為守則
包含各種規定，明列個人與群組間的權利義務。

protocol 外交禮節
非常正式的國際禮儀，鉅細靡遺的規定能避免跨國間的交往發生誤會，影響邦交。

摩根：嘿，先生，你知道發生什麼事了嗎？

瑞克：我今天在醫院裡醒來，回到家，只知道這些而已。

摩根：但你知道有死人，對吧？

瑞克：對，我看到好多屍體，都堆在卸貨區和卡車上。

摩根：不是，不是那些被他們殺掉的屍體，是那些沒倒下的——喪屍，就像我今天槍殺的那個。因為他們會攻擊你，想吃掉你，至少會咬下一些肉。嗯，我猜假如這是你第一次聽到，我知道第一次聽到的那種感覺。

瑞克：他們就在外面？在街上？

摩根：沒錯。他們有時候在天黑後更活躍。也許是因為天氣較涼爽，或是，該死，也許只是因為我今天開了槍。但我們只要安靜就不會有事，他們早上應該就會離開。不過，聽著，有一件事我是很肯定的，不要被咬到。我們是因為看到你的繃帶才害怕。被咬到會死。你會發高燒，但是過了一段時間……你會變成喪屍。

學英文 122

put down 殺掉（動物）
put down 是指殺死動物，尤其是生病受傷的家畜，以免牠繼續受折磨。

A: What happened to Ray's dog?
　　雷養的狗怎麼了？

B: He got rabies, and they had to put him down.
　　得了狂犬病，他們必須把牠解決掉。

看影集

汽車警報器響起,引來更多喪屍,其中一個是摩根的妻子。

Rick: That noise—won't it bring more of them?

Morgan: Nothing we can do about it now. Just have to **wait 'em out** till morning.

Duane: *[gasps]* She's here.

Morgan: Don't look. Get away from the windows. I said go. Go on. *[Duane starts crying]* Quiet. Come on, quiet now. Shh, shh. It's OK. Here, cry into the pillow. Do you remember? Shh. *[to Rick]* She, uh…she died in the other room, on that bed in there. There was nothing I could do about it. That fever, man—her skin gave off heat like a furnace. I should've…I should've put her down, man. I should've put her down, I know that. But I…you know what? I just didn't **have it in me**. She's the mother of my child.

瑞克:那個噪音,不會引來更多喪屍嗎?

摩根:我們現在無計可施了。只能等到天亮他們自己離開。

杜安:(倒抽一口氣)她來了。

摩根:別看。離開窗戶。我說走,快走。(杜安開始哭泣)安靜,拜託,安靜。噓,噓。沒關係,來,躲到枕頭裡哭。記得嗎?噓。(轉向瑞克)她,呃……她在另一個房間裡死的,在那張床上。我無能為力。她發著高燒,天哪,她的皮膚像火爐一樣燙。我應該……我應該殺掉她,天哪。我應該殺掉她,我知道。但是我……你知道嗎?我就是下不了手,她是我孩子的媽。

學英文 🎧 123

wait sth./sb. out 避風頭

句子對象是人的時候,表示在僵持無解的情況下故意拖延,等對方採取行動,或離開、放棄等。對象是事物的時候,表示靜待事件結束或發生之後再行動。也可以說 wait out sth./sb.。

A: We'll never be able to drive in this weather.
這種天氣我們沒辦法開車。

B: No. We'll just have to wait the storm out.
不行。我們只好等暴風雨結束再說。

have it in oneself (某人)辦得到

這裡的 it 是「成就某事所需的本事或勇氣」。

A: I've had it with the boss! I'm gonna threaten to quit unless he treats me better.
我受夠我的老闆了!如果不對我好一點,我要威脅他我要離職。

B: Wow! I didn't think you had it in you.
哇!我以為你不敢。

看影集

瑞克準備離開摩根和杜安,開車前往亞特蘭大。

Rick: You sure you won't come along?

Morgan: A few more days. By then Duane will know how to shoot and I won't be so rusty.

Rick: *[hands Morgan walkie-talkie]* You've got one better. I'll turn mine on a few minutes every day at dawn. You get up there, that's how you find me.

Morgan: You **think ahead**.

© AMC

Rick: Can't afford not to, not anymore.
Morgan: Listen, one thing. They may not seem like much one at a time, but in a group, all **riled up** and hungry—man, you watch your ass.
Rick: You too.

©AMC

瑞克：你確定你們不跟我一起走？
摩根：再過幾天吧，到時候杜安學會開槍，而且我也不那麼生疏以後。
瑞克：（將對講機拿給摩根）你最好也拿一個。我每天黎明時會打開幾分鐘。你來的時候就能聯絡到我。
摩根：你想得真周到。
瑞克：不多想點不行，再也不行。
摩根：聽著，還有一件事。他們單獨出現時或許威脅性不大，但是成群結隊的時候，像一群憤怒的惡鬼，老兄，你要小心。
瑞克：你也是。

** 學英文** 🎧124

think ahead 設想周到，未雨綢繆
think ahead 表示事情還沒發生就提前想到，預先為各種狀況作好準備。

A: Oh no—it's starting to rain.
糟糕，開始下雨了。
B: We should've thought ahead and brought an umbrella.
我們應該事先想到，帶把傘的。

rile sb. (up) 激怒
是指因冒犯或挑釁激起他人的怒氣。

A: Sarah's behavior really riles me up.
莎拉的行為真的把我惹毛了。
B: Yeah. She can be pretty annoying sometimes.
對啊。她有時候真的很討厭。

因本劇一炮而紅的諾曼瑞德斯（Norman Reedus）原本是參加另一個角色的試演，結果劇組和原著作者看到他之後靈感大發，乾脆幫他創造一個全新角色，還把他的角色寫得越來越酷。如果是從中間才開始看《陰屍路》的觀眾，甚至會以為主角是他飾演的戴瑞迪克森（Daryl Dixon），但其實是警長瑞奇格萊姆斯（Rick Grimes）。製播《陰屍路》的 AMC 公司已為熱愛騎機車的他量身製作真人秀 Ride With Norman Reedus（暫譯《跟諾曼瑞德斯一起追風》），大家終於可以好好欣賞他身上沒有血漬的俊俏身影了。

© Helga Esteb / Shutterstock.com

© HBO

TRUEBLOOD
噬血真愛

125

Adapted from a series of novels called the Southern [1]**Vampire** Mysteries, HBO's *True Blood* is a [2]**supernatural** drama set in the fictional town of Bon Temps, Louisiana. Two years before the story begins, Japanese scientists invented Tru Blood, a blood [3]**substitute** that allows vampires—who no longer need to drink human blood—to "come out of the [4]**coffin**." But true [5]**acceptance** takes time, especially in a small Southern town like Bon Temps.

HBO 的《噬血真愛》是一部超自然戲劇，由系列小說《南方吸血鬼謎案》改編，場景設在虛構的路易斯安納州小鎮，良辰鎮。故事開始前兩年，日本科學家發明了 Tru Blood，是一種能讓吸血鬼「出棺」的替代血液，這樣吸血鬼就可以不用再喝人類的血。不過，要真正接受吸血鬼仍需要一點時間，尤其是在像良辰鎮這樣的南方小鎮。

Sookie Stackhouse, the show's [6]**protagonist**, is a [7]**telepathic** waitress who works at Merlotte's Bar and [8]**Grill**. Always knowing what people are thinking makes it hard to have normal relationships, which is why Sookie is instantly attracted to a handsome stranger who walks into the bar one evening. She can't read his mind because he's a vampire—173-year-old Bill Compton, to be exact. But Sookie can read the minds of the couple at the next table, the Rattrays, who are planning on draining his blood and selling it. V-juice, as it's called, is an illegal drug that's [9]**addictive** to humans. Sookie tells her boss Sam, who's secretly in love with her, and her best friend Tara, who just quit her job—but they have no desire to help a vampire. Rushing outside, she saves Bill, who's tied up in silver chains, driving the couple away.

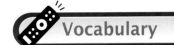
這部影集的主角蘇琪斯塔克豪斯是莫拉燒烤酒吧的女服務生，會讀心術。因為總是會知道其他人在想什麼，因此她很難有正常的人際關係，這也就是為什麼蘇琪會立刻被某天晚上走進酒吧的一位英俊陌生人所吸引。她無法感應到他的心，因為他是吸血鬼——確切來說，是一百七十三歲的比爾康普頓。但蘇琪可以讀到隔壁桌拉特瑞夫婦的心，他們打算抽乾他的血拿去賣。所謂吸血鬼汁是非法毒品，人類喝了會上癮。蘇琪將此事告訴暗戀她的老闆山姆，以及剛剛辭職的好友塔拉，但他們對拯救吸血鬼沒興趣。她急忙跑到店外，救了被銀鍊綁住的比爾，並將那對夫婦趕走。

Bill is not only ¹⁰⁾**grateful**, but attracted to Sookie as well, and soon ¹¹⁾**repays** the favor by killing the Rattrays when they return to the bar for ¹²⁾**revenge**. He also helps out when Sookie's brother Jason is arrested for the murder of Maudette Pickens, who's found strangled after their ¹³⁾**one-night stand**. Because Maudette was a fangbanger— a human who has sex with vampires—Bill takes Sookie to Fangtasia, a vampire bar in Shreveport ¹⁴⁾**run** by Eric Northman, a 2,000-year-old Viking vampire who is also sheriff of Area 5—the local vampire territory. Will Eric help her find the killer and prove her brother's innocence? Will her romance with Bill ¹⁵⁾**blossom**? You'll be sure to find *True Blood* just as addictive as V-juice!

© HBO

比爾不但心懷感激，同時還被蘇琪吸引，拉特瑞夫婦返回酒吧報仇時，比爾為了回報蘇琪，便殺了他們。蘇琪的哥哥傑森因涉嫌殺害穆戴皮肯斯被捕時，比爾也幫了蘇琪，皮肯斯是在跟傑森發生一夜情後，被發現遭人勒死。因為穆戴是吸血鬼迷——與吸血鬼發生性行為的人類——比爾帶蘇琪到什里夫波特市的「迷幻酒吧」，這個吸血鬼酒吧是由兩千多歲的艾瑞克諾特曼經營，他是維京吸血鬼，也是第五區的區長，第五區是當地吸血鬼的領土。艾瑞克是否能幫她找到真兇，證明她哥哥的清白？她和比爾的愛情是否能開花結果？你會發現《噬血真愛》就跟吸血鬼汁一樣，會讓人上癮！

1) **vampire** [ˋvæm͵paɪr] (n.) 吸血鬼
Do you believe in vampires?

2) **supernatural** [͵supɚˋnætʃərəl] (a.) 超自然的，靈異的
Molly believes in ghosts and other supernatural beings.

3) **substitute** [ˋsʌbstə͵tut] (n./v.) 替代的人事物；替代
You can use milk as a substitute for cream in the recipe.

4) **coffin** [ˋkɑfɪn] (n.) 棺材
The body was buried in a wooden coffin.

5) **acceptance** [əkˋsɛptəns] (n.) 接受，承認
The biologist's theory quickly won acceptance in the scientific community.

6) **protagonist** [proˋtægənɪst] (n.) 主角，主要人物
The protagonist is killed in the third act of the play.

7) **telepathic** [͵tɛləˋpæθɪk] (a.) 心電感應的
The movie is about a detective with telepathic powers.

8) **grill** [grɪl] (n./v.) 燒烤店，烤架；（用烤架）烤 (a.) grilled
We had steaks down at the local grill.

9) **addictive** [əˋdɪktɪv] (a.) 會使人上癮的
Video games can be addictive.

10) **grateful** [ˋgretfəl] (a.) 感激的，感謝的
We felt grateful to be alive after the earthquake.

11) **repay** [rɪˋpe] (v.) 償還，清償
I have six months to repay my loan.

12) **revenge** [rɪˋvɛndʒ] (n./v.) 報仇
The man swore revenge for his brother's murder.

13) **one-night stand** [ˋwʌn͵naɪt] [stænd] (phr.) 一夜情（的對象）
Stella had a one-night stand with a guy she met at the club.

14) **run** [rʌn] (v.) 經營，管理
The couple runs a small restaurant.

15) **blossom** [ˋblɑsəm] (v.) 成長，發展，開花結果
Cynthia is blossoming into a beautiful young woman.

吸血鬼名著

The Vampire Chronicles 《吸血鬼紀事》

作者安萊絲（Ann Rice）以《吸血鬼紀事》系列聞名，電影《夜訪吸血鬼》（*Interview with a Vampire*）是由系列第一本小說改編拍攝，為美國超自然（supernatural）文學的代表作家，全球暢銷上億冊，文壇地位無可取代。

Southern Vampire Mysteries 《南方吸血鬼謎案》

作者莎蓮哈里斯（Charlaine Harris）出身美國南方，長期致力於奇幻推理小說的創作，其中以《南方吸血鬼謎案》系列最受歡迎，一共出了十三本，曾創下全系列同時登上《紐約時報》暢銷榜的空前紀錄。

Twilight 《暮光之城》

作者史蒂芬妮梅爾（Stephenie Meyer）寫這部暢銷系列作品之前，完全沒有寫作經驗，儘管評價兩極，但因內容充滿少女情懷，廣受青少女喜愛，小說馬上被改拍為賣座的系列電影，被媒體譽為「J.K. 羅琳第二」。

© HBO

🎬 看影集

塔拉辭職後，在蘇琪上班時打電話給她。

Sookie: This had better be an emergency.
Tara: I just quit my job.
Sookie: Again?
Tara: I can't work for assholes.
Sookie: I'm glad you can afford to be so picky.
Tara: Oh, shut up! Sam is not an asshole and he's totally in love with you.
Sookie: Tara, he is my boss.
Tara: Jesus, Sookie! You need to **lighten up**.
Sookie: You know I hate it when you use **the J word**. Now I gotta go.
TarA: I'm coming over. I need a margarita…a big one!

蘇琪：妳最好是有急事。
塔拉：我剛剛辭職了。
蘇琪：又來了？
塔拉：我沒辦法幫混蛋工作。
蘇琪：我很高興妳有本事這麼挑。
塔拉：噢，閉嘴！山姆不是混蛋，而且他還很愛妳。
蘇琪：塔拉，他是我老闆。
塔拉：天啊，蘇琪！妳不要那麼嚴肅。
蘇琪：妳知道我討厭妳說 J 開頭的字。我要掛電話了。
塔拉：我過去找妳。我要一杯瑪格麗特，大杯的！

📖 學英文　🎧 127

lighten up 放輕鬆，別太認真
lighten 當動詞有「使變輕」或「使變亮」的意思，引申為「讓人變開心」。當我們叫人 lighten up 就是要他停止負面的情緒，不要再抱怨、苛責或消沉了。

A: Ken's negative attitude is starting to get on my nerves.
　肯恩的負面態度開始惹毛我了。
B: Yeah. He really needs to lighten up.
　對啊，他真的需要放輕鬆點。

🎬 看影集

蘇琪和塔拉的表哥拉法葉談話，他是酒吧裡的同性戀廚師。

Sookie: Onion rings. And if you drop a few of them on the floor…that's fine with me.
Lafayette: Got it. *[looks at Sookie]* Ooh, Sookie! You look like a porn star with that tan and pink lipstick. You got a date?
Sookie: No! When I wear makeup, I get bigger tips!
Lafayette: Yes, girl, that's it. These damn rednecks **are suckers for** packaging.
Sookie: And I get even bigger tips when I act like I don't have a brain in my head. But if I don't, they're all scared of me.
Lafayette: They ain't scared of you, honey child. They scared of what's between your legs.
Sookie: Lafayette! That's nasty talk! I won't listen to that!

蘇　琪：我要一份洋蔥圈。假如你掉了幾個在地上……我無所謂。
拉法葉：知道了。（看著蘇琪）噢，蘇琪！黝黑的膚色配上粉紅色口紅，讓妳看起來像個A片女星。妳要去約會嗎？
蘇　琪：沒有！我化妝可以拿到更多小費！
拉法葉：沒錯，丫頭，這就對了。那些該死的鄉巴佬對濃妝豔抹就是沒轍。

蘇　琪：而且我只要表現得像是腦袋空空的草包，就能拿到更多小費。但假如我不這樣做，他們都會怕我。

拉法葉：他們不是怕妳，親愛的，他們是怕妳兩腿之間的東西。

蘇　琪：拉法葉！下流！我不要聽！

be a sucker for... （某人）對……完全沒輒

sucker 是指容易上當受騙的人。for 後面接某事物，表示某人特別偏好某事物，一遇上此事物就完全沒輒。

A: You like Marilyn Monroe better than Audrey Hepburn?
你喜歡瑪麗蓮夢露更勝於奧黛莉赫本？

B: Yeah. I'm a sucker for blondes.
沒錯。我對金髮美女就是沒輒。

看影集

山姆因為離開酒吧去查看救比爾的蘇琪是否沒事，要塔拉幫他顧店，之後，山姆向塔拉道謝。

Sam: Thanks for helping me out tonight, Tara.

Tara: How much you gonna pay me?

Sam: Uh…20 bucks?

Tara: Sam, how do you expect me to work here for 20 bucks a night?

Sam: I don't expect you to work here, and you only covered tonight for what, an hour at the most?

Tara: Yeah, but Sam, if I did work here….

Sam: It'd be a matter of time before you **went off on somebody**. I don't want to drive my customers away.

Tara: I only go off on stupid people.

Sam: Most of my customers are stupid people.

Tara: Yeah, but I could help you keep an eye on Sookie. You see the way she was looking at that vampire? That is just trouble looking for a place to happen. She means too much to both of us to let anything happen to her.

Sam: Be here tomorrow at six. *[hands her a bartending book]* And learn this on your own! I don't have time to train you.

山姆：謝謝妳今天晚上幫我顧店，塔拉。

塔拉：你要付我多少錢？

山姆：呃……二十塊錢？

塔拉：山姆，你怎麼會認為我在這裡工作一晚只賺二十塊錢？

山姆：我沒想過妳會在這裡工作，而且只有今天晚上，最多一個小時吧？

塔拉：是啊，山姆，但假如我真的在這裡工作……

山姆：妳遲早會發飆罵人，我不想把客人趕走。

塔拉：我只罵笨蛋。

山姆：我的客人大部分都是笨蛋。

塔拉：是啊，但我可以幫你看著蘇琪。你看到她看著那個吸血鬼的樣子了嗎？遲早會惹來麻煩。她對我們來說都很重要，所以我們不能讓她出事。

山姆：明天六點來上班。（遞給她一本調酒書）自己學吧！我沒時間訓練妳。

go off on sb. 對人破口大罵

go off 有「爆炸」、「發出巨響」的意思，因此 go off on sb. 就是對著一個人發飆狂罵的意思。

A: What did you do to make Vicky so mad?
你做了什麼讓薇琪那麼生氣？

B: Nothing. She just went off on me for no reason.
沒什麼。她無緣無故就對我發飆。

the J word 以 J 開頭的字

對白中的 J word 是指 Tara 前一句說的 Jesus，因為虔誠的教徒是不會把 God、Jesus、Christ、Jesus Christ 這些字掛在嘴邊的，這在他們眼中是褻瀆神明的語言，hell、damn 這些也是跟宗教有關「不可說」的字。

下次迫不得已必須用到「不可說」的字時，可以學著用同樣的方法迴避：

・Jim got suspended for using the N word in class.
吉姆因為在班上說「黑鬼」（nigger）被停學處分。

・She slapped me when I called her the B word.
我叫她「婊子」（bitch），她賞了我一巴掌。

◎ 看影集

蘇琪和傑森說起她遇到拉特瑞夫婦的事，他從同事霍伊特那裡聽說此事。

Sookie: Well, did Hoyt tell you that Mack came after me with a knife?

Jason: Motherfucker! You want me to kick his ass?

Sookie: I already took care of that, thank you.

Jason: What are you doing **messing with** him anyway?

Sookie: Well, did you know that in addition to dealing drugs, the Rats also happen to be vampire drainers? Yep! One of my customers last night was a vampire, and they were draining him out in the parking lot. I couldn't have that.

Jason: Sookie, you do not want to **get mixed up with** vampires. Trust me!

Sookie: Oh, shut up! Even if you hate vampires, you can't let trash like the Rats go and drain them. It's not like siphoning gas out of a car. They would have left him in the woods to die.

Jason: Who fucking cares? He's already dead.

Sookie: That's not his fault.

Jason: What did he look like?

Sookie: Handsome…in a sort of old-fashioned way, like from a movie on TCM.

吸血鬼相關字彙

自古以來，世界各地都有形形色色吸血鬼的傳說，但一般大眾認知的吸血鬼，都是從電影裡看來的：

外型

吸血鬼的特徵就是一對獠牙（fangs），這是吃飯的工具。古裝電影中，衣冠楚楚的男吸血鬼都披一條黑色斗篷（cape），梳整整齊齊的油頭（slick hair）；時裝造型的吸血鬼已經不披斗篷，但還是一個個像要去走秀的模特兒。吸血鬼大多男的英俊、女的性感，臉色或許蒼白（pale），但嘴唇一定很紅潤。

剋星

吸血鬼怕大蒜的氣味。由於銀在古代被視為神聖金屬（holy metal），吸血鬼碰到銀器會灼傷，發射銀子彈（silver bullet）可以消滅吸血鬼。其他聖物如十字架（crucifix）、玫瑰念珠（rosary）、聖水（holy water）也能驅走吸血鬼。凡是鬼都見不得陽光，吸血鬼也不例外，只要曬到太陽，他們就化為灰燼。

蘇琪：嗯，霍伊特有告訴你麥克帶刀來對付我嗎？

傑森：混帳！你要我幫妳扁他嗎？

蘇琪：我已經處理過了，謝謝。

傑森：妳為什麼要惹他？

蘇琪：這個嘛，你知道除了販毒，拉特瑞夫婦也在吸取吸血鬼的血嗎？沒錯！昨天晚上我有一位客人是吸血鬼，他們在停車場開始吸取他的血。我不能放任不管。

傑森：蘇琪，不要跟吸血鬼扯上關係，相信我！

蘇琪：噢，閉嘴！就算你恨吸血鬼，也不能讓拉特瑞夫婦那種垃圾去吸他們的血。這不是把車子裡的汽油抽乾，他們會把他丟到樹林裡等死。

傑森：誰在乎？他本來就死了。

蘇琪：那不是他的錯。

傑森：他長得怎樣？

蘇琪：英俊……有點老派，就像從 TCM 經典電影台裡走出來一樣。

📢 學英文 🎧 130

mess with… 找……麻煩

mess with 是「找某人麻煩，跟某人挑釁」的意思，with 後接的是找麻煩的對象，通常用於否定祈使句中。

A: Do you think I can beat Jeff in a fight?
你認為我打得過傑夫嗎？

B: No. He's not the kind of guy you want to mess with.
打不過。那個傢伙不好惹。

get mixed up with 廝混

經常用於否定語氣，表示跟不務正業的人牽扯在一起，或是跟素行不良的人鬼混。

A: How did Michael end up in prison?
麥可怎麼會淪落到去坐牢？

B: He got mixed up with a bad crowd after he graduated from high school.
他高中畢業之後交到壞朋友。

看影集

警探安迪貝爾夫勒和警長巴德迪爾波在審問傑森。

安迪：　你到過穆戴的公寓找她嗎？

Andy:　You ever visit Maudette at her apartment?

Jason:　Me? No! Boys, I could do a lot better than Maudette Pickens, believe me.

Andy:　You weren't there last night?

Jason:　Last night…uh…OK, yeah! I was there last night.

Andy:　Yeah? Then why didn't you say so?

Jason:　Because I know she got killed, and I thought it would look bad me having been at her place.

Bud:　　Well, it does look bad, Jason.

Jason:　OK, look. I **hooked up with** Maudette last night, we had sex. That's all!

傑森：我？沒有！老兄，我可以找個比穆戴皮肯斯更正點的，相信我。

安迪：你昨天晚上不在那裡？

傑森：昨天晚上……呃……好吧，沒錯！昨天晚上我在那裡。

安迪：對吧？那你為什麼不承認？

傑森：因為我知道她被殺了，我想我要是說自己去過她家，會讓我看起來很可疑。

巴德：確實很可疑，傑森。

傑森：好，聽我說，我昨天晚上跟穆戴搭上，我們做愛了。就這樣而已！

飾演本劇女主角蘇琪的安娜派昆（Anna Paquin）來頭不小，她年僅十一歲時，就以《鋼琴師和她的情人》得到奧斯卡最佳女配角獎，之後一路演電影都有所斬獲。二〇〇七年接演《噬血真愛》，不但讓她於二〇〇九年贏得一座金球獎最佳戲劇類女主角，更贏到一個丈夫，跟飾演劇中男主角比爾的英國男星史蒂芬莫耶（Stephen Moyer）結為連理！

 學英文 131

hook up with sb. 跟人上床，與人結交

hook是「鉤住」或「與人產生關係」，表示與人交往聯繫，但通常如上面對白，解釋為跟人發生性關係。

A: Hey, do you want to get something to eat with us?
嘿，你想跟我們去吃點東西嗎？

B: No, I already ate, but I'll hook up with you guys later at the party.
不，我吃過了，但我晚點和你們在派對上碰頭。

A: Are you and Kathy going out?
你在跟凱西交往嗎？

B: Not really. We just hooked up a couple times.
不算是。只是上過幾次床。

© FOX

嘻哈 世家
Empire

132

Fox's *Empire*, a musical drama about the struggle for control of a family-run New York record label, has been called *Dynasty* for the hip-hop [1]**generation**. The show centers on Lucious Lyon, an orphan and former drug dealer from the mean streets of Philly who eventually became a successful rapper and founded [2]**Empire** [3]**Entertainment**. Just as the music [4]**mogul** is about to take the label public, however, he's [5]**diagnosed** with a [6]**fatal** illness and given at most three years to live.

福斯電視網的音樂劇《嘻哈世家》，已被稱為嘻哈世代的《朝代》（編註：美國一九八〇年代熱門肥皂劇，內容為富豪家族的恩怨情仇），描述紐約一個家族經營的唱片公司陷入權力鬥爭的故事。本劇的焦點人物路西斯萊恩是孤兒出身，曾經在費城街頭販毒，最後成為成功的嘻哈歌手，並創辦了帝國娛樂唱片公司。不過，就在這位音樂界大亨要將唱片公司上市時，他被診斷出患有絕症，最多只剩三年可活。

© FOX

Knowing his time is limited, Lucious [7]**summons** his three sons—Andre, Jamal and Hakeem—and tells them he plans on [8]**grooming** one of them to [9]**take over** the label. But before the struggle for power can even start, Lucious' ex-wife Cookie, who's just been released from prison after serving a 17-year sentence, shows up and **throws a monkey wrench into** the situation. Apparently, the label was started with money she made from a drug deal—the same deal that [10]**landed** her in jail—and now she wants half of the company. Lucious tells her that's impossible, and offers her a multi-million dollar salary instead.

知道自己時日不多後，路西斯將三個兒子召來——安德雷、賈莫、哈金——告訴他們要培養其中一人接手唱片公司。但在這場權力鬥爭開始前，路西斯剛服滿十七年刑期出獄的前妻庫琪出現，將一切都攪亂了。原來唱片公司當初創辦的資金是她販毒得來的，她也因為那次販毒而入獄，現在她要拿回公司一半的股份。路西斯告訴她不可能，但是願意給她數百萬元高薪。

But Cookie wants more than just money—she wants to [11]**regain** power and make [12]**hit** records too—and what better way to do that than through her sons. Oldest son Andre is an MBA with a head for business, but Lucious wants a [13]**celebrity** to take over the company. He seems set on grooming youngest son Hakeem, a talented if [14]**undisciplined** rapper, so Andre encourages Cookie to manage middle son Jamal, a sensitive singer-songwriter who lives with his gay lover. But this is easier said than done. Although Lucious doesn't approve of Jamal's lifestyle, he isn't willing to give up control of his career until Cookie threatens to reveal that the label was started with drug money. With Hakeem and Jamal as [15]**pawns**, the battle for the Empire throne now begins!

但庫琪要的不只是錢——她要奪回權力，也想製作暢銷唱片——而且沒有什麼辦法比透過自己兒子達到目的更好了。大兒子安德雷是企業管理碩士，有生意頭腦，但路西斯希望由名人來接管公司。他似乎要培養小兒子哈金接手，他是個有才華但放縱任性的嘻哈歌手，因此安德雷鼓勵庫琪當二兒子賈莫的經紀人，他是敏感的創作歌手，和同性戀人同居。但說的永遠比做的容易。雖然路西斯不認同賈莫的生活方式，但他仍不願意把賈莫的演藝生涯拱手讓人，直到庫琪威脅要揭露唱片公司的創辦資金是來自販毒。以哈金和賈莫為棋子，帝國唱片公司的奪權之戰才剛要開打！

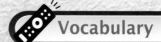
1) **generation** [ˌdʒɛnəˈreʃən] (n.) 代，世代
We should all do our part to preserve the planet for future generations.

2) **empire** [ˈɛmpaɪr] (n.) 帝國
The Roman Empire fell in the 5th century.

3) **entertainment** [ˌɛntəˈtenmənt] (n.) 娛樂，演藝
Hollywood is the center of America's entertainment industry.

4) **mogul** [ˈmoɡəl] (n.) 巨擘，大人物
The movie mogul has a mansion in Beverly Hills.

5) **diagnose** [ˈdaɪəɡˌnos] (v.) 診斷
More and more children are being diagnosed with diabetes.

6) **fatal** [ˈfetəl] (a.) 致命的
Brain tumors are often fatal.

7) **summon** [ˈsʌmən] (v.) 召喚，召集
The manager summoned the employee to his office.

8) **groom** [ɡrum] (v.)（為了特定目標）培養，訓練
Robert is being groomed for a management position.

9) **take over** [tek] [ˈovə] (phr.) 接管
Germany took over Poland in 1939.

10) **land (in)** [lænd] (v.) 使陷於
Your reckless behavior could land you in serious trouble.

11) **regain** [rɪˈɡen] (v.) 奪回，恢復
Government forces have regained control of the city.

12) **hit** [hɪt] (a./n.) 流行的，熱門的；成功、受歡迎的事物
Have you heard Jolin Tsai's latest hit single?

13) **celebrity** [səˈlɛbrɪti] (n.) 名人，名氣
Many celebrities attended the royal wedding.

14) **undisciplined** [ʌnˈdɪsəplɪnd] (a.) 缺乏自律的，不遵守紀律的
The coach yelled at the players for being lazy and undisciplined.

15) **pawn** [pɔn] (n.) 棋子，小卒，傀儡
Parents shouldn't use their children as pawns during a divorce.

134

throw a monkey wrench into
壞了好事

monkey wrench 是「活動扳手」，一把又大又重的活動扳手被扔進運行中的機器，鐵定整組機器都壞掉，這個說法因此引申為「妨礙計畫進行」、「造成失敗」。
A: I can't believe the boss is making us work this Saturday.
真不敢相信老闆要我們這個星期六來上班。
B: Yeah. He really threw a monkey wrench into my plans.
對啊。他把我的計畫全搞砸了。

看影集

路西斯將兒子們召回家裡，討論他的接班計畫。

© FOX

Lucious: I'm glad you're all here. And get your **big-ass** feet off my $40,000 table! I eat there! Your brother and I have been working hard to turn Empire into a publicly traded company. Now part of us going public means ensuring a legacy for this company, and right now it seems none of you are prepared to take over after I'm gone. Now, it won't happen today, nor tomorrow…but I will start grooming someone soon. And it can only be one of you.

Hakeem: What is this, we…we *King Lear* now?

Lucious: Call it what you want, **smart-ass**, but over the next several months….

Andre: Wait, wait. What are you saying? We're all in competition to be the future head of the company?

Lucious: In order for it to survive, I need one of you **Negroes** to **man up** and lead it. And nothing or no one is going to tear it down, hear me?

路西斯：我很高興你們都在這裡。把你的大腳丫從我的四萬塊桌子放下來！那是我吃飯的地方！我和你們大哥一直努力要讓帝國成為一家上市公司。那麼，上市的用意之一，是要讓這家公司能夠代代相傳。但現在你們沒一個看起來是準備好可以在我走之後接班的。雖然不是今天，也不是明天，但我很快會開始培養接班人，而且只會從你們之中選一人。

哈　金：什麼意思？我們……我們要上演《李爾王》了？

路西斯：隨便你怎麼說，自以為是的傢伙，但在接下來幾個月……

安德雷：等等，你在說什麼？我們都要競爭公司未來的負責人？

路西斯：為了公司的生存，我要你們其中一個黑人拿出魄力，領導公司，而且不能讓任何事或任何人破壞，聽到了嗎？

學英文　135

man up 像個男子漢

如同字面上的意思，就是要人「像個男子漢」，把事情扛起來。

A: Did you hear that Ryan got his girlfriend pregnant?
你有聽說萊恩讓他女友懷孕了嗎？

B: Yeah. He needs to man up and marry her.
對啊。他得負起男人的責任，把她娶回家。

把「屁股」掛嘴上

ass 經常用來跟一些字眼連用以加強語氣，big-ass 就是「大的，驚人的，了不起的」；dumb-ass 就是「笨蛋」；lame-ass 表示「爛透了」；smart-ass 即「自以為聰明的人，講話刻薄不留情面的人」，也可以說 wise-ass。

King Lear《李爾王》

《李爾王》（King Lear）與《馬克白》（Macbeth）、《哈姆雷特》（Hamlet）、《奧賽羅》（Othello）並列莎士比亞四大悲劇。《李爾王》故事敘述年老的李爾王想聽聽三個女兒誰比較愛他，他就傳位給誰。大女兒、二女兒滿口奉承，小女兒只說了經典的一句 "Love and be silent." 「我愛你，盡在不言中。」李爾王氣她不夠窩心，把她草草嫁到國外，將國土平分給另外兩個女兒。沒想到女兒們翻臉無情，結果老國王發瘋，女兒自相殘殺，最後以悲劇收場。

Negro 黑人

源自西班牙文及葡萄牙文。意指「黑色」。一九五○年代前，美國不論白人或黑人都會用 Negro 這個字，後來因被認為帶有殖民色彩而少用，只有黑人自己可用。

庫琪到帝國唱片公司與路西斯對質。

Cookie: You forgot about me the second you divorced me in there. You still owe me what's mine.

Lucious: What are you talking about?

Cookie: Half of this company. It was my 400,000 that started this bitch. You know it, and I know it. Did 17 hard years for that money, and I want half my company back.

Lucious: I'm sorry, Cookie, but it don't work like that.

Cookie: It don't work like what, honey?

Lucious: This company isn't the company that we started 17 years ago. As a matter of fact, I control maybe ten percent of this damn thing. I've got a board of directors, quarterly reports, **SEC** filings. And on top of it, we're about to **go public**, which is a **whole nother** monster in itself.

Cookie: Public? What the hell is public?

Lucious: Baby, I can give you a huge salary, but I can't give you half of my company.

Cookie: Your company?

Lucious: I can't give you any of it.

Cookie: This is my company, Lucious. I…I started this. You need to stop playing with me.

Lucious: I promise you, anything you want, you can get.

Cookie: Five million…a year, and I want to be head of **A&R**.

庫　琪：我入獄後你跟我離婚的那一刻你就忘記我了，你還欠我應得的。

路西斯：妳在說什麼？

庫　琪：公司一半的股份。因為有我的四十萬元才有這間公司。你知道，我也知道。為了那筆錢我蹲了十七年的苦牢，我要拿回屬於我的一半股份。

路西斯：我很遺憾，庫琪，但這事不能這樣。

庫　琪：不能怎樣？

路西斯：這間公司已經不是十七年前剛創辦時的樣子了。事實上，我只掌控百分之十的股份，我們有董事會、季度報告、證券交易所申報。而且最重要的是，我們要上市了，這完全是另一回事了。

庫　琪：上市？上市是什麼東西？

路西斯：寶貝，我可以給妳高薪，但我不能把我的公司分妳一半。

庫　琪：你的公司？

路西斯：我完全不能把公司分給妳。

庫　琪：這是我的公司，路西斯，我……我創辦的。你別想再耍我。

路西斯：我答應妳，只要妳想要的，妳都能得到。

庫　琪：五百萬……一年，而且我要當藝人開發部的負責人。

SEC
即 Securities and Exchange Commission「證券交易委員會」的縮寫，是美國證券業主管機構，負責美國證券的監督管理。

🗨 **學英文** 🎧 136

go public（公司）股票上市

go public 除了解釋為「將祕密公開」，還可以表示某公司股票正式掛牌上市，開放讓一般民眾投資購買該公司股票，巨額的資金湧入，將會為公司帶來可觀的財富。前面文章中的 take (the label) public 也是一樣的意思。

A: Why did the company go public?
為什麼這間公司要股票上市？

B: They wanted to raise money to expand their operations.
他們想募集資金擴大營運。

a whole nother 完全是另一回事

a whole nother 是 another whole 的口語說法，another 被拆開成 a 和 nother 兩部分，再把 whole 放在兩者中間。

A: What do you think of the team's new player?
你覺得這隊的新球員如何？

B: He's amazing. He's really taken their game to a whole nother level.
他太棒了。他真的讓球隊的比賽表現更上一層樓。

© FOX

看影集

© FOX

庫琪闖入公司會議後,路西斯帶她進他的辦公室。

Lucious: Are you out of your damn mind? I told you I was gonna **hook you up**.

Cookie: And I'm telling you that's not enough. I want Jamal, too.

Lucious: You can't have him.

Cookie: You messing with the wrong bitch, Lucious. I know things.

Lucious: What do you know?

Cookie: What if I were to disclose to the SEC that I was the original investor with $400,000 in drug money? Yeah. Your application for an IPO would be effectively denied. You know it's true.

Lucious: Baby, why are you doing this?

Cookie: **Don't you "baby" me**, you two-faced bastard. I've been living like a dog for 17 years and now I want what's mine. I want Jamal.

路西斯: 妳瘋了嗎?我告訴過妳我會幫妳做好安排。

庫　琪: 我要告訴你這還不夠。我還要賈莫。

路西斯: 賈莫不能歸你。

庫　琪: 你惹錯了人,路西斯,我知道你的秘密。

路西斯: 妳知道什麼?

庫　琪: 假如我向證券交易所透露我才是原本的投資人,那筆四十萬元是販毒來的呢?沒錯,你的首次公開募股申請會被拒絕。你知道這是事實。

路西斯: 寶貝,妳為什麼要這麼做?

庫　琪: 別再叫我寶貝,你這個雙面人,我這十七年活得像狗一樣,我現在要拿回屬於我的一切。我要賈莫。

音樂產業相關字彙

record label 唱片公司

在娛樂圈內,label 為 record label 的簡稱,也就是唱片公司(record company)。「大型唱片公司或集團」為 major record label,而 sublabel 則是指大型唱片公司旗下的「子公司」。

hip-hop 嘻哈

嘻哈是源自一九七〇年代紐約非裔及拉丁美洲裔青少年的次文化,透過音樂、舞蹈、服裝及塗鴉(graffiti)表現混跡街頭的生活形態。超粗金項鍊、超大金耳環的風格為其招牌。

rap 饒舌

饒舌也發源於一九七〇年代的紐約,是一種帶有節奏和押韻(rhyme)的說唱方式,押韻的歌詞充滿自誇驕傲的氣氛,再配上重複性強的節拍,與嘻哈文化有密不可分的關係。

singer-songwriter 創作歌手

所唱的歌曲都是自己作詞譜曲的歌手。一般流行歌手為了迎合大眾口味,會採用他人的創作,或是與人合作雕琢出最具賣相的歌曲;而 singer-songwriter 是要透過歌詞抒發人生觀、表達對社會議題的看法,經常以吉他或鋼琴自彈自唱,不會太過琢磨伴奏、編曲。

A&R 藝人開發

artist and repertoire(藝人及曲目規劃)的縮寫。repertoire 是指表演的「曲目/戲目」,在唱片業中,A&R 負責發掘培訓藝人,主動依照藝人的發展計畫向作曲者邀集新歌試聽帶(demo),籌組製作團隊。

record producer 唱片製作人

除了要指導藝人、監督錄音、混音、後製的技術工作,還要控制預算及進度。過去大多唱片製作人都是受唱片公司或藝人延攬雇用,現在有更多獨立製作人(independent producer)成立自己的公司,工作內容就需涵蓋 A&R,甚至親自參與詞曲創作。

studio musician 錄音室樂手

專門幫沒有固定班底的歌手伴奏錄音的樂手,也幫廣告、電影或是電視錄製配樂,經常隸屬於唱片公司或錄音室。studio musician 通常只做錄音室表演。

session musician 表演伴奏樂手

表演範圍較 studio musician 廣泛,除了在錄音室,也在演唱會現場表演(live show)擔任樂手。

音樂出版品相關字彙

demo 樣品帶，試聽帶

歌手／樂團的自製歌曲作品，寄給各表演場所或唱片公司，以爭取登台或簽約的機會。

album 專輯

音樂界細分為：

・**studio album** 錄音室專輯，在錄音室錄製的專輯，可於後製加入聲音效果或是伴奏，音質清晰完美。

・**live album** 現場專輯，表演現場錄製，藝人即興演出、與聽眾的互動都能完整呈現。

・**compilation** 合輯，將受歡迎的曲目集合在一起，集結多張專輯的經典曲目（vintage track）、現場實況錄音、重新混音歌曲（remix）。

EP 單曲專輯

即 extended play，但其實 EP 是介於單曲（single）和專輯之間的作品，也有人稱之為「小碟」，會收錄四到八首歌曲。

LP 專輯唱片

即 long play，又稱為 full-length，也可以說是「大碟」，曲目一般在十首歌以上。

bootleg 私製唱片

趁歌手、樂團現場演出時私自收音的聽眾自製唱片，雖然不合法，而且音質不佳，但因收錄許多專輯唱片聽不到的歌曲而廣受歡迎。

mixtape 混音專輯

饒舌歌手將喜歡的音樂，加上自創混音編曲，串連起來的合輯，在街上發放，以試探市場大眾對自己音樂的反應。

charts 排行榜

chart 原本是「圖表」，但在音樂界是「流行唱片排行榜」的意思。當一張專輯登上排行榜第一名，就可以說 reach number one on the charts。美國最具公信力的音樂排行榜為告示牌排行榜。

學英文 137

hook sb. up (with) 幫人弄到

這句話原本是指幫人牽線買毒品或是買春等等較為負面的用法。但後來也被引申在替人得到東西，像是幫人找到或是提供可以買到東西的方法。

A: Your new tattoo is awesome! Who did it?
你新刺的刺青真是太酷了！誰刺的？

B: This cool tattoo artist I know. I can hook you up if you want.
我認識的一個很棒的刺青師。如果你想要的話我可以幫你介紹。

don't "…" me 別叫得那麼親熱

當你火冒三丈，別人來安撫你的時候，經常會動用溫情攻勢，跟你稱兄道弟、直呼你的小名。說這句話就表示你不吃這一套。

A: But honey, I was just out having a drink with the guys.
可是親愛的，我只是去跟哥兒們喝一杯。

B: Don't "honey" me! You were probably out with some bimbo!
別叫得那麼親熱！你應該是跟哪個野女人出去吧！

© Featureflash Photo Agency / Shutterstock.com

飾演庫琪的泰拉姬漢森（Taraji P. Henson）曾在《班傑明的奇幻旅程》飾演班傑明的養母，還因這個角色獲得奧斯卡最佳女配角提名。後來在影集《疑犯追蹤》主演警探，非常受到影迷喜愛，卻在第三季忽然被編劇寫死，外界猜測是因為她要接演庫琪這個難得的角色，而美國電視圈又有不能同時主演兩部影集的行規，所以只好讓她退出《疑犯追蹤》了。

© glee wiki

glee 歡樂合唱團

138

Fox's musical comedy *Glee*, which aired from 2009 to 2015, [1]**revolves around** the colorful [2]**misfits** who make up the glee club at McKinley High in the small town of Lima, Ohio. By combining fun musical performances with serious drama—the show [3]**tackles** serious [4]**issues** like [5]**gender** identity, teen pregnancy and [6]**bullying**—*Glee* has attracted millions of loyal fans, known as "Gleeks." *Glee* has also won a number of Emmys and Golden Globes, and even set a record for hit singles—an amazing 207 songs from the show made it onto the Billboard Hot 100!

《歡樂合唱團》是福斯電視網的音樂喜劇，從二〇〇九年播映到二〇一五年，以俄亥俄州利馬小鎮的麥金利高中為場景，故事圍繞著校內合唱團中各種怪咖團員。本劇結合了有趣的音樂表演和嚴肅的劇情，探討性別認同、青少年懷孕和霸凌等嚴肅的問題。《歡樂合唱團》藉此吸引數百萬名忠實粉絲，這些粉絲自稱「歡樂客」。《歡樂合唱團》也獲得多次艾美獎和金球獎，甚至創下暢銷單曲紀錄──本劇有驚人的兩百零七首歌都登上告示牌百大單曲榜。

As the show begins, the head of McKinley High's glee club has just been fired for [7]**molesting** a student. When Spanish teacher Will Schuester learns what happened from guidance counselor Emma Pillsbury, he [8]**volunteers** to take over the glee club. Hoping to restore the club to its former glory, he holds [9]**auditions** and brings in new members—fame-hungry Rachel Barry, [10]**diva** Mercedes Jones, gay **tenor** Kurt Hummel, shy Asian American Tina Cohen-Chang and [11]**disabled** guitar player Artie Abrams. But [12]**rehearsals** are a disaster, and in an attempt to attract more talent,

© FOX

Will tries to [13]**recruit** kids from the [14]**cheerleading** and football teams. Unfortunately, cheerleading coach Sue Sylvester turns him down, and while football coach Ken Tanaka lets him talk to his players, none of them sign up.

本劇一開始，麥金利高中合唱團的團長因為猥褻學生而被解雇。西班牙語教師威爾舒斯特從輔導老師愛瑪皮爾斯伯里得知此事時，自願接手合唱團。為了恢復合唱團昔日的輝煌，他舉辦試唱會，招募新成員——渴望成名的瑞秋貝瑞、歌后梅塞迪絲瓊斯、同性戀男高音科特漢默爾、害羞的亞裔緹娜柯恩張，以及身障吉他手痞提艾布蘭斯。但練唱的情況簡直是一團糟，為了吸引更多人才，威爾想從啦啦隊和美式足球隊招收團員。不幸的是，他遭到啦啦隊教練蘇席維斯特拒絕，而美式足球隊教練肯田中雖然讓他和球員談，但沒有人願意報名。

Just as Will is about to give up, he hears quarterback Finn Hudson singing "Can't Fight This Feeling" in the shower and decides to [15]**blackmail** him into joining glee club—claiming that he found marijuana in his locker. With Finn and Rachel as leads, the group—now called New Directions—is starting to sound much better. But when Will takes them to see [16]**Vocal** [17]**Adrenaline**—their likely competition at Regionals—perform "[18]**Rehab**," they realize they have a *lot* of work to do. And then Will's wife Terri gets pregnant and convinces him to give up teaching and find a better paying job. What will happen to New Directions? Will they ever make it to Regionals, or even Sectionals? Be sure to [19]**tune in** and find out!

正當威爾要放棄時，他聽到四分衛菲恩哈德森在洗澡時唱「無法抗拒這種感覺」，決定要勒索他，好讓他加入合唱團——聲稱在他的置物櫃裡發現大麻。以菲恩和瑞秋為主唱，現在名叫「新方向」的合唱團開始越唱越好。但當威爾帶他們去看「激情美聲」——他們可能在地區賽遇到的競爭對手——表演「戒了吧」這首歌時，他們意識到自己還有許多進步的空間。然後威爾的妻子泰莉懷孕，說服他放棄教書，找一份薪水更高的工作。新方向合唱團的未來將會如何？他們能打進地區賽、還是連縣市區賽都打不贏？想知道的話務必收看本劇！

歌唱聲部

義大利是西洋音樂早期發展的中心地，因此樂理術語幾乎都是義大利文。聲部是以音域區分，基本分為：

soprano「女高音」、alto「女低音」、tenor「男高音」、bass「男低音」；mezzo-soprano 是指介於 soprano 和 alto 之間的音域，為「女中音」；介於 tenor 和 bass 間的音域是 baritone，即「男中音」。

Vocabulary 🎧139

1) **revolve around** [rɪˋvɑlv] [əˋraʊnd] (phr.) 以……為中心
   Mary's life revolves around her children.

2) **misfit** [ˋmɪsˏfɪt] (n.) 格格不入的人，怪胎
   Kevin was a bit of a misfit in high school.

3) **tackle** [ˋtækəl] (v.) 著手處理，對付
   The government has promised to tackle inflation.

4) **issue** [ˋɪʃu] (n.) 議題，問題
   We have several issues to discuss at today's meeting.

5) **gender** [ˋdʒɛndə] (n.) 性別
   Do you know the gender of your baby yet?

6) **bullying** [ˋbulɪɪŋ] (n.) 霸凌
   Students should report bullying to school officials.

7) **molest** [məˋlɛst] (v.) 猥褻（孩童），調戲（女性）
   The man was arrested for molesting his daughter.

8) **volunteer** [ˏvɑlənˋtɪr] (v./n.) 自願服務；志工
   John volunteered to join the army because he loved his country.

9) **audition** [ɔˋdɪʃən] (n./v.) 試鏡，試演，試唱
   Did you pass your audition for the play?

10) **diva** [ˋdivə] (n.)（歌劇）女主唱，（樂壇）天后，態度高傲的女子
    Who is your favorite pop diva?

11) **disabled** [dɪˋsebəld] (a.) 殘障的，有生理缺陷的
    The accident left Frank severely disabled.

12) **rehearsal** [rɪˋhɝsəl] (n.) 排練，排演
    When is the next rehearsal for the play?

13) **recruit** [rɪˋkrut] (v.) 招募，招收
    The company recruited new employees at the job fair.

14) **cheerleading** [ˋtʃɪrˏlidɪŋ] (n.) 啦啦隊運動 (n.) cheerleader 啦啦隊員
    Becky is thinking of trying out for cheerleading this year.

15) **blackmail** [ˋblækˏmel] (v./n.) 勒索，脅迫
    Someone is using nude photos of the actress to blackmail her.

16) **vocal** [ˋvokəl] (a./n.) 聲音的，歌唱的；（歌曲中）歌唱部份（常用複數）
    It takes years of vocal training to become an opera singer.

17) **adrenaline** [əˋdrɛnəlɪn] (n.) 腎上腺素
    The rollercoaster really got our adrenaline flowing.

18) **rehab** [ˋriˏhæb] (n.) 勒戒所（為 rehabilitation center 的簡稱）
    The judge gave the defendant a choice of either jail or rehab.

19) **tune in** [tun] [ɪn] (phr.) 選台收看、收聽，鎖定
    Be sure to tune in tomorrow for the final episode.

音樂喜劇

© 看影集

威爾在妻子工作的家居用品店遇到山迪，以前的合唱團團長。

Sandy: Well, hello. How are things? I hear you have taken over glee club.

Will: Yeah. I hope you're not too upset.

Sandy: Are you kidding? Getting out of that swirling eddy of despair—best thing that ever happened to me. **Don't get me wrong**. It wasn't easy at first. Being dismissed, and for what I was accused of. My long-distance girlfriend in Cleveland nearly broke up with me. *[holds up pillow with monkey on it]* Oh God, don't you love a good monkey? Took me weeks to get over my nervous breakdown.

Will: Did they put you on medication?

Sandy: Better—medical marijuana. It's genius. I just tell my **Dr. Feelgood** I'm having trouble sleeping, and he gives me all of it I want. I'm finding the whole system quite lucrative.

Will: You're a drug dealer?

Sandy: Oh, yeah—make five times more than when I was a teacher. I keep some for myself, and then I take money baths in the rest.

山迪：嘿，哈囉！最近如何？我聽說你接手合唱團了。

威爾：是啊，我希望你不會太難過。

山迪：你開什麼玩笑？能離開那個絕望的深淵，是我這輩子遇過最棒的事。別誤會，一開始當然很辛苦，被人解雇，還被指控那樣的罪名。我在克利夫蘭的遠距女友差點跟我分手。（舉起上面有猴子圖案的枕頭）喔，天哪！這猴子好可愛不是嗎？我崩潰了好幾個星期才釋懷。

威爾：他們有給你吃藥嗎？

山迪：比藥更好的，是藥用大麻。真是太妙了。只要跟我那拿錢開藥的醫生說晚上睡不著，我想要多少他都會開給我。我發現這整套機制相當有利可圖。

威爾：你在販毒？

山迪：喔，對啊，比當老師還多賺五倍。我留一點給自己用，剩下的賣掉賺了不少。

 學英文 🎧140

Don't get me wrong. 不要誤會我。

get 可以表示「理解」，所以 get someone wrong 就是「用錯誤的方式理解某人的意思」，這個片語幾乎都只用在 Don't get me wrong. 的情況。

A: You don't think David should get the promotion?
你不認為大衛應該被升職嗎？

B: Don't get me wrong. I think he has management potential—he's just not ready yet.
不要誤會我的意思。我覺得他有擔任主管的潛力——他只是還沒準備好。

© FOX

威爾來到蘇的辦公室。

Sue: So you want to talk to my Cheerios about joining glee club?

Will: Well, I need more kids—performers—and all the best ones are in the Cheerios, so I figured some of them might want to **double up**.

Sue: OK, so what you're doing right now is called **blurring the lines**. High school is a **caste system**. Kids fall into certain slots. Your jocks and your popular kids—up in the penthouse; the invisibles and the kids playing **live-action druids and trolls** out in the forest—bottom floor.

Will: And…where do the glee kids lie?

Sue: Sub-basement.

蘇： 你想跟我的啦啦隊談加入合唱團的事？

威爾：嗯，我需要更多孩子——表演者——最好的表演者都在啦啦隊裡，所以我想其中有幾個可能想要多一個發揮的地方。

蘇： 好，你現在做的，就是所謂的打破階級。高中是有等級制度的，學生們各自有各自的位置。運動員和受歡迎的學生在頂樓；無名小卒，還有在森林裡玩角色扮演的孩子，都在一樓。

威爾：那，合唱團的孩子在哪裡？

蘇： 地下二樓。

> **caste system 種姓制度**
> 是一種森嚴的階級區分體制，社群內會自動將人分類，認出自己所處的位階，彼此不相往來。最有名的是印度過去施行的卡斯特體系，以職業類別畫分社會階級。

💬 **學英文** 🎧 141

double up 同時做兩件事

一人同時做兩種不同的工作，或肩負兩種角色，就是 double up。

A: You're pursuing a double major in physics and economics?
你在攻讀物理和經濟雙主修？

B: Yeah. I really like both, so I decided to double up.
是啊。我兩科都很喜歡，就決定同時修兩科。

blur the line(s) 模糊界線

blur 是「讓東西變模糊」，使分界線變得不清不楚，也就無法清楚區分彼此，看不出差別在哪了，經常會說 blur the line between A and B。

A: What did you think of *Black Swan*?
你覺得電影《黑天鵝》如何？

B: Yeah. I really liked the way it blurs the line between fantasy and reality.
不錯。我很喜歡那部片讓幻想和現實難以分辨的手法。

宅男玩很大

tabletop role playing game
桌上角色扮演遊戲（簡稱 tabletop RPG 或 TRPG）是最初始的角色扮演遊戲，場景經常帶有魔幻色彩，一般需三到五名玩家，其中一人擔任 game master「遊戲主持者」（簡稱 GM，不同的遊戲會有不同的稱呼），其他玩家決定角色、能力、職業後，就開始玩。

整場遊戲是由 GM 主導，除了要講解劇情、決定故事走向，在遊戲進行中還要跑龍套，演出怪物、路人甲之類的角色，讓玩家更有身歷其境之感。玩家一邊聽 GM 講故事、一邊擲骰子玩遊戲、一邊跟 GM 及其他玩家互動，也算是故事的共同創作者。tabletop RPG 後來也演變成透過電腦網路進行的線上即時遊戲，劇本都已固定，GM 的角色就從編、導、演，變成網管人員了。

tabletop RPG 參加者常被視為有人際障礙，活在虛幻世界中的宅男／女，也就是 geek。

Dr. Feelgood
這個字可以表示「毒販」，因為毒癮發作時很難受，毒販就像能幫人 feel good 的醫生。而有些無良醫生違法收取費用，開立非醫療需要的處方簽，讓有毒癮的患者取得管制藥物，這種醫生就成了名符其實的 Dr. Feelgood，上面對白中即為這個意思。

live-action role playing game
臨場動態角色扮演遊戲（簡稱 LARP）參加者會打扮成遊戲角色，並以角色的身份進行實境任務。這種活動多由桌上角色扮演遊戲發展而成，規模有時非常驚人，甚至在森林裡搭建出整個中世紀村莊的場景。而有些玩家很認真準備行頭及道具，武器擬真到具有殺傷力，遊戲主持者（因規模太大，現場會有多位 GM）除了當導演，還要負責維安，以免有人太入戲而鬧出人命。

Dungeons & Dragons
《龍與地下城》（簡稱 D&D），初版於一九七四年推出，是史上第一個商業化的 tabletop RPG，對後來的 RPG 影響深遠。《龍與地下城》光聽名字就知道是以中古世紀的奇幻故事為背景，上面對白中所說的 druid「德魯伊」（源自克爾特神話）和 troll「巨魔」（源自北歐神話）都是遊戲中的角色。

© IanRedding / Shutterstock.com

看影集

回到家，威爾問泰莉是否想當監護人帶學生戶外教學，去看激情美聲的表演。

Terri: On Saturday? Oh, I can't. I had to pick up an extra shift at work, Will. We're **living paycheck to paycheck**, you know.

Will: And how much of that paycheck goes to your Pottery Barn credit card?

Terri: I don't know what you're talking about. [Will walks toward closet] Don't go in the Christmas closet!

Will: [opens closet, which is full of purchases] I was looking for my jacket the other day. Come on! We cannot afford this stuff, Terri.

Terri: But we could, Will. Yes, I am **a shoo-in** to be promoted during the Christmas week at Sheets-N-Things. You know, I reek of management potential. And they're hiring at H.W. Menken.

Will: My passion is teaching, Terri. For the last time, I don't want to be an accountant.

Terri: **Dr. Phil** said that people could change.

You know, it's not a bad thing to want a real life, Will, and to have a glue gun that works! You know, it's really hard for me not having the things that I need.

泰莉： 星期六嗎？喔，我不行。我要加班，威爾。我們是月光族，你知道的。

威爾： 妳的薪水有多少都拿去繳 Pottery Barn 家飾用品的聯名信用卡了？

泰莉： 我不知道你在說什麼。（威爾走向衣櫥）不要打開放聖誕禮物的衣櫥！

威爾： （打開衣櫥，裡面裝滿了購買的物品）我前幾天在找我的夾克。拜託，我們買不起這些東西，泰莉。

泰莉： 但我們要就可以，威爾。沒錯，Sheets-N-Things 家居用品店 聖誕節那週鐵定幫我升官。你知道，我有管理天賦。還有會計事務所 H.W. Menken 在徵人。

威爾： 我熱愛教書，泰莉。最後一次說，我不想當會計師。

泰莉： 費爾博士說人是會改變的。

Dr. Phil 費爾博士

心理學博士費爾麥格羅（Phil McGraw）是美國電視名人，他於一九九八年成為《歐普拉秀》的每週固定來賓，以兩性問題及自我激勵專家的身份進入電視圈，接下來四年連出四本相關書籍本本熱賣，使他成為暢銷作家，並於二〇〇二年開始主持自己的電視節目《費爾博士》（Dr. Phil），在節目中幫來賓面對人生困境，儘管獲得頗多專家惡評，但他麻辣的言論、煽情的節目內容還是受到廣大觀眾歡迎。

學英文 142

live paycheck to paycheck 薪水全花光

是指賺來的錢在下次領薪水之前就花光了，幾乎存不了錢，也就是我們常說的「月光族」，也可以寫做live from paycheck to paycheck。

A: You've decided to go back to school and finish your degree?
你已經決定要重回校園完成學業了嗎？

B: Yeah. I'm tired of living from paycheck to paycheck.
對。我再也不想當收入微薄的月光族了。

a shoo-in 穩贏的人

shoo-in 是指「必贏的候選人」，這個說法源自「賽馬場」racetrack，表示可以輕鬆贏得比賽的馬。後來引申為「內定、穩贏的人選」。

A: I'm betting on Shannon Briggs to win the fight.
我下注押夏南布吉斯贏得這場拳擊賽。

B: I'm putting my money on him, too. He's a shoo-in.
我也賭他贏。他穩贏的。

看影集

在校外教學時，瑞秋和菲恩在排隊買點心。

Rachel: You're very talented.

Finn: Really?

Rachel: Yeah. I would know. I'm very talented, too. I think the rest of the team expects us to become **an item**. You, the hot male lead, and me, the stunning young ingénue everyone **roots for**.

Finn: Well, I, uh, have a girlfriend.

Rachel: Really? Who?

Finn: Quinn Fabray.

Rachel: Cheerleader Quinn Fabray? The president of the Celibacy Club?

© s_bukley / Shutterstock.com

「情侶」相關英文

an item 一對
尤其是交往動態能成為花邊新聞的情侶，因為 item 這個字原本是指「報章雜誌上的一則簡短報導」。

a couple 一對
要說一對情侶在一起的樣子很甜蜜，很可愛，就說 a cute couple。

a match 一對
match 有「相稱的」的意思，因此要說一對情侶很登對，就說 a perfect match 或 a match made in heaven。

high school sweethearts 高中校園情侶
在同一所高中就讀進而交往的情侶。

瑞秋：你非常有天分。

菲恩：真的嗎？

瑞秋：是啊，我看得出來。我也非常有天分。我想其他團員都期待我們能變成一對。你成為性感男主角，而我，是大家都支持的純真美少女。

菲恩：嗯，我，呃，已經有女朋友了。

瑞秋：真的嗎？是誰？

菲恩：昆恩法布蕾。

瑞秋：啦啦隊的昆恩法布蕾？貞潔社團的團長？

學英文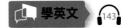

root for 支持

root 當動詞是「為人打氣加油」，當我們說 root for sb.，就代表支持某人、挺某人的意思。

A: Which team are you rooting for?
你支持哪個球隊？

B: Actually, I don't really care who wins.
其實，我根本不在意誰贏。

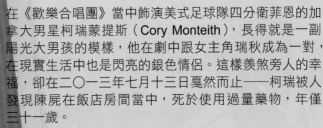

在《歡樂合唱團》當中飾演美式足球隊四分衛菲恩的加拿大男星柯瑞蒙提斯（Cory Monteith），長得就是一副陽光大男孩的模樣，他在劇中跟女主角瑞秋成為一對，在現實生活中也是閃亮的銀色情侶。這樣羨煞旁人的幸福，卻在二〇一三年七月十三日戛然而止——柯瑞被人發現陳屍在飯店房間當中，死於使用過量藥物，年僅三十一歲。

50 位 當代名人
與 他 們 的 那 些 小 東 西

ARTISTS, WRITERS, THINKERS, DREAMERS :
Portraits of Fifty Famous Folks & All Their Weird Stuff

作者 / 詹姆士·格列佛·漢考克
定價 / $350

特色 1：輕鬆有趣的經典名人小傳

從達文西、莫札特、愛因斯坦到香奈兒、卓別林、切格瓦拉……，本書精選 50 位橫跨世紀、極具現代影響力的經典人物，並透過簡介讓讀者具體了解他們的非凡成就、輕鬆認識這些每個人都該知道的世界名人。

特色 2：圖解名人小物，另類閱讀名人的生活

愛因斯坦最不喜歡穿什麼？安迪沃荷老是戴墨鏡的原因？柴契爾夫人發明了哪種甜品？每翻一頁人名會先看到幾個引發思考的名人相關問題，作者的構圖設計，讓讀者從名人的小物中更了解、更貼近成功名人的世界。

特色 3：最夯手繪風格，創意詮釋名臉

擺脫正經八百的名人傳記式人像，透過作者別具風格的眼光與獨特的手繪筆觸，詮釋每一位名人面貌與他們的隨身小物。

史上最好玩的名人傳記！

最有想像力的名人錄，
探索 50 位影響當代大眾文化的名人，
充實你的文化「識力」！

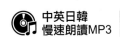

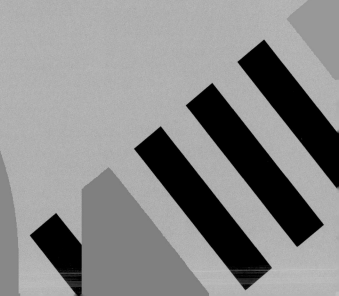
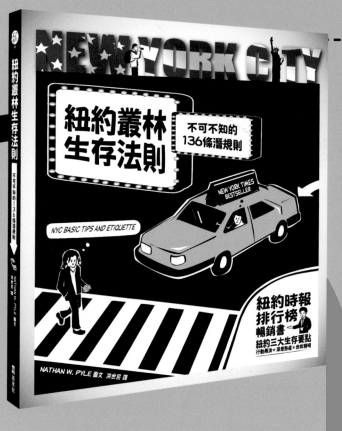

1. 在紐約最基本的生存法則是 …?

2. 搭計程車也是要看時間的

3. 佔位子是不被允許的！

4. 在紐約生存必備道具

我只知道，今天在紐約的某個地方，
某件美妙的事正在發生

5. 紐約生活的小確幸 ♥

EZ 叢書館 24

越追劇，英文越好 熱門影集
EZ TALK 總編嚴選特刊

越追劇，英文越好 熱門影集：EZ TALK 總編嚴選特刊 / EZ 叢書館編輯部作 . -- 初版 . -- 臺北市：日月文化，2016.06

144 面；21*28 公分

ISBN 978-986-248-562-0（平裝附光碟片）

1. 英語 2. 讀本

805.18   105007107

總　編　審：Judd Piggott
英　文　撰　稿　Judd Piggott
專案企劃執行：陳思容
主　　　　編：張玉芬
執　行　編　輯：盧晏星
封　面　設　計：徐歷弘
版　型　設　計：用視覺有限公司
視　覺　設　計：蕭彥伶
內　頁　排　版：健呈電腦排版公司
錄　音　後　製：純粹錄音後製有限公司
錄　音　員：Michael Tennant、Terri Pebsworth

發　行　人：洪祺祥
總　編　輯：林慧美
副　總　編　輯：王彥萍
法　律　顧　問：建大法律事務所
財　務　顧　問：高威會計師事務所
出　　　　版：日月文化出版股份有限公司
製　　　　作：EZ 叢書館
地　　　　址：臺北市信義路三段151號8樓
電　　　　話：(02)2708-5509
傳　　　　真：(02)2708-6157
客　服　信　箱：service@heliopolis.com.tw
網　　　　址：www.heliopolis.com.tw
郵　撥　帳　號：19716071日月文化出版股份有限公司

總　經　銷：聯合發行股份有限公司
電　　　　話：(02)2917-8022
傳　　　　真：(02)2915-7212
印　　　　刷：中原造像股份有限公司
初　版　一　刷：2016 年 6 月
定　　　　價：350 元
I　S　B　N：978-986-248-562-0

日月文化集團
HELIOPOLIS
CULTURE GROUP

客服專線 02-2708-5509
客服傳真 02-2708-6157
客服信箱 service@heliopolis.com.tw

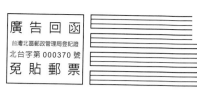

日月文化集團 讀者服務部 收

10658 台北市信義路三段151號8樓

對折黏貼後，即可直接郵寄

日月文化網址：**www.heliopolis.com.tw**

最新消息、活動，請參考 FB 粉絲團

大量訂購，另有折扣優惠，請洽客服中心（詳見本頁上方所示連絡方式）。

日月文化

EZ TALK

EZ Japan

EZ Korea

大好書屋・寶鼎出版・山岳文化・洪圖出版

感謝您購買 **越追劇，英文越好 熱門影集：EZTALK 總編嚴選特刊**

請詳細正楷填寫「讀者資料」並寄回「讀者回函卡」，（影印無效），即可參加「新世紀福爾摩斯 1-3 季套裝 DVD」乙份（市價 NT$2,500）抽獎活動，限量 3 名！活動時間：105/06/03~105/07/30 止（以郵戳為憑）

讀者資料（請詳細填寫以確保各項權益）

讀者姓名：＿＿＿＿＿＿＿　生日：＿＿＿年＿＿＿月＿＿＿日　　性別：□男 □女

電話：（日）＿＿＿＿＿＿＿（夜）＿＿＿＿＿＿＿＿　手機：＿＿＿＿＿＿＿＿＿＿＿

Email：（請務必填寫，以利及時通知訊息）＿＿＿＿＿＿＿＿＿＿＿＿＿＿＿＿＿＿＿＿＿＿

收件人地址：＿＿＿＿＿＿＿＿＿＿＿＿＿＿＿＿＿＿＿＿＿＿＿＿＿＿＿＿＿＿＿

您從何處購買本書：＿＿＿＿＿＿ 縣 / 市＿＿＿＿＿＿＿＿ 書店

您的職業：□製造 □金融 □軍公教 □服務 □資訊 □傳播 □學生 □自由業 □其他

您從何處得知這本書的消息：□書店 □網路 □報紙 □雜誌 □廣播 □電視 □他人推薦

您通常以何種方式購書：□書店 □網路 □傳真訂購 □郵政劃撥 □其他

您對本書的評價：（1. 非常滿意 2. 滿意 3. 普通 4. 不滿意 5. 非常不滿意）

書名＿＿＿＿ 內容＿＿＿＿ 封面設計＿＿＿＿ 版面編排＿＿＿＿ 文 / 譯筆

請給我們建議：＿＿＿＿＿＿＿＿＿＿＿＿＿＿＿＿＿＿＿＿＿＿＿＿＿＿＿

贈品介紹　得獎名單將於 **105 年 8 月 3 日公佈在 EZTalk 美語會話誌** Facebook：www.facebook.com/jiesi.EZTALK

注意事項：

1. 於 105/08/03 在 EZTalk 美語會話誌 Facebook 公布得獎名單；105/08/05 掛號寄出回函贈品 2. 如因資料填寫不完整及不正確以致無法連絡者，視同放棄中獎資格，本公司有權另抽出替補名額。3. 本活動贈品以實物為準，無法由中獎人挑選，亦不得折現或兌換其他商品。4. 本活動所有抽獎與兌換獎品，僅郵寄至台、澎、金、馬地區，不處理郵寄獎品至海外之事宜。 5. 對於您所提供予本公司之個人資料，將依個人資料保護法之規定來使用、保管，並維護您的隱私權。